MW01172139

Ghost Commando
Battle for Cavallo

A Adélard l' ombre Adventure

Fabio Tagliasacchi

ISBN: 9798860980044

DEDICATION

This book is dedicated to my Tagliasacchi family. To my parents and their parents, to my brother and sisters, to my children, and to their children, and to all the children yet to be born within our bloodline.

This book is also dedicated to those that have joined my family, that by their love and kindness are in every sense forever more part of the Tagliasacchi family.

**"Let the mirror be your judge,
the wind your guide, and
the horizon always beckon you."**

Fabio Tagliasacchi, 2023

Ghost Commando
Battle for Cavallo

CHAPTERS

Le Début

Chapter 27: Night Raid

0200 May 5th, Mayotte Island: 190 miles northwest of Madagascar in the western Indian Ocean.

12 divers moved with stealth and precision, making their way through the dark waters off the coast of Africa towards an unguarded port without leaving a trace of their passage.

The distant glow of a nearby dockyard and the hum of activity heightened their sense of urgency. As they reached their input locations, the two commando squad leaders carefully surfaced and assessed the situation above the water.

The area near the docks seemed peaceful, but even without armed guards, spotlights still swept across the buildings from time to time, leaving no room for error.

Under the cover of darkness, the two squads of French Commandos rose from the sea and made their way towards a featureless port warehouse on the island of Mayotte.

With hand signals exchanged between the men, Blue and Red squads moved swiftly and quietly, avoiding the spotlight's gaze. The atmosphere was tense, each breath calculated, their training taking over to ensure their movements were undetectable.

"Blue squad on target, perimeter clear. Two unidentified inside."

"Acknowledged."

"Red Squad, this is blue leader, thermal shows our 2, house guest taking a smoke break at the east entrance."

"Will neutralize."

"Much appreciated blue leader. Report when clear."

"Red Squad, move in. Locate 'Pune River Industries' crates and arm explosives.

One by one the red squad men disappeared into the warehouse found their targets and reported explosives ready to their squad leader.

"Blue Squad, this is red leader, fireworks in place."

"All clear red leader, our 2 guests are ignorant and taking a happy nap."

"All squads move to exit points. Red1 run backdoor, make sure we are still isolated."

"Heard commander."

"Red squad on exit."

"Blue squad on exit."

"Bring your backdoor in red leader and light the fuse."

"Red1 clear, all secure."

"Best cover your ears boys, New Years is coming early."

* * *

In an instant the warehouse erupted into a massive fireball, momentarily illuminating the sky over the port. The explosives aided by the ammunition secretly stored in the warehouse created a deafening roar echoing across the night air as the building and all within it obliterated into indistinguishable fragments, the explosion sending shockwaves through the surrounding area, causing windows to shatter and debris to fly in all directions.

The two squads watched from their concealed positions, their hearts pounding in their chests as they witnessed the successful execution of their mission. As the fire began to subside, they could see the chaos that had unfolded around them. Smoke and dust filled the air, obscuring the once sleepy dockyard in an eerie haze.

* * *

Later that morning, international news reported an industrial accident with no loss of life occurred on a small French island in the Indian ocean as chemicals in a port warehouse caught fire.

* * *

2 Weeks Earlier.
0900 Navel Command, Toulon, France
Confidential Threat Assessment Meeting
Rohan Akhil COO
COO Bugatti enterprises Indian Ocean
Étienne Vacheron VAE
Vice-Amiral d'escadr of the Navy
Gaston Bernardone COSG
Commandement des Opérations Spéciales COSG
Gérard Constantin SOF
Senior Operations Officer Bérets Verts

* * *

Vice Admiral Étienne Vacheron entered the naval offices at the Toulon seaport in the south of France, his expression one of mild annoyance. He was met by Gaston Bernardone, the Commandant of the special forces, who for his part appeared slightly anxious.

Vice Admiral Vacheron, was a difficult and intimidating officer. Old school to the core with a mouth that could make battle harden men whither.

"Good afternoon, Vice Admiral. Thank You for coming on such short notice." Gaston greeted, gesturing towards the office chairs. "Please, have a seat."

* * *

Vice Admiral Vacheron took a seat, mildly curious, although not entirely pleased with being dragged into an unexpected meeting. "Alright, Gaston, what is this about?" His manner and tone direct.

"Yes Sir." Gaston said, turning. "I would like to introduce you to Rohan Akhil COO Bugatti enterprises Indian Ocean."

With a minor nod of acknowledgement towards Rohan, the Vice Admiral again turned his inquisition towards the Commandant, seemingly more annoyed than when he entered.

"Fine, now Gaston please tell me why I am here? Why he is here? And what the hell does Bugatti have to do with it? I am running the Navy for gods' sake, not serving champaign and caviar to some rich kid."

"This is very serious Sir with many lives at stake." Gaston replied firmly. "Please give us a moment to brief you."

"Very well Gaston."

"Mr. Akhil, please share the events leading up to today that are of concern to France."

"Thank You Commandant Bernardone. Bugatti enterprises is a global company invested in hundreds of different businesses from over the horizon satellite communications to F1 racing. One of those companies is an Indian manufacturer of premium NATO grade ammunition as in the 5.56 mm as well as weapons which we sell to militaries and legitimate companies."

"French intelligence has informed us that a large shipment of our ammunition and weapons was purchased by what was on the surface a legitimate dealer and through a series of shell companies is now sitting in warehouse off the coast of Africa destined for a warlord in the Congo."

"Has any of this been verified?" Admiral Vacheron asked.

"Yes Sir, it has. I have spoken directly with Intelligence and with Armand Bugatti." Gérard, commanding officer of the Bérets Verts answered.

The Vice Admiral's jaw tightened, and he took a moment to process the gravity of the situation. "I see."
Standing up the Vice Admiral walked to the counter and poured himself a glass of water before continuing.

"Mr. Akhil, what exactly do you or Mr. Bugatti want the Navy to do?"

"He wants us to destroy it Sir." Gaston answered quickly.

"What? How? Where?" The Admiral asked.

"Mr. Bugatti owns the warehouse being used and most of the surrounding buildings. He wants it all destroyed, buildings, weapons all of it, without loss of life Sir."

"Mr. Bugatti is adamant and is willing to go to extremes that nothing he is involved in supports mass murders and psychotic warlords." Rohan told the vice admiral distinctly and with obvious pride in the request.

The Vice Admiral looked squarely at Gérard. "Can your teams do this, and how fast?" Admiral Étienne asked.
"Yes Sir, we can. Two weeks, three on the outside."

"What, say you, Gaston. Should we do this?"
"Yes Sir, we should."

Pausing to take another drink from his glass, the Vice Admiral considered all the details of the briefing and the judgement of two of his most trusted officers . . . as he had done many times before in battle, he made a decision.

"Very well gentlemen, let's make this happen."

"Mr. Akhil please tell your boss; we will be most happy to blow his building to hell and back."

Chapter 1: Pivot

1330 Cavallo island

"There has been a change in plans. Transport to Melusine is not coming. You and your men are ordered to stay on Cavallo and await further orders."

"Understood Sir. Is this part of the mission?" Adélard asked.

"No, Adélard it is not. That is the most I can share with you at this time."

"I am sending a boat from the camp tomorrow with some items for your men."

"Make certain only your squad unloads and opens tomorrow's shipment. I will personally brief you at 1400 hours tomorrow afternoon." Commander Ross continued.

"Understood, Commander." Adélard assured him.

"Good. One more thing Adélard, keep your eyes open and keep me informed of anything significant or out of the ordinary happening on Cavallo. Ross Out."

* * *

Graham exchanged a nervous glance and a nod, turning off the equipment. Adélard called the men together and relayed the briefing information.

Afterwards the men sat filled with a mixture of curiosity, apprehension, and disappointed for not returning to camp.

"Commander Ross specifically told you this change is not part of our training mission?" Noel asked Adélard.

"Correct." He answered.

"Ok, it's official. Now I am getting a little nervous." Jojo interjected.

"I could think of worse places to be." Henri said. "Seriously guys we are going to be stationed for the time being, at one of the most amazing homes in the entire French empire, with staff running around breaking their asses taking care of us. Until I know different, I for one am going to enjoy it."

"All true Henri, but this not being a training mission and a boat coming tomorrow carrying who know what for a mission we know nothing about. It makes me a little nervous as well." Graham threw his two cents in.

"Any Ideas Adélard?" Julio asked.

"Julio, the only thing I feel somewhat certain about is that whatever this is, it concerns either the Island or Mr. Bugatti or both."

Adélard answered earnestly looking at each man in the squad. "Nothing we can do today but get cleaned up and prepare to enjoy our dinner with Armand.

"Heard." The men answered in unison.

"Besides, Julio and I are awful hungry." Jojo mentioned smiling.

"I hear you, my skinny French pirate." Adélard chided him.

"Julio, I do think once we see what Commander Ross has sent us, it might give us a hint of what to expect." Adélard added. "So, until then, let's get ready to go eat."

"Right on your 6 mon capitaine. Let's go." Jojo said happily, jumping up.

* * *

1000 Cavallo Island, Bugatti hidden cove.
Long before they needed to be, eager to get to the cove and discover what the commander had sent them. Adélard ordered his men to get into the two Bugatti's Defenders.

François, the butler, had requested to come along for the ride, and Adélard gladly welcomed him, curious as to his motives and to any insights he might reveal.

Arriving at the hidden cove, the squad members walked down the small hill and gathered on the dock, awaiting the arrival of the Requin boat from camp Melusine.

The men were happy and relaxed, joking with each other and speculating about what surprises Commander Ross was sending them.

Adélard and François stood apart from the others, taking in the scenic beauty and the serene waters of the cove.

François cleared his throat, breaking the silence between them. "Monsieur Adélard, I must relay a message from Mr. Bugatti." He said, his demeanor composed as always.

"Something you could not share with me during the drive François?" Adélard asked, turning to face him with an edge to his voice.

Seeing the butler unable or unwilling to respond and still intrigued by what François might say.

Adélard softened his tone. "Forgive me, François. Please share with me Mr. Bugatti's message."

François cleared his throat again and continued, although this time with a less superior attitude. "Mr. Bugatti has requested that you and your men move into the Rousseau guest house on the estate."

"He is committed to providing you with the finest hospitality during your stay, which the Rousseau house is well equipped to do, but he needs your team to be there for reason which will become apparent in the fullness of time."

François paused for a moment before adding.

"Forgive me Sir, but I took the liberty of arranging for your bags and belongings to be moved to the guest house while we were driving here."

Adélard was taken aback, but quickly recovered. "That's incredibly generous of Mr. Bugatti . . . please convey our acceptance and heartfelt thanks to him."

François nodded, a faint smile playing on his lips. "I will, Monsieur Adélard. Mr. Bugatti is quite pleased to have you and your squad here, and he wants to ensure you have everything you need for your mission."

"Mr. Bugatti is a good man, and someone that I hope would look upon me as a friend." He replied sincerely. "My commando squad will treat the Rousseau house with the utmost respect."

François inclined his head in agreement. "I have no doubt that you will, Monsieur Adélard."

As the two men stood there, a shared sense of loyalty to Armand and some understanding passed between them.

With the Requin boat from Melusine approaching the cove, Adélard turned his attention back to the task at hand.

"Graham, see that all the cargo is loaded and secure. Jojo you and Noel take the second Defender that will give you more room for cargo. Everyone else will ride with François and me in the front vehicle."

"Heard." Both Graham and Jojo responded sharply.

As Range Rovers carried them over the trails, François feeling like an unofficial part of the squad enjoyed the opportunity to drop another surprise on the men.

"Ah, Monsieur Adélard, I forgot to mention one important detail." François said with a hint of excitement in his voice.

"The Rousseau house has a spacious basement that is perfect for your team to use in any manner you choose. You will, I am certain, find it quite suitable for your needs."

Adélard was intrigued by this unexpected information. "Rousseau house, a basement? That might be very useful for us, thank you, François."

"That's not all." François continued, a hint of mischief in his eyes. "The guest house also has another surprise that I believe you and your men will find intriguing."

Adélard turned the wheel passing the automatic gates and entering the compound. "Another surprise François?"

François smiled enigmatically. "The Rousseau house is connected to the Mansion by an underground tunnel."

The squad members in the back seat couldn't hide their surprise, and Adélard's eyes widened with astonishment. "An underground tunnel? That's incredible!" Julio exclaimed, trying to picture the hidden passageway.

François chuckled at their reaction. "Yes, it's a bit of a secret feature of the estate. Mr. Bugatti enjoys his privacy."

"So, we can move between the guest house and the main house without being seen?" Graham asked.

"Exactly, and to other locations on the compound as well." François confirmed with an uncharacteristic smile, then quickly returned to his dour manner.

" Monsieur Adélard, meals will still be served in the mansion, as per usual. Lunch for your men will be at noon today."

* * *

The squad members carefully unloaded the bags and crates from the Range Rover Defenders, following François' guidance to the large basement of the Rousseau guest house.

Adélard's eyes widened with amazement as he stepped into the spacious underground room, perfect for their equipment and supplies.

"Look at this place," Adélard said with a grin. "It's even bigger and better than I imagined."

"Let's get these bags and crates sorted." Adélard called out.

"Wait Adélard! Look over here." Henri called him surprised.

Lowering his crate to the ground Adélard walked over to where Henri was looking through an open door.

"This is unbelievable Adélard." Henri said shaking his head. "A double shooting range right here."

"I think I am going to like the Rousseau house." Adélard said patting Henri on the back. "Come, we got stuff to unpack."

First order of business; the squad started opening the 6 waterproof bags. The men were pleasantly surprised to find a complete set of new diving gear, each with extra tanks and complete dive, navigation, and communication tech.

GHOST COMMANDO – Battle for Cavallo

"Graham, check this out." Jojo called out, holding up a brand-new diving suit.

"This is top-of-the-line equipment!" Graham nodded, a sense of excitement filling him. "This is unbelievable!"

"Jojo you and Julio sort the dive gear by men according to size." Then put them over by the wall. Noel there is a locker with some tools in it I noticed by the stairs." Adélard ordered. "See if there is a crowbar. I want these crates opened next. Start with the small one first."

"Heard." Noel responded.

Adélard and Noel pried open the first crate while Graham and Julio started on the second much larger crate. Adélard was taken aback by what he found inside. Six commando bags each with one of their names stitched to the outside. And even more impressive, each bag contained multiple sets of uniforms, winter gear, and nondescript clothing for each man.

"Adélard whispered to Noel. "I don't think they put this together over night. Looks like command knew about our extended stay for a while."

"Guys, you won't believe this." Noel called to the others. "We've got uniforms, winter gear, and some civilian clothes as well. Looks like the Navy went shopping for us."

"Jojo, Julio come . . . " Before Adélard could finish his command Graham excitedly interrupted him. "Everyone, come see this."

The six men gathered, looking down into the large crate Graham had opened. Their surprise turned to astonishment as they discovered an array of weapons, pistols, assault rifles, grenade launchers, even the TOZ underwater guns.

Boxes and boxes of ammunition and in a separate compartment dozens of micro drones, and surveillance cameras. Julio's eyes opened even wider as he opened a smaller box. "Are these explosives Graham?"

"Yes, they are, the underwater kind. Be careful with those." He answered.

"This is some serious firepower gentlemen." Adélard commented. "Henri find a place down here where we can hide or lock up these weapons."

"How about the shooting range? We can secure that area." Henri suggested.

"Good, I like that idea." Adélard responded. "Make it happen Henri."

Graham carefully picked up one of the surveillance drones and marveled at the advanced technology. "This is cutting-edge equipment Adélard. High definition and infrared cameras as well as swarm capabilities. These babies will give us a significant advantage in gathering intel." He said, impressed.

"With all these toys, we'll be like super, secret agent commandos." Jojo joked, lightening the mood as they processed the significance of their new arsenal.

GHOST COMMANDO – Battle for Cavallo

Jojo pulled out and inspected one of the unfamiliar medical kits. "Adélard these med kits are far more than patch and go." Lifting a small bottle to demonstrate what he had found Jojo continued. "There are sedatives, narcotics, stuff I don't even know, and medical auto injectors in here."

"Seems the Navy wants us armed with more than just guns Jojo. Get with Henri and store these kits with the weapons."

"Heard Adélard."

Feeling the impact of all they discovered Adélard stopped inspecting and called the men together.

"Listen guys. None of us knows what we are going to be asked to do or what the purpose of any of this gear is for. But we all know these weapons are lethal in the extreme. Not to mention the surveillance toys and drugs we have been issued have their own danger associated."

Adélard paused reaching into the crate to pull out a HK416 assault rifle.

"One thing we all need to understand is that we cannot use or carry these weapons without a clear need or a distinct target. We must be careful with this gear beyond its use. It can also attract unwanted attention if we're not discreet." Adélard warned, ensuring the squad understood the responsibility that came with the advanced equipment.

Graham nodded in agreement. "You're right. We need to be strategic with displaying or even letting others know we have them and always maintain our covert protocols."

"So, you're saying no blowing shit up with the grenade launchers after lunch." Jojo jokingly asked.

Adélard couldn't help but laugh before answering. "Correct, and no running around intimidating the locals like pirate Jojo brandishing his assault rifle."

"Oui, oui mon Capitaine. Understood." Jojo replied.

"I think Commander Ross knew he could trust us to keep the Navies secrets." Graham commented.

Adélard acknowledged the weight of the responsibility they now carried in his face. "Our lives I fear, just got a lot more complex."

Returning the assault rifle to its place in the crate he quickly changed his demeanor forcing a broad grin across his face.

"Enough with the drama . . . you motley crew of commando wannabes. Let's stow these toys and go eat lunch."

"Hell yes!" Jojo happily replied.

* * *

Adélard and Julio decided to walk across the compound to the mansion for their lunch. The other four squad members decided it would be fun to try the secret underground tunnels and find their way there.

* * *

"I am a little worried about all that stuff we unpacked." Julio admitted walking next to Adélard.

"What do you mean Julio?"

"I mean . . . well I know I am a good shot, and . . . well I know what it means to be a commando . . . It's just . . . Adélard I have never shot a person and I am not sure . . ."

"You're not sure you will be able to. Is that what you mean Julio?"

"Sort of, yes. I just don't want to freeze up and let the squad down."

"I think we all feel that way."

"Listen Julio. I will tell you what my grandfather, a true warrior, told me.

'Killing is not a game, killing it is not a fun thing to do. Anyone that enjoys it should be locked up forever. But killing at times is a necessary thing and a real man understands that.' Understood?" Adélard Asked.

"Well sort of." Julio answered softly.

"Good enough for now mon ami, good enough for now."

Chapter 2: Clear and present Danger

1300 Cavallo island
"Adélard squad, this is command."

"Command this is Adélard, go ahead.

"New orders. You are to be at the Bugatti helo pad with two vehicles at 1400. No support required only two drivers. Command out."

"Received and understood." Adélard answered.

Adélard turned to Graham with a small smirk on his face.

"Looks like the Navy wants us to be Uber drivers today." Smiling, Graham nodded. "So, you and me and the Defenders?"

"Sounds about right. Let the others finish their lunch. You know how grumpy Jojo can be if you interrupt his eating." Adélard answered laughing.

* * *

Adélard and Graham stood leaning on the front of their vehicles at the Bugatti helo pad. Their eyes fixed on the sky as they awaited the arrival of the helicopter.

With the helicopter in sight and getting closer, the thump, thump of the rotor blades grew louder.

The men exchanged curious glances, and walked closer wondering who would be disembarking from the aircraft.

As the Helicopter touched down, Adélard was happy to see Armand Bugatti stepping out looking as elegant as ever, accompanied by a stunning woman and two young girls, followed closely behind by two of Mr. Bugatti's well-armed security men dressed in full black combat attire.

The surprises didn't end there; Commander Ross and another older gentleman also in uniform stepped out and began walking toward Adélard and Graham.

"Mr. Bugatti, this is quite the surprise." Adélard said, reaching out to shake Armand's hand, while trying to conceal his astonishment at the unexpected guests.

Armand Bugatti flashed a warm smile. "Ah, Adélard, my friend." He said, extending his hand. "I want to introduce you to my family. "Armand gestured with obvious love and pride. "This is my wife, Isabella, and these two lovely girls are our twin daughters; Reine and Taber."

Commander Ross stepped forward, causing Adélard and Graham to snap to attention. " At ease, it's good to see you again gentlemen. Allow me to introduce Gaston Bernardone Commandement des Opérations Spéciales COSG.

Adélard and Graham were momentarily shocked, realizing this older man was the senior officer in charge of all French Commandos. Both men instinctively snapped back to attention and saluted.

Gaston smiled graciously. "At ease gentlemen, it is my pleasure to finally meet you. Commander Ross and Mr. Bugatti have been singing your praises all morning."

"Thank You Sir." Adélard and Graham told their senior officer respectfully until he reached out offering each his hand in friendship. "I was a tadpole once upon a time myself. We be Kraken now. Yes?" Gaston asked.

"Yes Sir." The men answered smiling in unison.

Armand Bugatti then turned to Adélard and Graham. "Well with the introductions over, shall we move on gentlemen? My little girls are tired, and I could use a drink."

As the party prepared to depart, Adélard noted that both of Mr. Bugatti's security men followed his wife and children into Grahams Defender. Leaving the four of them to ride together back to the compound.

* * *

Driving back to the compound Commandant Gaston was the first to speak. "Adélard, first off, I want you to understand none of this is normal or routine. There is a clear and present danger to the lives of Mr. Bugatti and his family. That is why we are here and that is why I am elevating you and your men to active commando duty as of today."

Turning to look at Armand, Commandant Gaston continued. "Although I have over 50 battle tested squads ready, Mr. Bugatti was adamant in your squad being here. You can thank him for your promotions and the honor."

"Later Gaston and I will be briefing you and the entire squad with what we know and what we are up against. Commander Ross interjected.

Adélard kept driving, trying to process all that he had just been told and responded in the only way he knew how. "Thank you, Sirs."

"Thank you, Armand, for your faith in me and my squad." "I will NOT let you down!"

"Of that Adélard, I am quite certain." Armand answered.

* * *

The men of Adélard's squad gathered in Mr. Bugatti's private office, standing at ease, awaited the briefing from Commander Ross, Commandant Gaston, and Armand Bugatti himself.

Commandant Gaston stepped forward, his demeanor serious and composed. "Seven months ago." He began.

"We received intel indicating that weapons and ammunition produced by one of Mr. Bugatti's Indian subsidiaries were being diverted to a warlord in the Congo."

"At Mr. Bugatti's request, two of my commando squads conducted a covert operation and destroyed one of his warehouses off the coast of Africa, eliminating those munitions with, I might add, no loss of life or transparency. The incident was reported by international news as an accident caused by industrial chemicals."

Adélard and his men listened intently, understanding the gravity of the situation. "We believe that this action angered certain powerful entities, and that they are now seeking revenge aimed at Mr. Bugatti and his family."

Raising his hand Graham asked a question. "Commandant, if that mission went off without any transparency, why have they focused their anger at Mr. Bugatti?"

"Unfortunately, I may have caused that." Armand interrupted. "Once French intelligence informed me that my armaments were being redirected to a psychotic Warlord, I instructed Rohan Akhil my chief operating officer for Bugatti enterprises Indian Ocean to institute a change in the vetting of our clients. With that change in place, we currently only sell to European Union approved countries and NATO approved customers."

"So, with their supply chain for your guns turned off at the same time the warehouse was destroyed . . . they connected the dots to you Armand?" Adélard Asked.

"It seems the only logical explanations." Armand responded.

"At that point Israeli intelligence got involved." Commandant Gaston interrupted continuing the briefing.

"It seems that our Congo Warlord has close ties with a particular Palestinian terrorists' group that the Israeli's as a matter of course keep on eye on for their own safety."

"Communications were intercepted which described that the Warlord believes Mr. Bugatti was personally responsible for destroying the warehouse and is doubly angry that his 5 million Euro's went up in smoke."

"For their part, the Palestinian's confirmed his beliefs."

"They pointed out the fact that the supply chain the Warlord had carefully developed to get Mr. Bugatti's Indian weapons was permanently disrupted by actions Mr. Bugatti initiated himself."

"Understood Commandant." Adélard spoke up. "Can you share why we believe that Mr. Bugatti and his family face an imminent threat?"

"I can do that, Adélard." Commander Ross answered.

"Working with Israeli and French intelligence as well as our operatives on the ground in Mali. We have confirmed that the Warlord is hiring a group of mercenaries to attack this island and kill Armand and his family."

"Do we know when Sir?" Graham asked.

"Specifically, no, Graham, but we speculate the attack will happen in the next 3 to 4 weeks. We have eyes and ears on the mercenaries which have been gathering in Orangi Town near Karachi Pakistan." Commander Ross added.

"Therefore, we will have intel when they make their move?" Adélard asked.

"That is the assumption we are working with Adélard." Commander Ross answered.

"They are coming gentlemen, of that there is no doubt. The when, and the how is still unknown, but they are coming." Commandant Gaston told the men firmly.

"Adélard, Commander Ross and I, need to have a briefing with the Vice-Admiral. Afterwards I want to hear every bit of intel you have on the island and any thoughts on how an attack might happen and how we might prevent it. I have the entire core and the Navy's might at my disposal gentlemen. No Warlord will harm a French citizen on my watch. Am I clear." Commandant Gaston said, his voice becoming louder and his actions more animated.

"Yes Sir." All the men including Commander Ross answered sharply.

"Monsieur Gaston if I may make a suggestion." Armand interrupted.

"Let us pause for your briefing with the Admiral and also have dinner before we begin again. This will give us all time to collect our thoughts and possibly develop an interim plan."

"Very well, Armand." Commandant Gaston said in agreement.

"Gentlemen, I do ask one more indulgence. My wife and children will be joining us for dinner. I ask all of you not to discuss these matters at the table. My Isabella understands the threat we face, but my children do not need to know everything. Is that acceptable?"

"Certainly Armand." Commander Ross answered.

"Thank you, my friend. I will have dinner served in two hours' time."

* * *

1630 Toulon France. Navy headquarters and primary naval base.

"Gaston, do what you need to do!"

"I don't want this situation to suffer mission creep."

"I want those mercenaries gone and that Warlord dead or wishing he was."

"Do you read me loud and clear Gaston?"

Étienne Vacheron, vice-Amiral d'escadr of the Navy in forces asked with menace in his voice.

"Yes Sir! Will do Sir." Commandant Gaston replied.

* * *

Rousseau House
Adélard's squad gathered around a table, their faces serious and focused. The weight of the imminent threat hung heavily in the air, and they knew they had to plan carefully to ensure the safety of Armand Bugatti and his family.

Adélard started the discussion, his voice calm and measured.

"We need to determine the most likely points of attack. Sea or the air. If we can anticipate their approach, we can be better prepared to counter it. Let us begin by assuming they are our equal in training and capabilities."

"If they are, they would have eyes on the compound now."

"Agreed and if not already then soon. We need to know exactly who belongs on this island and who if any don't." Henri added.

"Graham, see what intel you can gather on who lives and works here and where. The good news is most of the mansions at this time of year are empty. Still there are folks around that belong here and we need to identify them and if possible, track them." Adélard ordered.

"If we can get a thermal imaging drone out of Toulon, I can tell you exactly how many souls are on this island and at least at night where they are." Graham suggested.

"Excellent, with that intel we can crosscheck any list we put together of who might belong here. I will put that as my first request tonight." Adélard responded energized by his squad's engagement.

"If the attack comes at night. That drone would give us an edge Adélard. 'Be where the enemy is not'." Noel added.

"Was that a little from the Art of War?" Graham asked, poking Noel.

"What? Surprised I read more that comic books." Noel answered poking him back.

"Excuse me children." Jojo interrupted smiling.
"Adélard, just my two cents, but if I were attacking this island, it wouldn't be by air. Too limited and mercenaries, no matter how well equipped, usually don't have air cover or aerial surveillance.

"Besides, we know for a fact it is near impossible to defend every inch of any coastline, even on an island this small. My bet is they will arrive by sea." Jojo added his mind racing barely ahead of his words.

"I agree with Jojo. Adélard, the probability of an aerial assault is slim and none. We should focus the sea." Graham said nodding to Jojo.

"Graham, can we set up those micro drones to help with gathering intel during the day and also swarm and be our eyes during an attack? Adélard asked.

"Yes, and even at night. They do not have thermal, but they are equipped with night vision. I can program the drones to conduct regular sweeps, we have 36 drones so I can keep 12 in the field at all times if we need to, but we will need to find a safe spot to launch them from." Graham added, already thinking about the logistics.

"I think Father Paulo's tunnels would be a good place to hide Graham. No one would go looking for him there and its almost isolated up on that hill." Julio said, looking at Adélard.

"I like it. Good thinking Julio. At tonight's briefing I will ask Armand to impose on Father Paulo with this request." Adélard responded.

Henri spoke up next. "Intel notwithstanding, we need to be actively searching for any mercenaries or potential attackers who might already be on the island. If they are here, we need to know. We can't get caught with our guard down."

"You're absolutely right." Adélard agreed. "We'll also need to keep a low profile while gathering information. We don't want to spook the locals and end up on national TV. Thoughts?"

Jojo raised his hand. "We have already been posing as Bugatti employees on vacation. Why not continue the charade, we can use bicycles to move around the island without drawing too much attention. It's a common sight on Cavallo and something tourist would do."

Adélard nodded, impressed by Jojo. "That's a great idea. All of us can take turns, it will give us eyes on the island without being too conspicuous. I will put bicycles on my Christmas list for tonight. Any other ideas on how to hide in plain sight."

"Not much to do on this island, but if I were on vacation here, I might want to do a little fishing. Might be a clever way for us to keep an eye on the shoreline." Noel suggested.

* * *

Bugatti Conference Room
"Vice-Admiral Étienne is a hard ass." Ross mentioned as they walked into a small private conference room.

"Absolutely, as hard as it gets, but he did just give us Carte Blanc. So, all in all I am good with it." Gaston commented winking at Commander Ross.

The two officers sat across from each other, studying maps of the Island and of the Congo, discussing the potential missions ahead.

GHOST COMMANDO – Battle for Cavallo

Commander Ross leaned forward; his brow furrowed with concern. "We are going to need a lot of assets Gaston. Gathering intel, protecting this island, and eliminating a well-protected Warlord not on French soil."

"We have an intelligence team from special forces on the ground in Orangi Town watching the mercenaries."

"They are reporting 15 to 20 men on site. Several Palestinians have been identified and one ex-Chechen officer. Navy Intelligence at Toulon suggest he may be in charge." Gaston informed him.

"That will outnumber Adélard squad by 2 maybe 3 to one." Ross stated the concern evident in his voice. "We both know Armand will not allow us to turn his home into a military camp, but we need to even the odds. Honestly, Gaston these men are good, but they have never faced battle."

"I am well aware of that fact." Gaston stated grimly.

"If any of those antique baby submarines you keep hidden at your base are operational . . . Can you house two of my squads at your precious Melusine?" Gaston asked, looking up at Ross with a slight grin.

"Excuse me, my submarines may be small, but they are not antiques, and they are fully operational at a moment's notice.

I have a skipper and a complete crew always on site. As far as housing your squads I will have the good china washed, and the silver polished for when they arrive." Commander Ross answered with a prideful smile.

"Good! I will order two of my best squads transported to Melusine tomorrow. Equipped for either land or sea assault. Inform the base on their needs."

Gaston nodded firmly.

"I assure you, Commander, whatever we order them to do, my commandos, the men you trained, can execute any operation with surgical precision. Adélard Squad will not be left holding the short end of the stick on this mission."

"Thank You." Commander Ross answered.

"I do think the attack will come most likely from the sea. If I was transporting 15 or 20 men as a mercenary, I wouldn't do it by air."

Standing up Commander Ross paced across the room.

"Too many obstacles in passing multination security bottlenecks and it is almost impossible to bring along serious weapons." Commander Ross added diving into the mission.

"Agreed, most likely they will use overland routes avoiding any boarder inspections to a Mediterranean port somewhere along the coast between Spain and Italy, most likely closer to Italy and then acquire some form of indiscreet boat for the attack." Gaston added, formulating his thoughts.

"We should inform your squads to be ready and equipped for a ship assault. If we are to attempt to keep this as low profile as possible, best we blow it out of the water. Accidents do happen, don't they?" Ross asked rhetorically.

Rousseau House

Adélard stood up walking around the table, his eyes locked on each member of his squad. "We need to think like them, we must put ourselves in their shoes, plan an attack on this island ourselves considering the resources that we would have available as them. They have a clear mission, to kill the Bugatti's and we are in their way. It will be far better to overestimate than to underestimate their abilities."

Adélard's paused sitting back down his words hung in the air, the weight of the situation sinking in.

"Gentlemen, I believe we need to prepare for two possible attack scenarios. First, let's assume the make their way onto the island with or without us realizing it and that they are planning for an all-out frontal ground assault designed to overpower Mr. Bugatti's security measures, eliminate any resistance, and cause as much destruction as possible enroute to murdering his family."

"Second, that all the above is true, but they also plan an additional assault from the sea either to back up the main plan or using the main attack as a diversion."

"I think, the second possibility is even more dangerous." Jojo commented. "They could feign a powerfully frontal assault while secretly planning a stealthy attack on the most challenging part of the compound. A place most would not expect an attack to be coming from . . . the cliff."

"If we were them, we would assume it would be the least protected due to its natural defense."

Graham nodded in agreement, "It's a classic diversion tactic, trying to draw attention away from their true objective."

"That would mean a water team scaling the cliff and entering the compound from the rear." Adélard added.

Jojo raised his hand and jumped in. "It doesn't matter if they plan that approach or not. It would be the smart move on their part. We need to establish a defensive plan for the back of the house and be ready to fight simultaneously two battles. One at the back and one at the front of the house. The sides I believe are safe considering the property."

Adélard nodded in the affirmative. "Exactly Jojo. Strengthen our defenses, set up surveillance systems, and be ready to counter any attack from either direction or both."

Adélard's eyes scanned the room, looking at each member of his squad. "We can't afford to underestimate them. They are hired professionals, killers. If they are here to harm the Bugatti family, they won't hesitate to use any means necessary to achieve their goal."

* * *

Bugatti Conference Room

"Gaston, you mentioned the possibility of taking the Warlord alive. Do you think that's even feasible? The Vice Admiral was pretty clear on what he wanted." Ross asked.

Gaston paused, considering the possibility. "It won't be easy, but if we can . . . the intel he could provide would be invaluable. He could be our Rosetta Stone to other terrorist organizations and gun smugglers. We could dismantle entire networks with that information."

"The benefit to keeping him alive is real, but not so real or important as to put our men at risk or gain transparency. Making the news invading a foreign power that is not exactly friendly with us to kill one of their own will not look good on our resume's." Commander Ross warned.

Gaston leaned back in his chair, a thoughtful expression on his face. " Gérard is working on a plan. To pull this off without revealing our identity as French commandos, we will need to rely on our intelligence assets on the ground. Local contacts who can provide support. We may also need to disguise our presence as something else entirely."

Ross considered the options. "Yes, that could work. We can collaborate with local contacts to maintain our anonymity. But we'll need to rely on others not to compromise our mission. That never makes me feel comfortable."

"Before we arrived here, Gérard Constantin, Senior Operations Officer Bérets Verts started working on an attack plan for this Warlord. He has an intel team nearby and two assault teams on the way."

Gaston paused to light a cigarette. "Gérard is an excellent field commander and a true warrior. His preparation and planning are the best I have ever been around. I promise you Commander, that the Warlord will not get away. Dead or alive he will never again kill innocent people!"

As the two naval officers continued to discuss the intricate details of the foreign mission, they both understood the gravity of the task ahead.

Taking down the warlord could have far-reaching implications for national and global security. They knew they couldn't leave anything to chance, the fate of countless lives rested on their shoulders.

Ross leaned forward; his eyes locked on the map spread out before them. "Gaston, we need to ensure that our attack on the warlord in the Congo is synchronized with the mercenaries' attack on Cavallo. If we move too fast in the Congo, it might interrupt the mercenaries attack temporarily. Right now, we have the advantage, we know who is attacking, why they are attacking, and where they are attacking. If the Congo mission erupts too early, we will lose that advantage."

Gaston nodded in agreement. "You're right, Ross. We can't afford any missteps. If our attack on the Warlord is not synchronized with the mercenaries' assault on the Bugatti family, it will give them a chance to regroup and evade capture."

"Exactly." Ross replied firmly. "If the mercenaries are busy executing their plan on Cavallo, they'll be less likely to notice our actions in the Congo until it's too late."

I will inform Gérard not to launch his attack until we give him, the clear to engage signal." Gaston said tapped his fingers on the table, deep in thought. "Coordinating two operations of this scale won't be easy, but I believe it's doable. We have to rely on our intelligence to provide real-time updates on the mercenaries' movements and adjust our timing accordingly."

Ross reached out shaking Gaston's hand firmly. "Let's make it happen. The Bugatti family and a lot of innocents in the Congo are depending on us. We can't let them down."

"We won't." Gaston replied with determination.

Commander Gaston leaned back in his chair, a hint of satisfaction in his voice. "The element of surprise will be on our side. We've trained our men well, and they are more than capable of executing these missions."

"Let's get to dinner. Maybe even catch Armand in the bar room beforehand." Commander Ross suggested.

"Heard." Gaston answered standing up.

* * *

Rousseau house

Mr. Bugatti's butler, who had been silently eavesdropping from just beyond the entrance, spoke up. "If I may, monsieur . . ." Hearing words from an unidentified source caused all six men to jump up and race towards the door, only to immediately come to a screeching halt as François poked his head around the corner.

"François!!!! You retarded son of a mannequin. You almost got yourself killed. Never, never ever sneak up on commandos." Jojo yelled, being the closest while poking his index finger repeatedly into the butler's chest emphasizing each syllable.

"Please stop Sir." François asked without losing any of his haute attitude.

Adélard walked up and smiled. "At ease Jojo. Until evidence proves otherwise, we shall consider François a friendly."

"Ok Adélard." Jojo said, turning his back on the butler and walking back catching a high five and a wink from Noel.

"Welcome, François, what brings you to our little gathering?" Adélard asked.

"I came to inform you that this being a very small and exclusive island many estates have staff. I would also remind you that nothing stays hidden from staff for very long."

"Oh, you mean, they all have big ears like you?" Henri asked rhetorically.

Ignoring the quip, he continued. "Therefore, I am here to volunteer their eyes and the ears to aid in your intelligence gathering. Truly little can happen on this island without my brethren seeing or knowing about it. Mr. Bugatti is well respected and beloved on this Island, and you will learn that many are . . . what did you call me - oh yes - you will find many are friendly(s)."

"We could use some experienced human intel, Adélard." Graham noted.

"These folks see and hear everything Adélard." Henri added. "Very well François, we accept your offer. Tell your friends to coordinate any intel with Graham. Is that understood?"

"Yes, Commander Adélard, quite clear."

"One more thing, when the shit hits the fan, your friends need to find cover and stay out of the way, you included François. We have enough Heros already."

"Yes, Commander Adélard, quite clear."

"Is it time to eat yet? My ribs are starting to show." Jojo asked, pulling up his shirt and sucking in his belly.

"Monsieur Jojo, please cover yourself. Dinner will be served in 16 minutes." François responded.

"Fine." Adélard answered standing up laughing.

"Julio help Henri lock up the weapons."

"Can I take a gun to dinner?" Jojo asked grinning.

"Mr. Bugatti's children will be joining you for dinner this evening. Your presence, monsieur Jojo will be traumatic enough for them. I recommend you do not come armed as well." François stated with a straight face causing everyone to laugh.

"Let's go to dinner guys." Adélard ordered grinning.

Chapter 3: Dinner and Drinks

Commander Ross and Gaston sat in comfortable overstuffed leather chairs enjoying a cocktail with Armand and Isabella, his wife. The cool drinks mixed with the soft lighting created a relaxed and comfortable ambiance, a brief respite from the seriousness that surrounded them.

"So, Armand, I hear you have quite a collection of vintage cars." Commandant Gaston remarked, trying to steer the conversation beyond the obvious.

Armand's eyes sparkled with enthusiasm. "Ah, yes, it's a bit of an obsession." He admitted with a smile. "There is just something about the craftsmanship and beauty of those classic automobiles that captivates me."

Isabella, who had been quietly listening, chimed in. "He is not kidding you Commandant. Our garage at home looks like a museum of automotive history!"

Loving the topic as much as his cars, Armand's eyes lit up as he described each vintage beauty in his collection, its history and how he came about finding and acquiring them.

"Tell them about your latest." Isabella softly told Armand while winking at the officers.

"My Latest?" Armand said laughing.

"Well gentlemen, for my birthday, my friend Elon Musk sent me the most extraordinary gift this year."

Isabella's eyes sparkled enjoying the moment while chiding her husband.

"Go ahead Armand, tell them about it. You know you're dying to."

"Elon sent me a special Tesla." Armand replied with a grin.

"A top-of-the-line Model S with all the latest bells and whistles. Painted in a stunning mirror deep navy blue with a luxurious tobacco leather interior."

Commander Ross was surprised and clearly impressed.

"That sounds fabulous Armand!"

"Just the thought of it, the living heir to the Bugatti automobile empire driving a Tesla had to make Elon smile."

"Agreed, it's a wonder he didn't put my photo in his new advertising campaign. Sadly, there is a problem with the automobile." Armand continued, looking at Isabella with a playful glint in his eye.

Isabella raised an eyebrow, already anticipating Armand's complaint. "And what would that be my husband?"

"I never get to drive it!" Armand exclaimed, feigning exasperation. "Do not be deceived Commanders by my wife's sweet continence and sophisticated persona. She is a blatant car thief! Every time I want to take the Tesla for a spin, it's already gone."

The table erupted in laughter, as Isabella playfully nudged Armand's shoulder. Armand chuckled, wrapping an arm around Isabella's shoulders. "One of these days, I will catch you off guard and sneak away with it."

Isabella grinned mischievously. "Challenge accepted, my love."

Just as the conversation reached a comfortable lull, François, the butler, entered the barroom. "Messieurs et ma dame, dinner is served."

As they rose from their seats, the relaxed atmosphere shifted slightly. Armand looked towards Isabella and then at the officers with a gracious smile. "Shall we?"

As they walked towards the dining room, their brief conversation had allowed them a fleeting moment of normalcy in the midst of their extraordinary circumstances.

* * *

The setting sun cast a magical glow through the tall, elegant windows of the dining room. Adélard's men took their seats next to Ross and Gaston joining Armand Bugatti, his wife Isabella, and their twin daughters, Reine, and Taber.

Respectful of Armands request to not discuss military matters in front his daughter, the men quietly enjoyed the delicious food as the stewards served them. Recognizing the unnatural and somewhat nervous silence Isabella began regaling everyone with stories of her daughters' accomplishments.

"Reine has always had a passion for horses." She said with pride. "My Reine has been taking riding lessons since she was 5 years old. Recently she and her horse Isis, have started training for show competitions.

"I love horses." Noel blurted out between bites.

"Reine, I look forward to watching you during the dressage competition at the Olympics." Graham said to Armands daughter smiling.

"Isis does all the work Monsieur Graham." Reine shyly spoke up.

"Excuse me but no dear girl. I have spent many a day upon my own horse outside of Paris riding the hills and trails. Your Isis would be happy nibbling the sweet grasses that sprout up after the rain. It is you Reine that motivates her, it is you she learns from, it is you and no one else that gives her grace." Graham said softly with a loving voice.

Reine smiled from ear to ear and leaned in as her mother Isabella reached down to kiss her head, never taking her eyes from Graham.

"You will not need to wait for the Olympics to watch a Bugatti compete Graham." Armand added proudly. "Taber is also a lively and accomplished athlete."

Taber smiled hearing the praise from her father, chimed in. "I'm playing third base for the national youth softball team! I can't wait for the upcoming championship tournament."

Isabella's eyes lit up with pride hearing Taber speak about her sports exploits. "Oh, and we mustn't forget to tell you about Taber's latest adventure." Isabella said with a smile. "Taber has taken up winter skiing! She has already moved up to black diamond rated slopes."

"I tried to keep up with her." Reine interrupted. "But Taber is fearless, she jumps the moguls like she has wings."

Jojo, ever the enthusiastic adventurer, could not resist joining the conversation. "Actually, I used to be an instructor at my parents' ski resort." He revealed with a grin. "Tell you the truth Reine, I rode down many a slope on my backside."

Taber laughed at Jojo's admission. "I still get a mouth full of snow now and then Monsieur Joeux."

"You can call me Jojo, Taber. All my friends do. Maybe someday, we can fly down the slopes together. I usually avoid hitting any trees, but I am not making any guarantees." Jojo said smiling, his usual witty remark causing Taber and Reine to both laugh aloud.

Isabella's eyes shone with gratitude as she looked at the young commando. "Thank you, Monsieur Jojo." I hope that someday is soon."

Commander Ross smiled warmly at the Bugatti's "Your daughters are both exceptional young women, as are their parents." He said sincerely.

Gaston stood up from the table, motioning for all the commandos to do so.

GHOST COMMANDO – Battle for Cavallo

"A Toast then." He said lifting his glass. "To Armand and Isabella Bugatti, to their two beautiful daughters Reine and Taber. And to the spirt of France that flows through their veins. Vive Bugatti!"

"Vive Bugatti!" The commandos cheered with gusto.

* * *

Adélard's squad joined Armand and Commanders Ross and Commandant Gaston's, in Mr. Bugatti's private office after dinner, ready to continue the planning session.

"Adélard, please start us off, begin your briefing." Commander Ross said.

"Thank You Commander." Adélard answered.

"Working under the premise that the mercenaries targeting Mr. Bugatti's family are our equals in training and skills, we have developed what we believe will be their mission plan."

"First, we are assuming they either have or will have people on the island doing recon."

"Learning the patterns of the Bugatti family and identifying the strengths and weaknesses of the compound and any security measures that can be identified."

"Second, we believe that they will use overland transport from Pakistan to somewhere along the coast."

"Then they will attempt their access to the island by boat."

"Lastly, we believe that the assault on the compound will be conducted on two fronts."

"The primary, a full-frontal assault seeking to break through the main gate and a second assault in the most unlikely spot at the rear of the compound from the cliffs."

"We have a list of requests from the navy and a favor from Mr. Bugatti that we will need in preparation to defend this island and the Bugatti family."

"Well done, Adélard. What are your requests?" Commandant Gaston asked impressed with the young man.

"Mr. Bugatti please arrange permission from Father Paulo for Graham to set up a communication/intelligence post in one of his underground spaces."

"We request Navy intelligence and other agencies needed to help us complete a list of every soul that should be on the island at this time. We will coordinate that data with locals and staff from other estates via François which has volunteered to act as the liaison with the local community."

"We request the Navy to assign a thermal imaging drone for our exclusive use during the mission maintained and operated from the mainland. With all data synchronized with Graham at our intel center. The purpose of the drone is twofold. One to help identify if the mercenaries have one or more people currently on the island doing recon and two to aid our forces during any attack which most likely with be under the cover of darkness."

"During the days prior to the assault, my squad will maintain the charade that we are Bugatti employees on vacation and do human intel collection on the ground and at sea in that manner. To do so we will need the Navy or Mr. Bugatti to arrange for at minimum 3 bicycles with trackers and a fishing boat to be at our disposal."

"We may have more needs moving forward but for now this is what we require." Adélard finished sitting down.

"What you need from me Adélard, you will have by tomorrow noon." Armand spoke up impressed and determined to be more than an observer.

"Well done. Adélard. My compliments to your entire squad." Commander Ross quickly added.

"Have you considered my wife and children Adélard?" Armand asked.

"Yes Armand, my thoughts are if the mercenaries have eyes on the island which we must assume they do, if we remove your family too early, they will redirect their efforts to follow them and attempt the assassination at another time."

"I believe your family must leave, but it must do so at the last possible safe moment in a covert manner. Most probably by boat in the dark of night."

"I do promise you Armand . . . any that come here intent on harming you or your family will not leave this island except in shackles or in a body bag."

"That sir is another reason we need the thermal drone at all times. The moment we identify the incursion on the island is underway you and your family will leave with all haste on one of your fastest boats in the hidden cove."

"We will have intel tech on the cove starting tomorrow but we need to have your personnel rotating there 24 hours a day asap to protect your exit. I recommend that all your armed personnel accompany you."

"If you wish Armand, I will have my boat master bring one of the Requin boats brought to your cove. They are armored, well-armed and faster than anything in the med. You and your family will be safe there." Commander Ross said to his friend.

"Thank you, Ross. I will take you up on that." Armand answered solemnly.

"With the thermal drone overhead and the swarm drones you have sent us. I will be able to track and identify any of our targets in real time. This will give us an advantage during any battle." Graham spoke up to aid Adélard.

"What of weapons Adélard?" Commander Ross asked.

"You have supplied us with all the light weapons my squad could possibly use. Heavy guns would add a sense of security but would devastate the island which is not what Mr. Bugatti, or the Navy would like to see happen, Sir."

"Agreed. So, nothing more?" Ross asked.
"Well, more ammo is always a good thing Sir." Adélard said.

Gaston leaned forward; his eyes fixed on Adélard. "Adélard, what if I were to tell you that there are 20 or more bad boys coming to crash your party?"

Adélard looked squarely at Commander Gaston, his face serious, his eyes clear and focused. "I would tell you to have two more squads in the air ready to helo jump onto this island and to bring body bags."

"If they come by water Adélard, commander Ross and I have already ordered a submarine and two commando squads to be ready at camp Melusine."

"I can assure you that boat will also never leave this island. With those men and the men, you requested for a helo assault, you will have 4 full commando squads to defend this island." Commandant Gaston informed him.

"Thank you, Sir." Adélard answered.
"Give me a moment gentleman. I want to contact Toulon and get two drones and their operators ready and communicating with Graham asap." Commandant Gaston told them standing up to leave the room.

"Adélard, you need to know. I am not leaving my Island." Armand softly told him.

"Excuse me Armando, but I do not agree. You would be much safer with Isabella and the girls." Adélard insisted.
"That is true mon ami, but safer is not always best." Armand responded by putting a hand on Adélard's shoulder.

"Why Armand?" Commander Ross asked.

"Because my friends." Armand began by looking at all the commandos in the room.

"Each of you is prepared to risk your life to protect my family. What kind of man would I be to desert you when the shooting starts."

"No, my friends, those men are coming for me, and I intend for them to find me."

"If you ever get tired of being a billionaire Armand, we might find an extra Green Beret for you." Jojo said smiling.

"I bet you would love my grenade launcher Armand." Noel said smiling.

* * *

François entered the room rolling a cart with coffee and petit sweets. "By the way gentlemen I intend to be here as well."

"Do you eavesdrop on everything that goes in this house, François?" Henri asked smiling.

"Yes, Monsieur Henri I do, although the bathroom doors have proven to be a bit difficult." François answered with the slightest smirk on his face causing Armand and all the men to laugh.

* * *

Commandant Gaston reentered the room as the laughter died down. Taking a cup of coffee from François, he sipped it and asked. "Do you have anything to sweeten this, maybe a good cognac or an American bourbon?"

"Certainly Sir." François answered and left to acquire them.

GHOST COMMANDO – Battle for Cavallo

"Good news gentlemen. By tomorrow morning we will have 3 high-definition thermal drones covering the island and the surrounding waters 24 hours a day."

"A squad of special forces commandos on a fast attack helicopter are being redirected to camp Melusine to be briefed on the mission and await further orders and last but not least a full intel team assigned to work with Graham to lock down every soul on this island and assist during any combat operations." Commandant Gaston told the men prideful at the response of his command.

* * *

"Sir if I may, can you brief us on the Congo mission?" Adélard asked.

"In a nutshell Adélard, Gérard Constantin our SOF is currently moving 5 full squads into the Congo as discreetly as possible. We have intel assets already on ground and in the air. As commander Ross and I discussed this afternoon, getting a fighting force in place is difficult although very doable. Eliminating the Warlord, his men and turning his headquarters into ruble is also very doable in a matter of minutes."

"Our main concern is that the Congo is not exactly a welcoming nation for us, and we might have a transparency problem which will cause everyone from TV talking heads to the UN condemning our actions."

"Monsieur Gaston. What if we turn the tables on this Warlord and hire our own Warlord to eliminate him?

"In business I have used this tactic between my competitors with great success." Armand suggested a thoughtful look on his face.

"He has a valid point sir." Adélard added. "Under the cover of two Warlords fighting a turf war, our forces can eliminate all our targets, destroy the facility, and walk away with none the wiser. Even our pay for the day Warlord would not know it was us helping them along."

"And Sir." Henri added. "The Warlord we hire will be enriched not only by our money, but also by the demise of our target. Regardless, it would put less of our men at risk and be a much cleaner operation."

Armand spoke up again. "Gaston, I can supply whatever financial resources that are required."

"There is merit in this idea Gaston." Commander Ross stated firmly.

Commandant Gaston listened carefully, absorbing every detail of the proposed idea. "I will speak with the Admiral and Commander Gérard. I like the idea of creating a Warlord-to-Warlord fight to cover our action."

"The timing of both these events is critical. We need to strike the Congo warlord at the same time as the attack on the island. That will be on you Graham." Gaston said firmly. "If we strike the Congo too early, the mercenaries might be spooked and abort the mission only to try another day."

"Our best chance to prevent mission creep as the Vice Admiral loves to say is to eliminate everything and everyone at the same time leaving as little transparency as possible."

Adélard and the squad nodded in agreement, fully understanding the importance of coordination. They knew that any delay could allow the mercenaries to slip through their fingers, putting innocent lives at risk.

François entered the room quietly walking up to Commandant Gaston.

"Well said Sir."
"Cognac?"

Chapter 4: Never too Early

The first rays of dawn kissed the open window on the second floor of the Rousseau guest house. Adélard l' ombre as usual was already up, standing at the bathroom sink with a razor in hand, carefully shaving his beard. The soft sound of running water filled the air causing Graham to stir in his bed.

"Adélard, do you have to make so much noise this early?" Graham half-joked, his voice laced with sleepiness.

Adélard chuckled, glancing over at his friend. "Sorry, Graham. I will use quieter water next time."

As Adélard continued to shave, there was a soft knock on the door. "Who the hell could that be?" Adélard questioned walking across the room wiping the shaving cream from his face with a towel.

"We did pay the rent this month. Didn't we?" Graham asked pulling a pillow over his head.

Opening the door, he discovered François, Mr. Bugatti's butler, standing there with a polite smile.

"Good morning, François." Adélard said finishing to wipe his face and throwing the towel over his shoulder.

"Good morning, Sir." François greeted him. "Please forgive the hour, but Monsieur Bugatti ask if you and Mr. Graham would join him on the pool deck before breakfast."

"Certainly François." Adélard assured him.

"And you Mr. Graham?" François asked, tilting his head looking past Adélard.

Graham poked his head out from under the covers glancing at the clock, rubbing his eyes. "Yes, yes I will be there." Graham answered. "Give me a minute."

François nodded and left the room, closing the door behind him. Adélard exchanged a glance with Graham, who was now fully awake. "Coffee by the pool doesn't sound too bad." Graham said, getting out of bed stretching his arms.

* * *

Armand Bugatti was seated at an ornate metal table enjoying the picturesque view of the ocean from his pool deck as the men walked across the lawn.

"Good morning, gentlemen." Armand greeted them with a friendly smile as they approached. "Please, have a seat." As the steward poured the coffee, Adélard couldn't help but admire the calmness Armand demonstrated even under the fear of losing all that he loved.

Now alone Armand set down his cup and looked at Adélard and Graham with seriousness in his eyes. "I destroyed a warehouse and half a dock to keep a Warlord from harming innocent people. Soon those that same evil will be here."

Armand paused to look over the horizon before continuing. "I do not care what you need to do, what you need to destroy. I want those men to no longer share the air my children breathe. I want my family and this island protected no matter the cost. Do I make myself clear gentlemen?"

"Yes Armand." Adélard answered, for both of them.

"I am concerned that with you at the church Graham, Adélard will only have a 5 man team to defend this island, until reinforcements arrive."

"It must start that way Armand, or the mercenaries will abort the mission and come hunting you and your family at another time, maybe at a different place. We have the advantage at this moment. We know the who, we know the place, we know the target, and with Graham running our intel we will precisely know the time." Adélard explained.

"The window will be tight Mr. Bugatti. There is no sugar coating the danger or the possibility of loss of life." Graham solemnly added.

Armand nodded his head in understanding, taking a long drink of his coffee again looking out past the horizon then placing his cup delicately in its saucer before responding.

"Well then Adélard, what is the first order of business? Armand asked.

"I need you and Graham to secure permission from Father Paulo at the church and establish our intel and communication center. "

"I need one of your vehicles for Henri and Jojo to place motion detectors and cameras at locations on the island and approaching your grounds according to a site map Graham and I developed earlier."

"I need those bicycles we spoke of last night for Julio to begin doing some undercover reconnaissance."

"Until Graham can give us some assurance that there are no mercs on the island we must all act as if we are being watched."

"What about guns Adélard?" Armand asked.

"Tourist and house guest don't walk around with assault rifles and leg holsters, so I am instructing my men and recommending you keep the Beretta 9mm you gifted us in waist holsters clipped in back where they are hidden."

If they are discovered by accident having, your logo on them will support the charade that we are all nothing more than your employees on vacation at the boss's house." Adélard answered.

"I have a convertible Volkswagen Beetle that my staff uses to run around the island for supplies. Have Jojo and Henri use that. It will fit the charade. Father Paulo holds mass every morning at 7am. I will go with Graham after breakfast and speak with him. Do not worry Father Paulo is a good man that understand the real world. He will be on our side in this." Armand assured.

"And the bicycles? Oh . . . and a fishing boat?"

"The fishing boat I will arrange before breakfast, the bicycles will take a little longer unless you want Julio to be peddling Tabers. I will have 3 adult bikes brought over later today from the mainland." Armand answered.

"Well then gentlemen, and with your permission Armand, let's get to it." Adélard said as the three men stood up to walk inside.

"You and Armand go ahead. I got a call coming in from intel at Toulon." Graham said sitting back down answering his phone.

* * *

As they walked side by side Adélard paused to look again at the beautiful ground of the mansion. "Armand that pool of yours has a clear view of the grounds all the way to the cliffs edge."

"That is true Adélard. Why? What are you thinking?" Armand asked.

"I am thinking one Ghost Commando could ambush an entire squadron from your pool and I have the perfect man for the job." Adélard answered.

"Ghost Commando?" Armand asked.
Laughing Adélard patted Armand on the back.
"I will explain later mon ami."

* * *

As Adélard finished his breakfast, François approached him with a polite bow and said softly. "Monsieur Adélard." He began. "There are two American gentlemen in the living room waiting to meet you.

Curious, Adélard excused himself and followed François to the living room, where he found two older men waiting. By their looks they were both about his father's age, physically imposing, with a no nonsense look about them.

"Monsieur Adélard, may I present Adam and David."

Adélard shook their hands firmly, immediately sensing the quiet strength in their grip. "Pleased to meet you both." He said with a nod. "What brings you to the Bugatti estate?"

Adam, a rugged man with a beard and piercing eyes, replied. "We've been informed about the situation here. Our employer, Mr. Musk, decided we should avail ourselves of some of our PTO time for the next few weeks."

"Since neither of us likes fishing we thought you might like another pair of operatives already emersed in the island culture."

"As I may have mentioned, monsieur Adélard, there are few secrets on this island." François reminded him.

David, equally imposing but with a kind smile, added. "Adam and I have worked together for many years, both in the military and in civilian security."

"We are not here for fame or money." Adam added his expression serious. "We're here to support you and ensure the safety of the Bugatti family and this island. Full stop!" Steeping closer David looked Adélard square in the eyes. "We are ready to face whatever comes our way. Count on us for your 6."

Adélard was immediately impressed by their straightforwardness and experience. "Thank you for stepping up." Adélard said sincerely. "Let's meet at 1400 in the Rousseau guest house and discuss this further."

"Graham, were you listening in?" Adélard asked.

"Yes Adélard, the whole squad was, hard not to with these plugs in our ears." Jojo added.

"Good to know you guys missed me. Graham, run these two down, you know as much as I do. See what you can find out." Adélard asked.

"Heard." Graham responded.

* * *

Armand and Graham drove towards Father Paulo's church in his perfectly restored 1951 Bugatti Type 101 sedan, Armand couldn't help but reminisce about the car.

"You know, Graham." Armand began, a glimmer of pride in his voice. "This car was a turning point for my family's company after the war years. It played a crucial role in rebooting our legacy."

Graham glanced over at Armand. "Please tell me more."

Armand smiled, the memories flooding back. "After the war, Bugatti was facing financial struggles." He explained. "Our factory was taken over during the occupation, and Bugatti as a company was severely disrupted."

"Once the war ended, my family was determined to revive the company's reputation for exquisite craftsmanship and engineering prowess.

Revving the engine over a small hill Armand winked at Graham before continuing.

GHOST COMMANDO – Battle for Cavallo

"Enter this car, the Bugatti Type 101." Armand continued.

"The 101 was a lady, the embodiment of luxury. A grand touring car that boasted a beautiful sensual design and exceptional performance."

"She certainly is magnificent. I never expected for us to be using a car like her today." Graham commented running his hand over the dash in appreciation.

"This car is close to my heart." Armand said with a smile. "It represents the resilience and passion that runs through my bloodline. Isabella says it's just another old car, but to me it represents the heart of Bugatti and everything I am."

The two men shared a moment of quiet admiration for the car's history as they parked outside Father Paulo's church. The Bugatti Type 101, an emblem of the Bugatti family's endurance, sat proudly amidst the surrounding landscape. Little did they know that it would soon embark on a journey of further significance as they continued to face the impending threat together.

* * *

As Armand and Graham stepped into Father Paulo's church, the priest greeted them warmly. "Ah, Monsieur Bugatti and Monsieur Graham, what brings you to my humble church today?" Father Paulo asked, a hint of curiosity in his eyes.

Graham wasted no time and began describing the imminent threat the island was facing. "Father, we have reason to believe that mercenaries are planning to attack the island. Their intention is to kill Mr. Bugatti and his entire family." He explained, concern evident in his voice.

Father Paulo's face grew serious as he absorbed the gravity of the situation. "Mio Dio! Questo è impensabile." He blurted out in his beloved Italian. "Ask of me anything. This cannot be allowed to happen."

Armand nodded solemnly. "That's why we've come to you Paulo. We need your assistance in securing a location for Graham to establish a command center. A secure place away from the mansion, where he can monitor the island, gather intelligence, and coordinate our efforts to safeguard my family and all the island's inhabitants."

"Yes, my son, with that I can help you. But I cannot allow my church to become a house of weapons." Paulo said with concern.

"No, father. There will be no weapons stored here. My sidearm will be the only weapon near your church I promise." Graham offered.

Father Paulo considered their request thoughtfully. "I understand the need for such a location. Fortunately for all of us, this church has a long history with the Knights Templar, and beneath us lies a network of tunnels."

"One of which you have seen Mr. Graham that I use as my document room, but there are many more, some of which have remained untouched for centuries."

Armand and Graham exchanged glances, intrigued by the revelation. "You mean there is more than just that one? Graham asked, surprised.

"Yes." Father Paulo confirmed. "There is an entire tunnel system under our feet. The Knights Templar once used these tunnels for various purposes, including protection and secrecy. I believe they can serve that purpose again for you."

With Father Paulo holding a flashlight and leading the way, the trio made their way to a hidden entrance and descended into a dark and ancient tunnel, and as they walked, the damp stone walls seemed to tell stories of ages past. After a long walk, they arrived at a spacious chamber deep underground.

Father Paulo gestured around them. "This chamber is one of the best-preserved parts of the tunnel system. We are directly beneath the church graveyard. I think this will be suitable for you as it has a separate secure entrance there." He pointed to an equally old yet impressive door. "That is well hidden at the surface."

Armand looked impressed. "This is beyond perfect Paulo. With this location, we can ensure Graham has a safe and strategic vantage point to protect the island."

"Graham text me a list of everything you need here, and I will have my people help you set up tonight after sunset." Armand stated, as he quickly diagnosed the actions required. A personal trait for which he was famous.

Father Paulo nodded in agreement. "It is my duty and my pleasure to protect the people of this island." Paulo said, bowing his head, offering a silent benediction for the mission Armand and Graham had before them.

"Miei cari figli, you have my full support."

Armand and Graham thanked Father Paulo profusely for his assistance and guidance. With the underground command center secured, they knew they had taken the first crucial step in preparing for the looming threat.

Leaving the church, Armand made an unexpected offer. "Would you like to drive her, Graham?" Before he could even answer Armand tossed him the keys. "Once around the block my brave Commando. Don't spare the horsepower, this lady likes to let her hair down."

* * *

"The church is secure Adélard. It is an amazing, perfect location for our command center." Graham reported.

"Excellent." Adélard answered feeling better at the sound of any positive news. "Toulon informed me Drones will be up and running by night fall and that additional monitoring and communication equipment is inbound by Helo. Eta 1300."

* * *

Adélard found Commandant Gaston sitting alone at a corner table inside Mr. Bugatti's barroom. "You asked to see me Sir?"

"At ease, Adélard. Please sit down." Gaston said taking a sip of his drink while leaning back into his chair, his gaze serious.

"Adélard, I want to inform you of steps I have put into motion for the extraction of the Bugatti family."

Putting the glass down, Gaston leaned in closer to Adélard, his voice hushed but filled with authority.

"As soon as we receive confirmation that the mercenaries have left Pakistan and are enroute to this island, I have ordered Master Philippe to bring one of the Requin boats to the Bugatti Cove. On board will be a full squad of my seasoned Commandos whose primary mission is to secure the cove and the road leading there. That door must remain open for any extraction to work."

Adélard's eyes narrowed, acknowledging the importance of protecting the cove. "Understood." He replied, his mind racing already processing the logistics. "I'll inform my squad to cooperate fully with Captain Philippe and offer whatever support he might require from us."

"Once the Bugatti family and personnel are safely on board the Requin, I have ordered four members of my squad, trained in the offensive firepower of the boat, to accompany Mrs. Bugatti. Those men, with that boat will be capable of delivering a lethal response to any potential threats."

"And the remaining two members?" Adélard asked.

Gaston's gaze remained unwavering. "They will be under your command and assigned to reinforce your squad."

Adélard took a moment to absorb the information. "The timing will be most important Sir. Too early we may endanger the family in the future. Too late and we endanger them today."

"You understand the issue well Mr. Adélard." Commandant Gaston said leaning in closer, his voice low and confidential even thought they were alone.

"Adélard, there is a change in plan. I have decided the Requin boat will not be taking the Bugatti family to the naval base at Toulon as originally planned. Instead, I have decided to send it to my home in the south of Corsica."

Adélard's eyes widened in surprise as Gaston revealed his plan. "Redirecting the Requin boat to your home in Corsica? We are weeks away sir. Isn't it too early to make these changes?" He asked, trying to grasp the implications of the decision.

"No Adélard it is not. It's never too early to be prepared. This information is strictly need-to-know." Gaston emphasized. "Only you, me, and Armand are aware of this change in plan. Not even Master Philippe on the boat will be informed until they are out at sea away from Cavallo."

Adélard nodded once more. "Yes Sir. Understood."
"Good. This is a delicate situation for many reasons, but I trust my wife Genevieve to take care of the Bugatti's and keep them safe."

Adélard's eyes widened even further in amazement as he absorbed the revelation. "Wait, Genevieve is your wife?" He exclaimed, unable to hide his surprise. "And those two girls, Sylvie and Arlette, are your daughters?"

Gaston nodded, a faint smile tugging at the corner of his lips. "Yes, Adélard they are. My family is my everything Adélard."

The officer paused to take another sip of his drink, which by now Adélard realized was not water and spoke volumes to the tension within his Commandant.

GHOST COMMANDO – Battle for Cavallo

"Adélard, one day you will come to understand, our profession is a dangerous one. We make enemies along the way. I keep my family's existence on a need-to-know basis to protect them, and I expect you to keep my secret as well."

Regaining his focus on the mission Gaston continued.

"I am risking my own family with this change in plans. Taking Isabella and the children to Toulon is too obvious. If it was you or me leading the mercs we would be prepared for that. We can't risk any potential ambush from secondary mercenary assets. Genevieve's home on the south of Corsica is secure, and she'll be able to provide the Bugatti family with the protection and the care they need."

Adélard nodded, understanding the gravity of the situation. "Understood Commandant." He said earnestly. "Your family's anonymity is safe with me."

Adélard took a deep breath, feeling the weight of the responsibility placed upon him. He admired Gaston's strategic thinking and dedication to protecting his family.

"Sir, you are a remarkable man. I am humbled that you have honored me with your trust."

"That honor young man will most certainly put you in harm's way." Gaston told him, finishing his drink. "Reports are the merc force coming is large and well-armed."

"Are you ready for the shitstorm coming our way Adélard?"

"Yes Sir. I am!"

Chapter 5: Enemy of my Enemy

The Bugatti once tranquil estate now buzzed with an air of urgency and anticipation. A large Naval helicopter, adorned with the French flag, had just landed on the helipad, its rotors still spinning as Graham and Adélard approached.

Graham's eyes widened in amazement as the side door opened and he saw the abundance of electronics and communication equipment loaded inside the helicopter.

Captain Auclair stepped out smiling. "Adélard, Graham, good to see you both again!"
"Captain Auclair, always a pleasure. Thank you for coming." Adélard said, reaching out his hand.
"Indeed, thank you, Captain." Graham added, unable to take his eyes from the boxes inside the helicopter.

Captain Auclair turned to the two naval officers now standing at his side. "Allow me to introduce Lieutenant Dupont and Lieutenant Laurent, both from the Counterintelligence Division. They will be staying here during the rest of the mission. Their orders are to assist Graham with surveillance and communication."

Lieutenant Dupont extended his hand to both Adélard and Graham. "We look forward to working together gentlemen."

Lieutenant Laurent followed, shaking both their hands, and added. "Yes, Captain Auclair has told us you youngsters are a bit special. Calls you the Ghost Squad."

Adélard answered grinning." Welcome to the dance Sirs."

Lieutenant Dupont spoke directly to Graham, his voice formal and yet friendly. "We've been briefed on the situation and have some valuable intel to share. But first, let's get the equipment unloaded and to your command center. We only had broad strokes on the requirements for this mission so we brought everything Toulon would let us steal."

"Yes Sir. But first you will need to change out of those uniforms and lose the weapons. Our orders are not to invade this Island and scare the locals, but to operate as Bugatti employees on holiday." Adélard firmly told them.

"See what I told you Lieutenant, this boy is no tadpole." Captain Auclair said smiling at Adélard.

* * *

Commandant Gaston and Armand approached the helicopter in deep conversation, their voices low and determined. They both looked up seeing the five men gathered, giving them a nod of acknowledgement.

"These are my two new house guest I presume." Armand whispered. "They are good men Armand; you will like them." Gaston answered back quietly.

* * *

"Ah, there you are." Gaston said loudly his hand held wide apart, gesturing towards the men. "This is all for you, Graham. The navy has pulled out all the stops to help you set up and operate the Bugatti command center." Turning to smile at the two officers Gaston added. "I picked these two officers out myself Graham. Lieutenants Dupont and Laurent are fellow techy super nerds so I think you will all get along just fine." He finished smiling.

"Yes Sir. Thank you, Sir." Graham said as the rest of the men chuckled.

* * *

The sun was high in the sky warming the winter chill on the island as Graham and the two officers arrived at the church.

"Father Paulo, it's good to see you again. Thank you for welcoming us to your church." Graham said smiling. "This is Lieutenant Dupont and Lieutenant Laurent. They are both with the Navy and they will be helping for the duration of the mission here at your church."

Father Paulo smiled warmly. "You are always welcome here, my son. Do your friends know the rules?"
"Yes Father, no uniforms or weapons."

"Grazie mio dolce Ragazzo! Now let me show you the way."

As they walked through the peaceful graveyard, Father Paulo leads the men to a small mausoleum covered with ivy. Pressing a concealed stone, the wall swings open, revealing a narrow passage leading underground.

"This is quite impressive, Father." Lieutenant Laurent commented. "The Knights were very serious about keeping their secrets hidden." Graham added as they entered.

Father Paulo chuckled. "Indeed, they were. Now, follow me, but be careful, the steps they are far older than me." A large chamber came into view, illuminated by soft candlelight. Father Paulo had hung tapestries on some of the walls making it feel more inviting and much quieter than Graham's last visit. "Wow." The officers said almost as one.

"Thank you, Father, you have outdone yourself." Graham said in all honesty.

"This is incredible. I never thought we'd be working from a Knights Templar transit station." Dupont whispered. "It's like stepping back in time." Lieutenant Laurent said in awe.

With the men ready to go back to the surface and get under way. Father Paulo stopped them for a moment of prayer and benediction. The men bowed their heads in silent prayer as Father Paulo voiced a benediction and asked for God's mercy and protection to these brave young men.

Later as they set up their equipment and prepared the command center, the men are struck by the weight of history and the significance of their task. This sacred place, once used to protect Christians from harm, would now be the heart of their efforts to protect innocent lives from evil.

Hours passed as the command center came alive with the hum of electronics and the chatter of communication. The sound of the portable generator hummed softly in the background and the led lamps added much needed light as they finished setting up and checking their equipment.

Graham was in his element, expertly navigating the equipment and setting up the surveillance network. Satisfied with their efforts Graham stopped, looking over the command center with pride.

"I'll say this, fellas. For a thousand-year-old grotto, this is as fine an example of a surveillance and communication center as I have ever seen."

"Agreed." The officers said standing next to him looking over their handy work. "What's next Mr. Graham."

"Showers and then Dinner at the mansion. You don't want to miss that, trust me! And for dessert we will come back here and put this stuff through its paces. I am anxious to link to the thermal drones and get eyes on this island."

"Come along Sirs." Graham said, leading the way up the stairs. "Mr. Bugatti does not like late comers to his table."

* * *

It had been a busy afternoon on the compound as men and supplies arrived and departed. Armand and Adélard stood watching from a distance, their eyes following the Naval helicopter as it lifted into the sky, its rotors slicing through the air until it disappeared.

"Quite a sight, isn't it?" Armand said, breaking the silence. "I always find helicopters fascinating."

Adélard nodded, a small smile playing on his lips. "They are useful, no doubt, but for me it always feels like I am a rock in the sky waiting to fall, only held in the air by magic and fairy wings."

"Magic and fairy wings? I will ask my pilot to look for those." Armand said laughing as they watched the Bugatti helicopter arrive and gently touch down.

Together the men walked towards the helicopter pad. Armand was obviously excited. He couldn't wait to show Adélard the surprises he had in store for him and his squad.

GHOST COMMANDO – Battle for Cavallo

Bugatti employees bustled around, unloading the 2 sleek and powerful Ducati Scrambler Night Shift black out motorcycles and 3 Ducati TK-01RR All Terrain E-Bikes. The five bikes gleamed under the afternoon sun, a testament to their Italian design and craftsmanship.

"These, my dear Mr. Adélard, are the latest offerings from Ducati." Armand said proudly. "They were more than happy to provide these bikes for us, considering our close friendship."

Adélard's eyes widened with surprise and admiration as he examined the bikes. "These are incredible." He remarked.
As Adélard stood in awe beside the Ducati motorcycles, Armand couldn't help but chuckle. "I thought your squad would appreciate not having to pedal so much." He said with a playful grin. "That's why I got you the all-terrain E-Bikes. And as for Graham, well, I figured he needed a fast way to get around, so the Night Shift motorcycle is for him."

Adélard laughed, shaking his head in amusement. "You always know exactly what needs to be done. These bikes will be incredibly helpful during our reconnaissance missions."

The Bugatti employees completed unloading and preparing the bikes, Adélard turned to Armand with a curious expression. "There are two of the Ducati Night Shift Motorcycles, what is the second one for?" He asked.

Armand's eyes twinkled mischievously. "For me, of course!" He replied, with a hint of excitement in his voice. "I couldn't resist the temptation. Don't tell Isabella."

Noel and Julio had joined them, seeing the excitement of the delivery. They stood chuckling at Armand's remark. Your secret is safe with us Mr. Bugatti." Julio spoke up smiling.

"Thank you, Armand." Adélard said sincerely. "These bikes are more than we could have asked for. They'll be put to good use, I assure you."

Just then, Jojo and Henri came running across the compound, their eyes widened with excitement as they saw the two sleek black Ducati motorcycles being unloaded from the helicopter. Jojo couldn't contain his enthusiasm and immediately jumped on one of the motorcycles. He looked up at Armand with a grin and said, "To support the mission readiness, Henri and I should field test the motorcycles first, don't you think?"

Armand and Adélard both chuckled at Jojo's unabashed boldness. "Go ahead, Jojo," Armand said, waving his arm towards the open gate. "Enjoy yourselves but be careful!"

Without wasting a moment, Jojo revved the engine, the powerful motor humming beneath him, and he zoomed off with Henri right behind him. The two men raced across the compound and out the open gate, the motorcycles effortlessly gliding through the terrain.

As the excitement settled, Adélard's phone buzzed, and he saw a text message from Commandant Gaston. He read the message and then looked up at Armand. " Commander Gérard wants to hold a video briefing update on the Congo mission at 1500," Adélard informed him. "He requests you and me to be present. It's a need-to-know briefing, so we'll need to find a secure location."

GHOST COMMANDO – Battle for Cavallo

* * *

1500 Armand's private office. Cavallo Island

Armand and Adélard were already waiting when Commander Ross and Commandant Gaston entered Armand's private office. The room was dimly lit, with the soft glow of the desk lamps casting a warm ambiance.

A large conference table dominated the center of the room, adorned with maps detailing all the structures on Cavallo Island. The men sat down saying few words recognizing the gravity of the moment. As the minutes passed, the tension in the room intensified. But the four men remained resolute, their focus unwavering.

Finally, the video call screen illuminated, signaling the arrival of Commander Gérard. The room fell silent once more as they eagerly waited for the Commander to speak.

"Good afternoon, gentlemen." Commander Gérard began. "I have positive news to report from our operatives in the Congo. We have been successful in locating a local Rebel leader who is willing to challenge the Warlord that poses a threat to Mr. Bugatti and his family. This leader is highly motivated and has strong support in the region. With our assistance, she can mount an effective attack.

"That's excellent news, Gérard." Armand said relieved. "Please, tell us more about this leader and the plan."

"Of course, Armand. The leader's name is Aziza Samira. She has developed a considerable following in the region. For the last 8 months, she has been quietly gathering international support and resources while building a large rebel force."

"Aziza Samira. I have heard of her and her efforts to protect the thousands of refugees in the Congo. She is a charismatic and popular leader. But I'm surprised to hear she has put together a rebel force and more surprised to hear she is willing to take on our Warlord." Armanda commented, sharing what information he knew with the others.

Does she know it's France that is asking for her help?" Adélard asked.

"Let me answer your question first Adélard. Aziza is only aware that our field operatives are French nationals. She believes them to be undercover agents representing rogue elements within the Congo political establishment. She is not aware that this request is part of an official French effort. We have been successful so far in keeping our involvement discreet. Our intelligence teams have been extremely cautious in keeping our involvement non-transparent."

"A question Sir." Commander Ross asked. "What is motivating Aziza to take on such a powerful Warlord, and more importantly what have we committed to?"

"Always right to the heart of it, commander Ross." Commander Gérard said, a small smile crossing his eyes. "Aziza's motivation stems from her deep-rooted hatred for the Congo Warlord. For years, his cruelty and disregard for human life has inflicted pain on her people. Her camps in the Congo are home to tens of thousands of refugees who fled the Burundi civil war, seeking safety and protection. This piece of shit Warlord (her words) frequently raids these camps, subjecting the people to unspeakable horrors."

Children are murdered in the streets for target practice as entertainment. Women are taken as sex slaves, and young men are forced into becoming soldiers for his army."

"Oh, mon dieu le diable règne." Armand blurted out.

"Indeed, Armand Indeed. I do not wish you a moment of living under this threat, but I would gladly fight this battle to rid the world of such trash regardless." Commander Gérard said to Armand, his jaw tight with venom.

"Aziza has made it her mission to protect these vulnerable refugees and to challenge the Warlord's reign of terror. That is why she formed her rebel army and that is why with us or without us Aziza wants him dead. She seeks justice for those who have suffered at his hands." Gérard added.

"As to your question Ross. Aziza asks for humanitarian and medical supplies for her people, but her main request is for heavy weapons and the financial means to strengthen her rebel group. She sees this as an opportunity to strike a decisive blow against the Congo Warlord and possibly gain an upper hand in the Burundi civil war."

"She is the perfect partner I think." Armand said aloud.

"Not exactly someone to add to your social circle my friend." Commander Ross stated solemnly. "Make no mistake on another day it may be her we need to fight, for she has no love for France or us. But for today she is the enemy of our enemy and as such has earned our favor."

"Well said Commander." Gaston said directly to Ross.

"Our primary commitment at this point is to provide Aziza with intelligence and logistical support. We'll share information on the Warlord's movements and activities. Additionally, we will arrange through various sources that she has access to medical supplies, food, and other essential resources for her camps."

Commander Gérard paused for a moment, moving out of range of the video camera, then continued.

"You should also know, that thanks to a little arm twisting and calling in some overdue markers from old friends of mine Russian heavy weapons from friendly Polish sources are already enroute to the Aziza rebel group. This promise of weapons has emboldened her, and she has begun mobilizing her soldiers for the impending assault. However, she remains steadfast in her demand for 10 million Euro's to be securely deposited before she begins any attack."

"We have contacts in the banking industry who can manage the transaction with utmost confidentiality. We can ensure that the funds are safely transferred to Aziza's accounts without leaving any trace." Commandant Gaston added.

Armand stood up with a dark resolve etched on his face. "Commandant I will have the money ready in 24 hours and will transfer it from one of my Asian manufacturing companies to any account Gérard specifies. I believe using this path will further help conceal the nation of France and my family of any involvement."

"Sirs, this money roadblock works in our favor. Let us not rush to give Aziza the money."

GHOST COMMANDO – Battle for Cavallo

Adélard added jumping into the conversation. "Aziza being unwilling to start any attack until getting paid is perfect for the mission of defending Cavallo and the Bugatti family. We are all agreed that the timing of the Congo assault is critical and that their attack on the Warlord must not take place before the mercenaries attack this island."

Adélard smiled. "It is fortunate for us that Aziza is not willing to proceed until the payment is made. This puts the timing of the Congo assault in our hands. We can ensure that both operations occur simultaneously."

"Agreed." Armand voiced his thoughts. "This cannot be allowed to go on and on. We must rid the world of this evil all at once."

"I have two full squads of attack Commando's making their way to the Congo as we speak Commandant and more planned. What then will be their mission?" Gérard asked, then paused but for only a moment. "We must be prepared to intervene if Aziza's attack fails, or the Warlord seeks to retreat."

"Exactly, Commander. Our teams on the ground must be ready to execute the mission and eliminate the Warlord. We are all in on this gentleman even if it means transparency. We must not fail! With respects to Armand, there are more lives at stake than just the Bugatti's."

"Commander Gérard, I promise you, no one on this island with evil intent will ever threaten anyone again." Adélard stated boldly, looking squarely at Armand.

"You are very confident in yourself for someone fresh out of training with no combat experience aren't you Mr. Adélard?" Gérard asked, his eyes smiling at Adélard.

"Yes Sir, of myself and my men."

"I will vouch for Adélard and his men." Commandant Gaston interjected.

"Well then. Good hunting young man." The Commander said, ending the video call.

* * *

Graham entered his room at the guest house, feeling a mix of excitement and satisfaction after building the new Bugatti command center. He found Adélard in the midst of changing his clothes for dinner, and he couldn't help but share his enthusiasm.

"Adélard, you won't believe how incredible the grotto looks." Graham exclaimed, a large smile playing on his lips. "The setup is top-notch, and the communications and surveillance equipment are state-of-the-art. We even have our own power source. We'll have complete control over the island's security, no matter what happens."

Adélard grinned back at him. "That's fantastic news, Graham! I knew we could count on Father Paulo's secret chamber to serve us well. And what about the two officers? Are they as good as Gaston made them out to be?"

"Oh, absolutely," Graham replied, nodding.

GHOST COMMANDO – Battle for Cavallo

"Dupont and Laurent are both sharp, highly skilled, and well-versed in counterintelligence tactics. With their help, I will have eyes and ears all over this island 24 hours a day."

"Oh, by the way," Graham added, almost as an afterthought.

"I received the report on the two Americans, Adam and David, who volunteered. They've got quite a history."

"Excellent, give it to me. I am interested it what kind of men they are." Adélard said.

Graham's expression turned professional as he relayed the information to Adélard. "I've completed the vetting on those two Americans, Adam and David." He began, his voice low and measured. "Everything they've told us checks out. They are indeed combat veterans with a long history of wet work and private security assignments. However, there's a catch."

Adélard raised an eyebrow. "What's the catch?"

"They have a reputation for being a bit... excessive." Graham continued. "Multiple reprimands for going beyond their mission parameters, being too brutal in their methods. They are effective, no doubt, but they are also known for pushing the boundaries and playing superheroes."

Adélard nodded thoughtfully. "So, they're not exactly by-the-book, go above and beyond, complete missions, and also try to do some good. Is that it in a nutshell?" He surmised.

Graham shook his head lightly laughing. "Yes Adélard. How nice of you to abstract my work for me."

"I do however have an idea of how we can best utilize their military experience and their intimate knowledge of this island for everyone's benefit if you want to hear it."

"By all means, but let's be quick about it. I am hungry."

"We need someone to take charge of the non-combatants on this island. People we are responsible to protect and keep from harm just as much as the Bugatti family. If or when an attack comes, we can't have civilians running around and getting caught in the crossfire."

"Agreed. Adam and David can coordinate with François and your surveillance, keeping them sheltered in place or moving to other safe locations as required. Be where the Enemy is not. I believe that tactic is called. And once the threat has passed those two superheroes can assist us from outside the perimeter" Adélard told Graham smiling.

Graham smiled, appreciating Adélard's pragmatic approach. "Shall I inform them of their part in our mission." He said putting his hands together as if asking for permission "I promise to make sure they understand the importance of keeping the civilians safe above all else."

"Perfect Graham you do that. Oh, and remind them they have my personal permission to kill every son of a bitch that assaults this island. I would be most happy just sipping coffee and watching their wet work." Adélard said smiling.

"Heard . . . Adélard, is it too late to change your nickname from Ghost Commando to Silly Ass Commando?" Graham asked slapping Adélard on the shoulder.

Adélard stood opening the door and bending over imitating an overly dramatic butler. "Dinner is being served Sir."

"Why thank you Mr. Adélard, please ask Milady de Winter to join me." Graham said doing his best d'Artagnan imitation.

* * *

The dining room of the Bugatti mansion was a picture of elegance, with a long table adorned with fine china, crystal glasses, and flickering candles. The squad members including Dupont, and Laurent, along with Commander Ross and Commandant Gaston, entered the room and found their chairs, joining Armand, Isabella, and their two daughters, Reine and Taber, who were already seated.

Armand stood up, raising his glass, and smiled warmly at everyone. " Mesdames et Messieurs, let us raise our glasses to celebrate the latest addition to our celebration, messieurs Dupont, and Laurent. Welcome to the Bugatti Household gentlemen."

Everyone around the table echoed the toast, clinking their glasses together. The atmosphere was lively and filled with camaraderie, a stark contrast to the tense discussions they had earlier in the day.

Throughout the dinner, conversation flowed freely. Isabella regaled the group with stories of her daughters' accomplishments and aspirations, and the squad members shared their own experiences and backgrounds.

Taber, the sporty and spirited daughter, chatted animatedly with Jojo and Henri about their various adventures, while Reine, the gentle and artistic soul, found common ground with Noel, discussing her love for horses and painting and the island's beautiful landscapes.

Commander Ross and Commandant Gaston also joined in the lively discussions, sharing nonviolent anecdotes from their time in the military.

Taber and Reine were both thrilled listening to Gaston tell stories of his adventures aboard a submarine and sailing across the Pacific when he was a young naval officer.

Armand listened intently to the conversations, pride evident in his eyes as he looked at his family and the commandos. "I must say." He began with a smile. "Having all of you men here breaking bread together with my family does bring so much joy and excitement into this house."

Leaning over to kiss his wife Armand spoke loudly and asked playfully. "Isabella would it alright if we adopted all these fine men?"

"I would not wish to offend the mothers of such fine men my husband. Certainly, men such as these have mothers whose ferocity in protecting their young would overpower any defense we could establish." Isabella answered clearly.

Isabella rose and faced the room of commandos. "My sweet husband would propose we adopt you all. Armand can be a bit excessive at times. I on the other hand offer this, an open invitation to the house Bugatti for each glorious man here."

At first the men sat quiet not knowing how to respond then seeing Armand smiling and motioning them happily with his hands they all stood up and started cheering.

"Vive Isabella, Vive Bugatti"

Adélard, seated next to Armand, nodded warmly. "We are honored to be here and to stand by your side, Armand."

As the dinner continued, the atmosphere became even more relaxed, with laughter and shared stories bonding the guests together as they found common ground, bridging the gap between their different worlds and backgrounds.

* * *

As the laughter and conversation continued to fill the dining room, Graham, Dupont, and Laurent exchanged glances, sensing that it was time for them to attend to their responsibilities. Graham leaned over to Adélard and spoke in a hushed tone. "Adélard, Toulon has the thermal drones flying overhead right now. It is time for us to go and start testing the capabilities of our equipment."

Adélard smiled and nodded. "Of course, Graham. You three go ahead and get to work. We'll catch up later."

As the trio bid thanks to the Bugatti family for the delightful dinner, Isabella smiled warmly, her gratitude evident in her eyes. "Thank you all for joining us. It's been such a pleasure having you here."

With that, the trio of Graham, Dupont, and Laurent bid their goodbyes to the Bugatti family and made their way to exit the mansion.

The night sky was clear, and the stars shone brightly overhead as they stepped outside. Walking across the compound towards the Range Rover Armand had assigned them, Laurent looked back at the mansion, a sense of responsibility settling on his shoulders. "It is incredible how warm they are to us, even with all that is going on."

Graham nodded in agreement. "Yeah, they've got that way about them that makes you feel like family, and you know something guys. With them it's real."

Graham drove them away ready to begin the task of testing all the new equipment and ensuring that their surveillance capabilities were fully optimized. Meanwhile, back in the dining room, Adélard and the remaining squad members continued to enjoy the company of the Bugatti family, cherishing the moments of peace and unity amidst the storm of impending danger. The night was far from over, and the challenges ahead loomed large, but for now, they all found solace in each other's company.

* * *

Graham, Dupont, and Laurent sat in the underground command center, the multiple screens in front of them alive, displaying thermal images of the island. The heat signatures of every living soul, even the pets, were clearly visible, providing an unparalleled view of the island's activity.

They worked together seamlessly continuing to fine-tune the equipment bringing the images into even finer focus. The weight of the upcoming mission was evident, although with each passing moment and minor improvement so was their confidence in the plan, they had meticulously crafted.

GHOST COMMANDO – Battle for Cavallo

"Look at that," Graham exclaimed, his excitement palpable.

"This is incredible! Tomorrow, we'll start cross referencing what we see with the intel of who belongs here and who doesn't. Then tomorrow night we can test the micro swarm drones and their night vision."

Dupont nodded in agreement, studying the screens intently. "Yes, it's remarkable. With that level of surveillance, we'll be able to see everyone and everything. We will be able anticipate and report any move the mercenaries make."

Laurent chimed in. "Indeed, Graham, I have to hand it to you. This is by far the most comprehensive and well executed surveillance plan I've ever been a part of."

"We have used this equipment many times, but never in such a coordinated and targeted manner."

Graham smiled humbly. "Thank you."

Graham looked at his colleagues with pride. "Tomorrow will be another critical day, but I have faith in what we are doing. I am sure with our help Adélard will send those mercenaries to hell in a hurry."

Dupont and Laurent both nodded in the affirmative.

"The highest priority we have is finding out if there are any bad guys on the Island right now. Even a half-backed plan would include a recon unit prior to any attack. The question command wants us to answer is, are they on the island now and if not, to know when they arrive." Graham stated.

Chapter 6: The Eyes have it

With breakfast concluded Adélard excused himself and the men as he had scheduled a briefing to begin at 9am.

"It is always disappointing when you leave our table." Isabella Bugatti said reaching out to hold Armand hand. "They are Catholics Isabella; they don't need you to add more guilt." Armand added chuckling.

"Monsieur Adélard." Taber said, running over to stand next to him. "Noel promised me a ride on that new motorcycle. Can we go now? Please, Monsieur Adélard, please."

"Taber?" Isabella spoke out scolded her softly.

"Momma, please. I promise to be very careful." Taber pleaded then turned again looking up at Adélard.

"Who among you mighty warriors can resist that face?" Armand asked waving his hand to all the Commandos. "You see Isabella, it is not just I."

"Well, Adélard?" Isabella asked.

"If your parents approve then yes. Let's see if your negotiating skills are as good as your fathers." Adélard answered looking down at her and smiling.

"Adélard, shame on you for giving into her so easy."

"I see you are infected with the same virus as my husband." Isabella said painting a fake scolding frown on her face.

"10 minutes and no more." Armand said. "Oh, and Noel do be careful."

"Yes Sir, Mr. Bugatti." Noel answered sheepishly.

"You men are absolutely insufferable." Isabella said unable to hold back her laughter.

* * *

The sun had just begun to warm the cold winter morning over the Bugatti compound as Adélard and his squad, along with Lieutenants Dupont and Laurent, made their way to the basement of the Rousseau guest house.

As they settled into their chairs, Adélard glanced around at the familiar faces of his squad and the two experienced naval officers.

He then turned his attention to the newest addition, Luigi Battista, the head of Bugatti security on the island. Luigi was a seasoned professional with a stern demeanor, known for his unwavering dedication to his role and unquestioned loyalty to the Bugatti family.

"Welcome Luigi, I am happy you could join us. Part of today's briefing includes you and your men."

"Gentlemen since we are waiting for Noel to arrive." Adélard stated. "I will begin with Luigi. When we have confirmation that the mercenary forces are enroute to the island, a well-armed high-speed boat will arrive to extract Mrs. Bugatti and the girls and take them to safety."

"How much lead time will we have?" Luigi asked.

"We are assuming the attack will come from the sea therefore our surveillance will give us a window of 1 to 2 hours Luigi." Graham interjected.

"That is not much time for little girls to pack." Luigi answered.

"Packing is the least of my concern. When I give you the signal to leave, I want you rolling in 15 minutes. Am I clear Luigi?" Adélard told the older man his face stern, the authority in his voice undeniable."

"Yes, it is very clear now." Luigi answered, stiffening his jaw.

"Don't get a case of the ass Luigi." Jojo jumped in. "Every man here has pledged their life to protecting the family just as you have all these years."

"Did I miss anything?" Noel asked, stepping into the basement.
"Only Adélard and Luigi arm wrestling with their chins." Jojo answered joking.

"Ok let's get back to it." Adélard said, throwing a smile and a wink to Jojo.

That boat will carry a Commando squad of six men. Four of those men will disembark and take the high ground guarding the cove directly with two more guarding the road access. "

"Are we expecting the Cove to be attacked Adélard?" Henri asked.

"No Henri we don't, but we want to cover every possible threat to our plan. We must make sure the exit is protected if any evacuation is going to be successful."

"The very reason we are waiting to evacuate the family is to hide their escape."

"If they left earlier, like today or any day while the mercenaries are in transit . . . then there is the possibility, that the merc's would discover they had left and redirect their forces to hunt the family down at a different place and time or to try and interdict our boat while in transit."

"How will we get to the Cove?" Luigi asked, his ego no longer bruised.

"One of my commandos, Julio, will drive the family and your entire security team using Armands special Defender. It will be a little tight but necessary."

"Luigi, I do not expect your men to get into a firefight at any time. Your mission as always is to protect the family at all costs. Make no mistake, you and your men are their human shield." "We are on the same page." Luigi answered.

"Once you are on board, the boat will leave the cove. Four of the commandos will accompany you, to add offensive might if needed using the hidden firepower of that boat on which they are well trained. The captain of that boat is Master Philippe. He is a crafty devil and an able warrior."

"That leaves two unaccounted for. What of those other Commandos?" Lieutenant Laurent inquired.

"Those two will stay on the Island and reinforce our squad." Adélard answered.

"Oh good, I was starting to feel like I had joined the 7 Samuri." Jojo quipped.

"Do you want me to smack you?" Noel asked, turning to Jojo.

Set off balance by the squad's usual banter Luigi shook his head and asked another question. "Where will we be going?"

Your destination is the main naval base at Toulon France. There is no safer place in the French empire than that base." Adélard said feeling the lie sting as it left his mouth.

"Are we all clear on the extraction part of the mission?"

"Yes Sir." Every man in the room answered.

* * *

"Very well then let's get to the defense of the compound and the protection of the innocents on this Island. There are 3 primary and 1 secondary location."

"Allow me to interrupt." Lieutenant Dupont added. "French intel has given us a list of all known individuals currently on this island. Not counting us and the souls at the Bugatti compound that number is 36."

"Coordinating that information with François and the two Americans, by the end of tonight, Adélard, we will have every one of them located using our thermal drones. Once we do, we will be able to tell you if there are any unwanted guests on the island and where they are." Graham added.

"And we can cross validate that information with our high-definition swarm drone that are night vision capable." Dupont added.

"Well done, gentlemen. The sooner we have a clean head count the better." Adélard said complimenting the men.

"Now as to the deployment of our onsite forces." Adélard began again.

"Noel you and the two Commandos from the Requin boat will set up behind the walls to the west side of the main gate. Julio after you drop off the commandos you are to join Henri and I on the east side of the gate."

"Did you forget me?" Jojo asked.

"No, my son of a Kraken you will be in the pool." Adélard answered smiling.

"In the pool at this time of year?" Jojo cracked a smile.

"Jojo, everyone here knows that the smart play in attacking this compound can come in two forms. One a frontal attack with everything they got and two splitting their forces and using the frontal attack as a diversion with a secondary action coming up and over the cliffs attacking from the rear."

"Day or night we will be able to warn you of any attack via the cliffs Adélard." Graham interjected.

"We have enough motion detectors to cover every inch at the rear of the compound to back up the drones." Lieutenant Laurent added.

"I am counting on it." Adélard stated seriously.

"As for the innocents on the Island I am assigning the task of organizing and if need be, moving any in harm's way to François and the Americans. The three of them will be connected to our communication systems at Graham's command center. The innocents will be connected to François using text messages on their cell phones."

"There are one or two other private security men besides the Americans on the Island as well Adélard." Luigi told him.

"We don't want to risk them in wet work, but do you think they will help protect the innocents?" Adélard asked Luigi.
"I am certain of it. They all know something of what the Bugatti's are facing." He answered.

"As I have been told many times, very little on this island happens in secret." Adélard said grinning. "Just to be clear, we are not running around dressed as Bugatti employees to deceive them. The locals know why we are here and what we will be doing. We only keep performing this charade to hide from unfriendly eyes."

"Graham take Jojo and the officers with you. I want every motion detector and camera placed today." Adélard ordered.
"Heard." Graham responded quickly.

"Noel you and Julio break out all the weapons and ammo. Sort them into two sets, one for the east side defense and the other for the west. I want every clip loaded and all the weapons tested in the range before we need them. Put aside two assault rifles, clips loaded with waterproof rounds."
"Heard." Noel added.

"I assume that those water guns are for me." Jojo asked smiling.

"For both of us Jojo, both of us." Adélard smiled reassuring him.

* * *

1400 Toulon France, Naval Headquarter

A hushed excitement filled the naval base in Toulon as an aide rushed into Vice Admiral Étienne Vacheron's office. The aid could barely contain his enthusiasm as he delivered the news.

"Admiral Vacheron, I have an urgent update from Commander Gérard at Special Operation command." The aide exclaimed, catching his breath. "He reports that two of our squads have successfully infiltrated the Congo and are coordinating with the intel team on the ground. They have managed to remain completely anonymous to the locals."

The vice admiral's eyes widened with interest. "That's excellent news." He replied, sitting up straighter in his chair. "Any further details?"

"Yes, sir." The aide continued. "COSG Gaston Bernardone has assigned the code name 'Ides of March' to the mission. It seems fitting, considering the purpose of this operation."

Étienne Vacheron nodded thoughtfully, recognizing the historical reference. "Indeed, the 'Ides of March' is appropriate but maybe not as you might think ensign. The 'Ides of March' is the Roman time to settle all outstanding debts. Gaston is a very clever man."

The aide nodded eagerly. "Yes, sir, it does seem that way."

"Keep me updated on any further developments." The vice admiral ordered. "I want to know the moment there is any new information from the field."

"Yes, sir." The ensign replied, saluting smartly before exiting the room.

* * *

1600 Toulon France, Naval Headquarter
Emergency Video Conference Call

"Gaston, what is this all about?" Commander Ross at camp Melusine asked. "Hold on, let's get Adélard and Armand online first." He answered. Gaston watched as all three heads popped up on the screen.

"Gentlemen. Are you in secure locations?" He asked. "Yes." Commander Ross answered from camp Melusine. "Go ahead." Armand answered standing next to Adélard.

"French intel in Pakistan reports that a convoy of mercenaries, totaling 20 to 25 men, has left Orangi Town at 1800 local time." Gaston paused, letting the words sink in. "They are heading north through Iran, and their estimated arrival at a seaport, most likely Genoa, is within 5 to 7 days, 10 at the outside.

"Oh, mon Dieu, they really are coming." Armand said a slight tremor in his voice as his mind raced with every possible outcome.

"Do not worry Armand. We have the entire French Navy and the full support of all naval assets at our command. You and your family will be safe." Gaston said, trying to comfort his friend.

"That is more than enough time for us to be ready at Cavallo Sir." Adélard reported.

Commander Ross at camp Melusine started slowly talking, his voice soft but his eyes as cold as ice.

"Gaston, the submarine is fully stocked and ready. Send me the two combat squads and we will shove off the moment the merc's arrive at whatever port."

"Will do. Expect them in 48 hours, brief them on the timeline and tell my helicopter pilot and the attack squad you are housing at the camp to be ready to go at any time. I will fly over in a few days to lead them myself. We will launch the moment Graham confirms an imminent attack. Point to point we should be on the ground in 30 minutes."

"Excuse me Sir, but 30 minutes is a long time in a firefight." Adélard commented, bringing a realistic tone to the plan.

"It is an eternity. The minute your intel reports them on the island I want to know. Your men will not be left holding the bag Mr. Adélard, I promise you that." Gaston told him.

"There is no power in heaven or earth that will stop us from eliminating that scum from Cavallo. Am I clear?" Gaston asked.

"Understood." All three men answered.

"Good." Gaston replied. "There are still some holes, mostly in Iran, but our intel assets are being coordinated to track their movements. The closest likely seaports are from Monico to Northern Italy. We will have eyes on everything. I will keep you updated on their progress."

Adélard nodded. "Sir we have no medical personnel or supplies other than our med kits on the island."

"Understood." I will send two medics with the squads for Ross. They can fly in with me on the chopper."

"Thank You Sir." Adélard said, with a somber voice.

Gaston concluded. "I trust in our abilities, I trust in the might of the righteous, I trust in the power of determination. In two weeks,' time, we will gather and celebrate the end of this chapter. You can bet the house on that."

"Toulon out."

As the call ended, the reality of the coming battle heightened the tension. Each man knew that the next few days would be critical, and that the success of their mission hinged on the faith they had in each other.

* * *

"Armand it's not too late to change your mind."

"There is no shame in you leaving the Island with your wife and the girls. It would make Isabella and Luigi very happy if you did." Adélard mentioned softly.

"And leave my champagne in the hands of those ruffians? No Adélard, this is my home, my people, my responsibility. I am staying." Armand said, regaining a bit of his swagger.

The two men silently walked outside. The cold wind from the sea adding to the chill of the pending battle.

"Where do you want me to be when the attack comes Adélard?" Armand asked.

"Anywhere you feel comfortable and safe. If it was me Armand, I would be in your bar with a large glass of Cognac." He answered.

Armand nodded looking out over the horizon.

"I think I will go for a ride on my new Ducati. Would you like to go with me, Adélard? I did buy two." Armand asked.

"Not today my friend. I have a lot to do." He answered.

The two men stood together bound by their mutual respect and affection. Fate and circumstances had united the billionaire and the warrior into brothers.

"7 days Adélard, maybe less." Armand said quietly.

"Yes, mon ami." Adélard answered putting a hand on his friend's shoulder.

"By the way. Did you know Ross had a submarine?" Adélard asked.

"No, I didn't." Armand responded.

"That son of a bitch keeps a lot of secrets." Adélard commented causing them both to laugh as they walked across the compound.

* * *

Graham looked up from his phone. His face belayed a sense of shock, but it quickly passed. Committed to his role, he called Dupont and Laurent over.

"Adélard just received word that the mercenaries are on the move. They are traveling by car, and it is assumed they will arrive here by boat. ETA Cavallo in 5 to 7 days."

Dupont spoke his words with calculated and deliberate care.

"If the mercenaries are enroute, it is highly probable that they have someone here or coming here as an advance recon unit. Our top priority right now is to find out if there's a spy on this island."

Laurent chimed in. "Agreed. We need to coordinate the intel we received with our surveillance."

"We need to account for every person. All our equipment is live and in place. Motion detectors, surveillance cameras, and the drones from Toulon are over us as we speak. We are ready Graham; we can do this. We will not let anyone slip through the cracks."

GHOST COMMANDO – Battle for Cavallo

Graham nodded in agreement. "Exactly and we don't have days to do it. We won't leave here tonight until we've identified every person on this island and if possible, have eyes on them as well. We want no surprises."

Just then, Father Paulo appeared with a tray of sandwiches, cookies, and steaming cups of coffee. "Good evening my children. The good ladies of my church thought you might enjoy this. I thought you might be working late so I asked them to help." He said with a smile as he set the tray down.

Graham was taken aback. "Father . . . How did you know?"

Father Paulo chuckled raising his arm and pointing his index finger straight up. "You are not the only ones keeping an Eye on my island."

Dupont and Laurent exchanged surprised glances before joining in the laughter while enjoying the cookies and coffee.

Chapter 7: The face of the Storm

Congo, Rebel Headquarters

In the heart of the Congo refugee camp, the undercover French Intelligence operative, Martine Boulanger met with Aziza Samira, the Burundian Rebel leader. Although the meeting was for just the two of them, 7 men also occupied the room. All seasoned guerilla fighters by the looks of them with all but one focus it seemed on him!

They sat or stood in various locations about the room silently watching his every move, like lions about to strike, ready to kill him at a moment's notice if they even suspected him of harming Aziza.

Aziza smiled with gratitude as she looked down at the latest shipment of Russian weapons, particularly the shoulder held rocket launchers.

"Thank you for these powerful weapons Mr. Boulanger." She said, her voice full of anger and hatred. "They will be instrumental in putting an end to that scum of a Warlord."

Martine nodded "You are most welcome. My friends and I simply want to support you in your fight for justice and the liberation of your people."

"Yes, it seems you do. Amazingly, shipments of food and medical supplies from the UN and Red Cross have started to arrive and have already made a difference to the suffering of my people. I am told more will be coming?" Aziza asked cunningly.

"It seems you have a number of powerful friends."

"There will be more of everything Aziza just as I promised." Agent Boulanger told her, masking his real purpose for his visit. Aziza's eyes gleamed with anticipation as she inquired. "And when can we expect the money, the 10 million Euro you promised?"

"It will be soon, within the next three to four days. Everything is being arranged, and the transfer will be discreet." Martine reassured her smiling.

Aziza nodded, satisfied with the response. "Good. Once we have the money, we can move forward with our plans."
"We have the means to support your cause, but I do need to know the size and skills of your rebel force. How big is your army?" He asked.

Aziza hesitated for a moment before answering. "We have 500 rebels armed and ready to fight with more joining every day. Among them, 50 of my most trusted men and women are already in position, poised to strike at the Warlord's heart in the town."

The operative nodded, impressed by Aziza's preparation and dedication. "That's a formidable force. And how soon after the money is delivered do you plan to attack?"

Aziza leaned forward, curious as to why the timing would be of interest, but her resolve and determination overshadowing any concern she had. "On the morning after we get the money, we will unleash hell on that Warlord. He will learn the cost of oppressing innocent people."

Aziza nodded, a sense of purpose emanating from her. "I will not rest until we liberate our people and put an end to that Warlord's reign of terror."

Then Aziza quickly jumped up from her chair, walking in circles around the table waving to the men in the room.

"Whoever you truly are Mr. Boulanger, and whoever your true masters are." Aziza said stopping to bend down and confront Martine mere inches from his face. "You can tell them from me that I will eat his still beating heart and celebrate with my people when that day is done."

* * *

Cave5 Melusine Camp, Corsica Island

Commander Ross gripped the railing tightly as he descended the narrow ladder through the outer hatch of the submarine. "Officer on deck." A crew man sounded as he reached the bottom of the ladder. and stepped onto the cold metal floor of the command deck.

Ross took his last step releasing his hold on the railing and turned to see the ship's captain and his command crew, all standing at attention and saluting.

The command crew stood with unwavering discipline, their dedication to duty evident in their sharp uniforms and focused expressions. Ross could feel the energy and readiness in the air, a palpable sense of purpose that comes from starting a mission.

"Commander Ross, welcome aboard the Liberté." Captain Louis Renault said with a crisp salute.

Ross returned the salute, a sense of pride swelling within him. "Thank you, Captain. It is good to be here. At ease gentlemen."

The captain gestured to two of his crew. "This is Lieutenant Patel, my executive officer." He said, pointing to a young officer with a determined look in his eyes. "And this is Lieutenant Donato, our chief engineer." He continued, motioning to another officer with a confident demeanor.

As Ross shook hands with each officer, he could sense their commitment to their roles on the submarine.

Submariners in general are always a tight knit team, each man knowing their responsibilities and trusting in one another to carry them out flawlessly. The Liberté and her Captain, Louis Renault, were no exception and if anything, the ship was the icon of what a submarine should look and act like.

"Let us get to it Captain Renault. Have my officers arrived?"

"Yes Sir. They are waiting for you in the mess." The captain acknowledged.

"Excellent, bring Lieutenant's Patel and Donato along they have an active part in all of this."

Commander Ross was the first to enter and took a seat at the end of the metal dining table. "Coffee Sir?" Lieutenant Nickalos, one of his Melusine officers offered.

"Yes, please." Commander Ross answered as he waited for the rest of the men to be seated.

"Gentlemen." Commander Ross began. "Our mission has four elements, first of which will be to locate an unknown vessel enroute to Cavallo Island from a yet to be known port somewhere between France and Italy."

"That's a pretty big area Commander." Captain Renault stated.

"Yes, it is Captain, but we do not need to canvas the entire sea. Their destination is Cavallo Island therefore we shall go there and lay in wait. Once we are alerted to their proximity our primary mission will be search and destroy."

"Tomorrow two Commando squads will be flown in from Toulon. Lieutenant Coop I want you to prepare one squad for underwater demolition work. Fully covert. I want enough explosives placed on the hull on that ship to launch it into space." "Understood Commander." Coop acknowledged.

"Lieutenant Nickalos, I want you to have the other squad ready for an assault on the island. When we eliminate that ship, we will surface, then you will take your squad in on the inflatables."

"What should we expect onshore Sir?" Nickalos asked.

"I do not expect any resistance to us landing on the beach, although we should be prepared for a live fire assault if needed. What I do expect is that our men already on that island will be in a shitstorm defending the Bugatti compound and outnumbered 3 to 1."

"Your mission Nickalos is to reinforce those men and eliminate any hostiles with extreme prejudice."

"By our men Sir, do you mean the Adélard training squad we sent there?" Lieutenant Coop asked.

"Yes, Lieutenant I do, although they received a field promotion and are now an active commando squad. Which I might add has been impressive in their preparation, execution, and leadership for this mission."

"The commandant and I, both have a lot of faith in those men." Commander Ross answered with his voice firm.

"Still Sir, they have never faced live combat before. Being outnumbered 3 to 1 against paid mercenaries . . . facing your first shitstorm. That's a lot of faith to put on those young men Sir." Nickalos commented, his concern evident.

"True Lieutenant, but if I were to guess I would say every man on that squad will rise to the occasion and show that they are true Kraken Commandos."

Turning to face Captain Renault the Commander continued.

"Luis this is your ship, and you are in command, but we will need your first officer to make sure we have no logistic hangups, launching and retrieving one squad underwater and another from the surface in short order."

"We will make that happen commander." Captain Renault said, turning to look at his first officer. "Yes Sir, no problem, Sir." Lieutenant Patel answered loud and clear.

"Time is the critical element on this mission. We cannot launch our men underwater until after we are certain the ship contains hostiles and not just a bunch of drunks. Which means that before our squad places the charges on the hull of that ship, the assault on the island will have begun."

"We are going to need to be close Captain to make this happen in time to support Adélard on the Island." Commander Ross told him.

"That may prove to be more difficult than we would like Commander." Chief engineer Donato interrupted. "Depending on where that ship parks the sea near the narrows is full of rock formations."

"And if it does anchor amongst the rocks, can we still get close Donato?" Captain Renault asked.

"Oh yes Sir, I might scrape the paint a little, but I will get Liberté close enough to throw spitballs at it." Donato answered his confidence visible in his smile.

Commander Ross nodded, satisfied with their responses.
"Very good gentlemen. Coop, Nickalos, the performance, and speed of your teams will be critical. Captain Renault will put us in the right place at the right time, of that you can have no doubt, but it is up to you to deliver the blows."

"I want to make myself perfectly clear in case you still have questions. Together we are going to blow that ship to hell and remove any vermin we find on Cavallo. Understood?"

"Sir. Yes, Sir." The men responded enthusiastically.

GHOST COMMANDO – Battle for Cavallo

* * *

0900 Toulon France, Naval Headquarter
The Admiral's ensign ran through the halls of the Naval senior offices, earning more than one reproach as he passed by. Pushing the door open without asking permission, he burst into Vice Admiral Étienne Vacheron's office disrupting a meeting of senior staff.

"Admiral Vacheron, they're in Turkey." The aide blurted out breathless.

"Ensign, have you lost your mind?? The admiral asked.

"Sorry Sir, but . . ." The ensign tried to continue but couldn't catch his breath.

"Here son, drink some water, first." The Admiral ordered, handing him a glass from the conference table.

"Thank you, Sir, French intelligence just reported that the convoy from Pakistan has crossed Afghanistan and Iran. They were observed crossing the Turkish border at 1100 local time. Intelligence estimates at this pace the convoy will reach the coast of Italy in two days."

The vice admiral nodded. "Well done ensign. Does Gaston have this intel?" "Yes, Sir he does." The aide responded. "Very well. Dismissed." The aid saluted and sharply turned to leave but before he reached the door the Admiral called out. "Ensign, I want you in PT every morning."

"Yes Sir. Understood." The ensign answered obviously unhappy with that order.

Graham and Laurent hurriedly approached Adélard as he walked across the Bugatti compound. Seeing them approach Adélard stopped and waited, the urgency in their steps told him something was up.

"Good morning fellas."

"Not so good Adélard." Graham told him, walking closer.

"We just intercepted some intel communication to Toulon."

Graham said, his voice urgent. "The mercenary convoy has crossed into Turkey ahead of the estimate. It looks like they might arrive on the Italian coast in the next 48 hours."

Adélard's eyes narrowed as he processed the information. "That's sooner than expected. 2 days and most likely on our Island in 3." He replied, a sense of concern creeping into his voice. "Did the intel specify their destination on the coast?"

Laurent nodded. "Highest probability is still Genoa, but we will know better in the next 24 hours."

Adélard sighed, realizing the gravity of the situation. "I have a feeling Armand already knows about this. I was summoned to a video meeting with him by Commandant Gaston."

"There is more Adélard. It gets worse." Graham said.

"Worse than 2 dozen murders coming to hunt us?" Adélard asked him, tilting his head to the side.

"No, but not good news." Graham added.

GHOST COMMANDO – Battle for Cavallo

"We've successfully located and identified everyone on this island Adélard. All our systems have worked to perfection."

"Then, what do you mean, not good news. That is excellent news." Adélard replied, feeling a sense of relief wash over him. However, before the celebration of their successful intel gathering could fully set in, Laurent's interruption changed the atmosphere.

"Late last night, an unknown person showed up on our thermal images." Laurent said, his voice tense with concern.

Adélard's eyes narrowed, he exchanged a concerned glance with Graham. "Are you certain it's not a false reading? Someone maybe out having a smoke or cheating on his wife?".

Laurent shook his head. "No such luck, we have checked and double checked, cross-referenced all previous data, even pulled up the video record from the drones for the last 36 hours. This is definitely a new presence."

Adélard's mind raced as he considered the possibilities. "Have you been able to pinpoint the location of this person?" He asked.

Laurent nodded. "Yes Sir. We have."

Graham chimed in. "We have been able to track them most of the time. They are constantly on the move, obviously reconning, the island and the compound."

"What have we learned?" Adélard asked.

"Whomever they are they have been methodical and deliberate. Moving between unoccupied buildings to stay out of sight and never returning to the same place twice to rest or eat. For one person, they are doing a respectable job."

"Do you think they are in communication with the mercenaries Lieutenant?" Adélard asked.

"Yes, I do, he wouldn't be of much use to if they weren't."

"Are we sure it's a man?"

"Our swarm drones caught some night vision video, and it does appear to be a man." Laurent said.

Adélard crossed his arms and looked up into the winter sky.

"We can't eliminate him right now. If he is in contact with the mercenaries that would tip them off and possibly disrupt their plans to something unknown to us."

"So, we do nothing and let him continue to gather intel?" Graham asked incredulously.

"In a manner of speaking, yes. We let him see what we want him to see. With you three watching him, when we want to do any preparations that we want to keep secret we will only do so when you give us all clear. He cannot be everywhere at once, but your eyes can."

"What happens if he gets too close or threatens the family in some manner Adélard?" Graham asked.

"Then we eliminate him immediately and then go hunting for the mercenaries ourselves before they get here."

"Understood." Both men told Adélard.

Adélard left the men and continued to walk toward the mansion for his meeting with Armand. With the mercenaries' arrival imminent and a mysterious figure lurking in the shadows, Adélard knew that the coming days would test their skills, and his patience.

* * *

The atmosphere in Armand's private office was tense as Adélard joined him for the conference call with Gaston and Ross. The screen flickered to life, showing the stern expressions of the two officers.

Gaston wasted no time in delivering the urgent news, "The mercenaries are advancing faster than expected. Intel suggests the attack on Cavallo is likely to happen in 3 days."

Armand's face tightened with concern, and he glanced at Adélard, who nodded in understanding. "Thank you for the update, Sir." Adélard said firmly. "We will be ready."
"You don't seem surprised Adélard." Commander Ross questioned. "No commander, I am not. Graham and his team briefed me on the way here."

"Gentlemen the two commando squads will arrive at the camp tomorrow. The Melusine submarine will be dispatched within 24 hours with myself and two of my officers aboard. We will patrol the waters near Cavallo, ready to intercept and perform our part of the mission." Commander Ross stated.

Adélard nodded gratefully. "Thank you, Commander Ross for coming yourself. Knowing you are out there will provide a morale boost to my squad." Adélard turned to wink at Armand. "Not to mention the 2 squads you are bringing. Be nice to have some company in the shitstorm."

"You may want to add a few more plates to the table Armand. I am coming as well. I have an attack helo ready at Melusine with a full combat squad and two medics ready now. We are on standby until the attack on Cavallo begins."

"That is good to hear Monsieur Gaston, but what of the evacuation plan for my wife and children? Armand asked his concern and pain clearly heard.

Commander Ross answered that question "My Requin boat with a full squad will also be dispatched and is expected to arrive at the cove after dark tomorrow night. And I have been informed that Adélard and your security chef Luigi have a solid plan to evacuate your wife and deal with any unexpected occurrences."

Armand visibly relaxed. "Thank you, Ross."

Adélard spoke up owning the moment. "Commanders, thanks to you both. We are well equipped and prepared to safeguard the Bugatti family and this island. We are utilizing local assets curtesy of Elon Musk to protect the innocents on the island with a high probability of no loss of life."

"My men are young and as some of you have whispered not battle tested, but I assure you will we stand and protect this island with honor."

Gaston's expression was solemn as he nodded. "I have complete faith in your abilities, Adélard. I know you and your squad will do what is necessary to defend the island."

"Commander Ross, I would beg for one more thing." Adélard asked.

"Name it and it is yours." Ross replied.

"Please Sir try to convince Armand to leave on the Requin." "I have been trying to convince him for 3 weeks Adélard. It is of no use." Ross admitted.

Armand's gaze shifted between the three men; tears filled his eyes with gratitude. "Gaston, Ross, Adélard, I am blessed to be your friend. Thank you all for your dedication."

* * *

The screen went blank as the conference call ended leaving Armand and Adélard alone in his office.

Swiveling in his office chair to face the bookcase Armand opened a small cabinet door.

Reaching in he removed a bottle of 1858 Croizet Cuvee Leonie exclusive Cognac and two glasses.

Opening the near priceless bottle Armand poured two healthy drinks and passed one to Adélard.

"Looks like your stuck with me mon ami."

Chapter 8: Once upon a midnight Clear

0730 Bugatti Mansion, Cavallo Island

The Bugatti dining room was a sight to behold every morning, an exquisite blend of elegance and warmth. The room itself was bathed in soft, natural light, filtering in through a pair of floor-to-ceiling windows accented with delicate lace curtains. The walls here and there were adorned with tasteful artwork. A large, embossed map of the Mediterranean overlooking the table added to the refined yet welcoming atmosphere.

The highlight of the room, a long, polished mahogany table took center stage, meticulously set with a fine white linen tablecloth and napkins. Each place setting arranged with polished silver cutlery, delicate china plates, and crystal glasses. Three small vases of fresh flowers lined up along the length of the table adding a pop of color and a touch of nature to the room.

At one end of the room upon a matching serving table stood two silver urns, exuding the rich aroma of freshly brewed coffee. Next to them were elegant glass carafes, inviting guests to indulge in Armand's favorite grapefruit juice.

As usual the breakfast spread was nothing short of a culinary symphony to delight the senses. A variety of eggs, cooked to perfection and served any way the guests desired, could be found at the side buffet. With fresh bread, still warm from the oven, carefully displayed in woven baskets, tempting guests with its enticing aroma. Platters of assorted cheeses and pastries and the specialty of the house.

The Bugatti sausage handcrafted on their family farm in France, was another delightful option, its rich and savory flavor tantalizing the taste buds.

* * *

The room was filled with a sense of friendship as the Bugatti family and the commandos gathered around the table. Conversations flowed effortlessly, laughter rang out, and smiles adorned the faces of all present.

Despite the impending threat, breakfast time in the Bugatti dining room was always a moment of unity and joy in the face of adversity.

* * *

Nearing the end of breakfast Reine leaned over and whispered to her sister. Nodding her understanding Taber reached out with her foot under table and lightly kicked commando Noel sitting next to her and motioned with her head towards her parents at the end of the table, as if asking for him to do something.

Noel, with a warm smile, turned to Armand and Isabella. "Mrs. Bugatti, I wanted to ask if it would be alright if I took your daughters for an eBike ride around the island after breakfast? They have bewitched me with promises of hidden treasures and untold beauty they are willing to show me.

Armand and Isabella exchanged a knowing look before nodding with approval. "Of course, Noel. That sounds like a wonderful idea." Armand said, his voice filled with appreciation. "The girls will be thrilled; they are the Bugatti explorer team. There isn't a nook or cranny on this island they are not aware of." He finished winking at his daughters.

Isabella smiled her approval and added. "Of course, Noel, you may take the girls for a ride. But do make sure you are all back by lunch at 1pm. I have a surprise planned.

The girls' faces lit up with joy and excitedly started chatting with each other at light speed. "Thank you both! I promise to make sure they have a great time and return home on time." Noel said smiling.

"A surprise, my love? You have my interest now. What have you got up your sleeve?" Armand asked curiously.

Isabella smiled playfully at her husband. "Well, my dear Armand, it wouldn't be a surprise if I told you, would it? You and the boys will have to wait and see!"

Turning to Adélard Isabella continued. "I do expect all of your men to be here at 1pm Mr. Adélard, no exceptions."

"Yes Mrs. Bugatti. We will all comply, wont we gentlemen?"
"Yes, yes." The men answered enthusiastically.

As the table conversation continued to other topics, Adélard couldn't help but admire the camaraderie that had grown between the squad and the Bugatti family. Despite the imminent danger, they had found moments of normalcy and connection, reminding them of the importance of protecting these innocent lives.

After breakfast, the two girls, Reine and Taber, each excitedly took one of Noel's hands as he walked them out of the house to the eBikes parked nearby. Armand and Isabella smiled watching as the trio set off on their adventure.

GHOST COMMANDO – Battle for Cavallo

Isabella and François approached the group of men gathered in front of the mansion, just in time to see Noel and the girls ride off on their eBike adventure. Isabella's smile was radiant, her eyes filled with affection as she watched them go.

"They are such a wonderful trio, aren't they?" Isabella commented joyfully.

"Indeed, Madame. He has a way with the girls, and they respond to him so positively." François added.

Isabella stepped closer to Adélard watching Noel and the girls ride off. "They adore him, you know. If he were not a 245-pound commando, I would hire him as their nanny in a heartbeat."

"Please, Isabella, don't tell him that. He might take you up on the offer!" Adélard told her grinning.

"Well when all this is over. I just might." Isabella laughed.

"But for now, we have some business to address. So, all of you, including my husband, need to go away and let François and me prepare.

Armand wrapped his arm around his wife's waist pulling her a bit closer. "Come on, Isabella, just a little hint about the surprise? You know waiting is not my strong suite."

"No Armand!" Isabella giggled, pulling out of his grasp. "No hints! It would not be a surprise if I told you now, would it? You will find out soon enough. Now, off with you all! Go and do boy stuff but be back at the compound by 1pm."

Graham, Laurent, and Dupont, along with the rest of the squad, chuckled as they dispersed, heading off to various activities. Adélard lingered for a moment, looking at Isabella with admiration.

"Isabella, you truly have a gift for making everyone feel special. Armand is lucky to have you, and we are lucky to know your grace."

With that, Adélard joined the others, leaving Isabella and François to make their preparations. As the morning sun warmed the Bugatti compound, the commandos could not help but feel grateful for the moments of joy that Isabella brought to their lives on the eve of battle.

Watching the squad members disperse, Isabella and François exchanged a knowing look, excited to put the finishing touches to their surprise.

* * *

1100 Camp Melusine, Corsica
As the NH90 Caiman naval helicopter from Toulon drew closer the men aboard could see a tall man standing alone waiting for them near the Melusine helipad.

Noticing the man as well, the helicopter pilot instantly recognized that rigid stance and commanding presence even from the 1000 feet in the air. He keyed his shipboard microphone to talk to the men in back.

"You boys must be special." The Pilot told them. "Looks like Commander Ross himself has come to meet you."

GHOST COMMANDO – Battle for Cavallo

Commander Ross stood alone; his face impassive while his mind raced with every detail of his responsibility in the mission ahead. He looked up, feeling his pulse quicken, watching the arrival of the commando squads he needed to put his plans in motion.

The rhythmic thumping of helicopter blades echoed through the air, and soon enough, the chopper descended gracefully onto the helipad. The dust kicked up, swirling around as the engines powered down. Out stepped twelve of Frances finest commandos. They quickly formed into squad ranks and came to attention saluting Commander Ross sharply.

"At ease gentlemen, welcome to Melusine." Ross said, raising his voice over the noise of the still running twin turbines of the helicopter.

The two squad leaders stepped forward shaking his hand. "Good to be back Commander."

"Good to have you back. We are mission critical with hostiles enroute to assassinate a French national and his family." Commander Ross wasted no time in telling them.

"I have assigned lieutenants Coop and Nickalos, which you are both familiar with as they were your Kraken instructors, to your units. They are fully briefed on each of your squads' responsibilities for this assignment and are prepared to join as active members. Understood?"

"Yes, Sir Commander." Both men said in unison. "Sir headquarter has assigned us designations; Toulon2 and Toulon3 for this mission."

"Toulon2 and 3, then who the hell is Toulon1?" Ross asked raising an eyebrow.

"Commandant Gaston Sir."

Shaking his head with a small smile on his face Commander Ross commented. "The commandant can be a bit of a prima donna at times." To which the two squad leaders did not choose to comment with more than a grin.

"Have your men pull their gear from the Caiman and be ready to hump to Cave5 in 10 minutes. Coop and Nickalos are already onboard, and Captain Renault is preparing to get underway at 1800."

"Prior to our departure I will conduct a mission briefing in the Melusine command center. I want you both there at 1630."

"Yes Sir." The men answered. "Commander will you be joining us?"

"Definitely, I have good men on that island, and I intend to join them." Commander Ross answered the cold look of a warrior returning to his eyes.

* * *

Bugatti Mansion, Cavallo
Isabella strolled through the compound. Her eyes sparkled with delight seeing her dream for the party come to life.

The Bugatti compound had been transformed into a vibrant and lively celebration site, awash with the colors of spring.

Tents adorned with fluttering, colorful banners stretched across the open space, creating a whimsical atmosphere.

The central tent stood as the focal point of the celebration, draped in flowing fabric in shades of green and pastel hues. The canopy created an inviting shelter where guests could gather and enjoy the company of friends and family.

In the heart of the tent, a large, intricately decorated cake took center stage, a masterpiece symbolizing the blossoming of new beginnings.

Walking up to her butler overseeing some decorations, Isabella gushed her happiness. "Oh, François, everything looks absolutely perfect!"

"It was not just our people Madame. A lot of credit needs to be given to the many ladies and men of the island that helped erect the tents and decorate." François said.

"And Armand is none the wiser. Wait until he sees this, that man for once in his life will be speechless." Isabella said laughing aloud.

As the sun rose high in the sky, the island's inhabitants started to arrive, each person bringing an air of anticipation and joy to the gathering. Isabella took it upon herself to personally greet them with real warmth and affection.

"Welcome, dear friends!" Isabella beamed as she shook hands and embraced those who approached. "Thank you for being a part of this special day."

The surprise Spring Equinox party was in full swing when the men returned. Armand and the commandos arrived back precisely at 1 pm.

As they entered the compound, they were taken aback by what they saw. The once quiet family estate was now a lively and exuberant celebration, teeming with all the residents of the island, singing and dancing together.

"What has happened here?" Armand exclaimed, his eyes widening in amazement. "My Isabella, where is my Isabella?"

"Come on fella's . . . it's time to party." Jojo said jumping into the crowd followed closely by Henri and Noel. Mixing with the crowd, they soon learned that the residents had spent days preparing for the surprise party.

"Isabella!" Armand exclaimed loudly, finding her dishing out slices of cake for some children.
"Oh, my dear amazing wife, this is all beyond belief."

Seeing the pure joy on her husband's face made Isabella smile. "Life my husband is to be cherished." She said stepping up to kiss him deeply much to the delight of the giggling children. "Dance with me Armand." Isabella said, pulling him towards the music tent holding his hand.

Now, with the entire island in attendance, the music intensified, and everyone swayed to the rhythmic beats, even those sitting. Children ran around with painted faces, and elders shared tall tales and taller glasses of wine.

Isabella moved gracefully among her guests, ensuring that everyone felt comfortable and included.

Armand stood by her side, beaming with pride at his wife's ability to bring people together and feel cherished.

Together they watched with joy in their hearts as the islanders reveled in the festivities. Isabella's surprise Equinox party had not only brought happiness but had also strengthened the bonds of love and friendship among the people of the island and their gallant protectors.

Adélard found himself laughing and dancing alongside the islanders, feeling a sense of belonging he had only experienced at home. In that moment, he knew that protecting this community was not just a job but an honor.

* * *

1630 Melusine Command Center, Corsica
Inside the Melusine command center, Commander Ross projected a map on the screen, showing the European coastline and their target area northeast of Cavallo Island.

"We do not know the precise location, or which port the merc's will use or the type and description of the boat. What we do know is their destination, here at Cavallo island." He said pointing to the spot on the map. "Therefore, regardless of which port they leave from their course will ultimately bring them somewhere in this area near the island."

"At 1800 hours today, we will set sail and be onsite patrolling the area by midnight." Ross announced, his voice steady and determined.

Captain Renault raised an eyebrow, his salt-and-pepper beard giving him an air of wisdom. "Commander, why are we leaving so early? There has been no indication that the merchantries are at sea yet, which gives us at minimum a full day of leeway before we need to go."

"Captain, I want you to run simulated test of the submarine's ability to launch and retrieve our commandos underwater."

"Sir, both the squads have trained for assault missions from submarines." Lieutenant Nickalos added.

"Yes, Lieutenant they have, but my Submarine Liberté has not. Therefore, we will run underwater drills until I am satisfied with the ship and the team's performance. Is that clear?"

"Yes Sir." Nickalos answered sharply.

"Master Philippe you will captain our best Requin boat with a full commando squad for our extraction portion of the mission. I want you onsite at the Bugatti cove at minimum 24 hours prior to any attack to establish security forces at the cove to ensure that Mrs. Bugatti and her children can in fact get to the boat."

Clearing his throat Commander Ross looked sympathetically at the boat captain. "Philippe your extraction window will be very tight. We cannot pull the Bugatti family out until we are certain the attack is imminent, or we risk altering the merc's to the fact that she is not there."

"When do you want us at the Cove Sir?" Philippe asked.

GHOST COMMANDO – Battle for Cavallo

"Tomorrow night under the cover of darkness. I recommend leaving Melusine at sunset and running without lights to help shield you from prying eyes. Assumming Intel has their estimates correct that should put you onsite between 12 and 36 hours prior to the extraction." Commander Ross told him.

"And once I have them on the Requin Sir?" Master Phillip asked.

"Once you have them on your boat, I want you to get out to sea as fast as you can and run that boat like a scalded dog to Toulon blowing anything in your way out of the water. Clear?" Ross asked his trusted Captain.

"Oh. Yes Sir, very clear." Philippe said smiling.

* * *

Bugatti Mansion, Cavallo
With the party over and most of the cleanup done Armand and Isabella finally settled into their cozy bed, feeling both physically exhausted and emotionally fulfilled after the grand celebration.

Armand let out a contented sigh. "Isabella, you are truly incredible." He said, his voice filled with admiration.

"I am amazed at how you pulled off such a magnificent affair and also kept it a secret from me. Thanks to you this whole island came alive. It was a wonderful day, and everyone had a great time, even the old timers that fell asleep in their chairs." He said chuckling.

Isabella smiled, resting her head on his chest. "Thank you, my love. But I could not have done it alone. So many people on the island pitched in to make it a success. They all deserve credit for the beautiful atmosphere and joyful spirit."

Armand chuckled. "You're right. Maybe I should throw them a party to thank them."

Isabella laughed softly. "You're funny, Armand. I think I have already done that."

As Isabella snuggled up closer to Armand, preparing to close her eyes, then whispered softly in his ear. "Besides my darling, the party was also a subtle way to deceive anyone who might be watching us into thinking that we are completely unaware of their plans."

Armand smiled. "You my darling have a devious mind. I think we should check if you have any Machiavelli in your family history."

"Maybe so my husband, maybe so." Isabella answered falling asleep.

* * *

Graham, Dupont, and Laurent made their way back to their underground surveillance grotto beneath the church graveyard. The dimly lit space was filled with screens showing live feeds from the Toulon drones that had deployed during their absence at Isabella's surprise event.

Dupont took a seat in front of one of the screens and began to review the recorded footage. "Graham, Laurent, you need to see this." He said, his voice tense.

Graham and Laurent rolled their chair over quickly and leaned in, their eyes fixed on the screen.

As they watched, a figure appeared on the display, walking around the island's only marina. The same unknown person they had previously identified on the island, the one they suspected of being connected to the merchantries. "Looks like our Peeping Tom" Dupont added.

"Did we get anything on the night vision cameras we placed at the marina?" Graham asked.

"Hold on, let me locate the same time stamp as the drone." Dupont said pulling up the video. "Bingo, we got him on the docks and visiting some of the empty boats."

Laurent frowned. "What's he doing there? Why would he be reconnoitering the marina?"

Graham shook his head, studying the footage carefully. "It's puzzling. The marina is not a center of activity at this time of year. We have only seen one boat come and go beside the Bugatti fishing boat with Noel on it."

Dupont tapped a few keys on the keyboard, bringing up additional video of the Peeping Tom by the marina.

Laurent crossed his arms, deep in thought. "Maybe he is searching for potential means to escape the island if needed."

Graham nodded, considering the possibility. "It's plausible, but for certain we need to ramp up our work at the marina. There might be more to this than meets the eye."

Without wasting any time, Graham reached for the communication device on the table and called Adélard. He quickly summarized the situation and the latest footage they had obtained.

"Adélard, we spotted the same mercenary near the marina." Graham reported. "We believe he might be scoping it out, but we can't ascertain the reason just yet."

Adélard's voice came through the device, firm and authoritative. "I'll be there in 20 minutes. See if you can get eyes on him, I want to know where that SOB is."

* * *

The next morning, after breakfast, Armand and Adélard asked to speak with Isabella in private. As they entered Armand's private office, Adélard began.

"Isabella, we need to talk about the upcoming situation. The attack on the island is imminent, less than two days away, and we must be prepared. You and the girls need to be ready to leave the island at any moment starting tonight."

"Tonight? But why so soon? You said two days." Isabella asked confused at the timing.

Adélard nodded his understanding. "It is, but we don't know exactly when you and the girls will need to leave, and therefore we must be prepared to do so starting today. Captain Philippe's boat that will take you and the girls to safely arrived last night from Melusine. At this very moment, other commandos are guarding the cove and the access road to ensure a safe passage for your evacuation."

GHOST COMMANDO – Battle for Cavallo

"Isabella, my darling, when we get the word, speed will become the most important part you can help with." Armand told his wife gently.

Isabella resolved to the urgency required asked. "So, what do you suggest?"

"You need to pack travel bags for yourself and our daughters today and keep them close by, ready to go when the signal comes." Armand told his wife.

"If the attack is at night, there will be no time for dressing Reine and Taber. You will need to grab your bags and leave the mansion in your robes, it is essential that you move quickly, for your own safety and that of your daughters." Adélard instructed her.

"But it is so cold at night now?" Isabella asked of no one in particular. "Please understand Isabella, we will have no more than 15 minutes from the time we get the signal to the time you need to be in the truck driving to the Cove. Once you are on the boat and safely away from the island, you can change." Adélard told her very seriously.

"When the time comes, you, the girls, and our security team led by Luigi will leave the mansion together. Commando Julio will be waiting at the side of the house by the kitchen door in one of our new armored Defenders."
"He will drive you straight to the hidden cove, where the Requin boat will be waiting. I promise you that there you will be safe, for it is more than just another boat, it is a naval gunship capable of defending itself in any situation." Armand told his wife firmly yet with love in his voice.

Isabella answered, taking a deep breath first. "I understand. I will have everything ready as soon as possible, but I am not telling the girls until later."

"But what about you, my husband?" She asked with tears welling in her eyes. "What will you and the others do?"

"I will stay and with Adélard's help defend our home and the good people of this island, Isabella."

"Oh Armand." Isabella said, breaking down into tears.

* * *

The moonless sky helped cloak the Liberté as the submarine approached the island of Cavallo riding on the surface. Captain Louis Renault stood on the bridge, peering out into the distance as the executive officer, Lieutenant Patel, approached.

"Captain, we have arrived at the edge of the mission area, and a suitable rock outcropping for our practice target has been located." The officer informed him.

Captain Renault nodded, taking one last look at the horizon. "Very well, Lieutenant, prepare the ship to submerge. Tell the helm to take us to 30feet and keep the course near your target. I want to look over the maps with you below."

"Yes Sir." The lieutenant answered waving the spotters below as the ship sounded the dive signal.

As was his style, the exec was the last man to enter the submarine pulling the watertight hatch closed behind him.

GHOST COMMANDO – Battle for Cavallo

The Liberté slowly submerged, disappearing into the cold Mediterranean water with only the slightest evidence it had ever existed on the surface.

Lieutenant Patel quickly went to work, plotting the coordinates on the map as Captain Renault leaned over to review it.

Under the red lights of the command deck, Captain Renault studied the maps and the target Lieutenant Patel had identified. "Yes, that should do nicely. Inform Lieutenant's Coop and Nickalos to get the Toulon squads ready for dive operations. Mr. Patel, I want you to personally oversee all dive operations during this mission. Clear?"

"Yes Sir, understood Sir. I'll inform the squads immediately." Patel answered with a quick salute then turned to leave the command deck.

As Lieutenant Patel made the necessary arrangements, Captain Renault turned to the chief engineer, Lieutenant Donato, who was overseeing the controls. "Mr. Donato, take the boat at 50 feet and steer us approximately 100 meters out from the practice target.

Lieutenant Donato acknowledged. "Aye, Captain. Leveling the boat to 50 feet and heading towards the target."

The submarine glided smoothly through the water, positioning itself for the practice target. Inside, the members of Toulon2 and 3 squads were preparing for their dive operations. The atmosphere on board was tense yet focused with each man aboard the Liberté understanding their roll.

"Commander Ross?"

"Yes Captain."

"We are within the mission area and are ready for dive operations."

"Well done, Captain, let's proceed with the practice." Ross commanded. "Launch the first team of commandos, and Captain I want a clock on this operation. Time is crucial on this mission."

One after the other both squads exited the submarine swam to the practice target, simulated placing demotion charges, and then returned to the ship all while still submerged.

After two sets of practice runs Commander Ross was not happy with the timing. The divers had performed flawlessly but the distance was too great for the time allowed.

"This is taking too long Captain." Commander Ross told him in a matter-of-fact tone. "Tell Mr. Donato to take us in closer, much closer, say 10 meters from the target and then run both squads again." He ordered.

"Sir that is too close for demolition charges." The captain reminded him.

"Agreed Mr. Renault, it is too close to ignite the charges, but it is not too close to set them. Let us try to see how fast we can make it happen."

"Yes Sir. Will do." The captain answered with a small smile.

"Sir. forgive me for saying so, but you really are a sneaky bastard."

"Correction Louis, I am a sneaky commando bastard." Commander Ross answered with a broad grin on his face.

"Now enough small talk. Get those men in the water."
"Yes Sir."

Chapter 9: In Harm's Way

0900 Toulon France, Naval Headquarter

Dressed in a crisp white uniform, the young ensign briskly walked down the corridor of Naval headquarters. Reaching the Admiral's door, he paused briefly to compose himself before raising his hand to knock firmly.

"Come ahead." The Admiral called out.

With a deep breath, he pushed open the door and stepped into the office. The ensign snapped into a smart salute, holding it until the Admiral returned the gesture.

"Ensign, what brings you here today?" the Admiral inquired, his tone firm yet welcoming.

"Sir, I have an urgent update." The ensign replied, his voice clear and unwavering. "The mercenary convoy from Pakistan crossed the border into northern Italy at 0500 this morning local time. They are reported enroute to Genoa."

Vice Admiral Étienne did not reply at once, instead he walked over to the window and stood quietly with his arms crossed behind his back looking out at the sprawling naval base and the ships in port.

"Thank you, Ensign. Confirm Commandant Gaston is aware of this intel immediately. I believe he is on Corsica at the camp." Étienne said without turning around.

"Yes, Sir. I will relay the information right away."
"Dismissed." The admiral said, still looking out the window.

GHOST COMMANDO – Battle for Cavallo

* * *

Submarine Liberté's, near Cavallo Island

In the confines of the submarines command deck, the crew diligently performed their duties, with the captain, Louis Renault, overseeing ships status and preparations for the mission ahead. Suddenly, a communication officer approached the captain. "Captain, it's Commandant Gaston calling from Melusine, he wishes to speak with you and Commander Ross on an urgent matter."

Captain Renault nodded. "Find Commander Ross and tell him to meet me in my quarters, then put the call through."

* * *

Commandant Gaston's voice echoed through the speaker. "Captain, I have an update regarding the mercenary convoy."

"Go ahead, Commandant." Captain Renault replied, while Commander Ross stood beside him, listening intently.

"The convoy has advanced into Italy and is confirmed enroute to Genoa Harbor." Gaston informed them.

"We anticipate their arrival Cavallo within 12 to 24 hours."

Commander Ross exchanged a quick glance with Captain Renault, understanding the significance of the news.

"Thank you for the update, Commandant." Captain Renault said. "We are currently submersed northeast of the island. There are only two access points from the sea. On the east side of the island is its only beach and in the southwest corner is a marina. We believe it will be a beach assault Sir."

Commander Ross chimed in. "Gaston we are locked down and tight. Two squads ready, and the sub able and willing."

"Good to hear commander." The commandant responded. "I am on Melusine, my squad and two medics are ready to go the minute Graham reports the mercs are in the water. By the way, your sergeant Moreau is pestering me to go along. Says the Adélard squad are his boys."

"He is a good man in a fight Gaston." Ross added quickly.

"Very well commander I'll bring him along." Gaston's voice remained serious yet friendly. "Captain how soon after you disable the merc boat will you be able to put men on shore?" "20 minutes, 30 on the outside Commandant." Captain Renault answered.

"Going to be tight gentlemen. Including himself, Adélard, has only seven commandos available to fight, facing as many as thirty hostiles until we reinforce him." Gaston said, worry evident in his voice.

"I don't want to lose those young men because we are late to the party Commander. Am I clear?"

"Yes Sir. He will hold Gaston. I have faith in that young man." Commander Ross answered.

"Very well. Gaston Out."

* * *

"Can he hold commander." Captain Renault asked.

"I hope so Louis, or this could all go south in a hurry.

GHOST COMMANDO – Battle for Cavallo

Congo, Rebel Headquarters

"Good morning Mr. Boulanger, what good news do you have for me today?" Aziza Samira the Burundian Rebal leader asked playfully.

"The funding you requested will be deposited into your accounts today. Is that enough good news for today?" Boulanger asked mimicking her playful manner.

"Excellent. Then we will attack the warlord in the morning."
"Not at night Aziza? In the morning?" The intelligence operative asked.

"Yes, yes, Mr. Boulanger in the full light and glory of God's sun. My people have identified 17 businesses and buildings outside the Warlords camp that actively support his evil world." Aziza paused to laugh aloud. "It will be glorious . . . we will destroy it all."

"What of the innocents Aziza?"

"There are no innocents." Aziza continued laughing, disconnecting the call.

* * *

Bugatti Mansion, Cavallo Island

In the quiet confines of Armand's office, Adélard sat with Armand and Isabella, discussing the grave news they had just received. The atmosphere was tense, and Adélard could see the concern in their eyes.

"Armand, Isabella." Adélard began. "I just received a critical update from Commandant Gaston."

"The mercenaries have crossed into Italy, and based on their current pace, it's highly likely they will attempt their assault on the island late tonight."

Armand's face tensed, and Isabella placed a hand on his shoulder, offering reassurance. "We knew this moment would come." Isabella said softly.

Adélard nodded, acknowledging their courage. "Indeed, we have Isabella. Try not to alarm the girls but tonight you will leave for Toulon. Once your safely away from this island, the rest of us will be free to do all that boys stuff you really don't want to know or see."

Armand looked at Adélard with a determined expression. "You may be underestimating this mother lioness mon ami. Regardless, I agree with you, I will feel much better knowing my family is out of harm's way."

Adélard leaned forward, his gaze steady. "I took the liberty of ordering my squad to come to your dining room for a briefing. We will need everyone to be on the same page, know their responsibility, and be ready to act at a moment's notice. Additionally, I would like you Armand, Luigi your security chef, and François to attend the briefing as well."

"Certainly." Both Armand and Isabella nodded in agreement.

Adélard gave a reassuring smile. "Excellent. I'll go make the arrangements, and we'll meet in the dining room in 45 minutes."

GHOST COMMANDO – Battle for Cavallo

As Armand and Isabella stood to leave, Adélard placed a hand on Armand's shoulder and asked him to stay behind. "You knew this already, didn't you?"

"Not exactly, but yesterday Gaston asked me to transfer the 10 million Euro for the rebel leader in the Congo, so I knew things were happening fast and I assumed the scum coming to hurt my family were getting close." Armand answered then paused. "Thank you, Adélard, I am grateful to have you and the men of your squad by my side."

"You could have asked for a seasoned squad Armand. It might have been the better call." Adélard told his friend.

"Yes, mon ami. That is true, but I had a feeling about you and your men. Call it divine intervention or just the madness of ignorance and hubris. But my Isabella and I . . . we trust you and believe you are the right man at the right time."

"Well Armand, for both are sakes . . . I hope you were right."

With that, they left the office, and Adélard quickly set about arranging the briefing with François. The squad members were the first to arrive followed by Luigi, Captain Philippe from the Requin, and the American Adam. As the sounds of hushed conversations and the scent of fresh coffee filled the air, Adélard understood how critical this briefing would be. The danger was imminent, the time to act was now.

"Gentlemen, this morning French intelligence confirmed the mercenary force has entered Italy and is traveling towards Genoa harbor." Adélard began, then paused seeing Graham had something to add.

"Adélard, we just received a report courtesy of the Italian intelligence agency AISE that a large fishing boat has disappeared from Genoa harbor. Our French intelligence has confirmed that it is work of the Pakistan mercenaries we have been tracking. Local police have reported two sailors were found dead with their throats cut near the docks, and marina camera's recorded 25 to 30 men boarding the stolen craft." Graham informed the room.

"Thanks Graham. Is Commander Ross aware of this?" Adélard asked.

"Yes, he is and Commandant Gaston at Melusine as well."

Adélard stood up facing the men. "It's tonight then gentlemen."

"Luigi, are your men ready to evacuate Mrs. Bugatti and the girls?"

"Yes, Monsieur Adélard. I have taken the liberty of loading Isabella and girl's bags already in the Defender. Monsieur Julio and my men have agreed to sleep in the mansion to make the evacuation as fast as possible."

"Full combat gear Julio. Understood?" Adélard ordered. "Understood." Julio responded very seriously.

"Captain Philippe, is your boat and the commandos ready?"

"Yes, we are Adélard and the two commandos staying behind know their assignments and are well armed."

GHOST COMMANDO – Battle for Cavallo

"Excellent Master Philippe. Commandant Gaston wants you to contact him after our briefing." Adélard informed him.

"Will do." Philippe answered.

"Adam, have you been successful in coordinating the island people to keep them out of harm's way?"

"Yes and No Adélard. François has set up a group text that includes every non-combatant on the island and David and I have spoken to every household telling them we may need to move during the assault, but some of the older people are not willing to move. They say they will fight to protect their homes."

"Right, like winning an argument with my father. I understand, Adam, we still need to do our best to avoid them getting involved. Frying Pans are no match for AK 47's." Adélard stated.

"Graham, I want every person in this room connected with ear buds. Communication will be the key to surviving tonight, I expect minimal chatter even from you Jojo, we need Graham and his team to keep us all informed in real time."

"It's always me. Why is it always me?" Jojo asked just before Noel smacked him on the shoulder.

Adélard's face had to break a small smile before he continued. "All intel aside, gentlemen we are facing a water assault either from the beach on the east or the marina.

Based on what Graham has told us and the distance from Genoa we should expect them to arrive early tomorrow morning before sunrise. Therefore, we need to know the minute that fishing boat approaches the island and confirm that the merc are onboard."

"Graham can your thermal drone give us an estimate of how many men will be on that boat. We only need a number to confirm that it is them. I doubt 25 or 30 tourists will be coming to fish here in March.?" Adélard asked.

"Can do Adélard, Toulon is assigning a second drone to me. So, we will have eyes at sea and eyes of the island every minute."

"That is a bit of good news. Then I want confirmation the moment you can get me a head count."

"Julio, Luigi, Captain Philippe and Commander Ross on the sub will need to be notified when that boat is ten miles out and in which direction it's heading."

"Julio, Luigi that call will be your go signal. You will have 15 minutes to get to the cove. Captain Philippe be ready."

"Excuse me, Adélard." Armand interrupted. "Can we not destroy the boat with the submarine before it gets here?"

"Yes, Armand we could. The issue is one of ethics and our military is bound by ethics. This is not war! We cannot indiscriminately kill 30 men simply because we think they are bad people. We must wait for them to attempt some violent act and then send them to hell." Adélard answered firmly.

"Yes, I understand, forgive me Adélard, forgive me all of you, it is just very difficult for me to wait for those devils to make the first move when my wife and children are at risk."

* * *

"Commandant Gaston, you wished to speak with me?" Captain Philippe asked alone after the briefing.

"Yes, old friend, I did. Do not take Mrs. Bugatti to Toulon. Set your course for Genevieve's home on Corsica. Tell no one of the change until it is obvious."

"To your wife Gaston?"
"Yes, Philippe, although the people on your boat do not need to know that. Do you understand mon ami?"

"You know your secret as always been safe with me Gaston. But why?" Captain Philippe asked obviously, genuinely concerned with the change in plans and the risk involved.

"I fear that we could have underestimated the warlord or his hired thugs. They might have guessed we would have an escape plan and have ready a second force to ambush you."
"I understand that by doing this eventually the truth that Genevieve is my wife will be known and that will put my family at risk in the future. But I must take that risk now to protect the Bugatti's."

"Understood. I will do as you asked. Have no fear, the Bugatti family and yours are safe in my hands." Philippe stated confidently.

"Of that I have no doubt. Gaston out."

Naval Headquarters, Toulon France

The phone on Vice Admiral Étienne Vacheron's desk rang, and he picked it up with a sense of urgency. The voice at the other end was that of Mr. Boulanger, his trusted intelligence operative overseeing the rebel forces in the Congo.

"Étienne, we have a problem." Boulanger began. "That rebel leader Aziza is proving to be far more unstable and violent than we initially anticipated. Sir, she will unleash her army to do as much damage as possible regardless of collateral damage or innocents. Admiral, straight up, this mission is going south fast."

The vice admiral listened intently; concern etched across his face. "What do you suggest?" Étienne asked, his voice low.

"Sir I suggest that France gets the hell out of here and has no active part in this shitshow. I believe it is in our best interest to have our commando forces fall back and not participate in the attack."

"Our mission is to eliminate the Warlord who is targeting French citizens, how is pulling out going enable that mission?" The Admiral Asked.

Mr. Boulanger replied. "Trust me Sir when I tell you, tomorrow morning there is going to be a bloodbath of epic proportions."

"The chances of that Warlord surviving the day are slim and that is without our active involvement in the attack, risking our men's lives, or involving our nation directly."

GHOST COMMANDO – Battle for Cavallo

Taking a deep breath Boulanger continued. "Étienne, I promise you, if that scum survives the day, I will hunt him down and eliminate him myself."

The admiral weighed the information carefully before responding. "You may be right. Our priority is to ensure the safety of our citizens and achieve our mission objectives without undue risk or transparency. Hold the line. I will issue a standdown order to the commando forces immediately."

With those words, the admiral put Boulanger on hold, called Gérard in charge of all the commando's forces in the Congo and began issuing the orders. The tension between the men was palpable as he conveyed the decision to stand down the commando forces from the Ides of March operation. At the same time, he made it clear that the intel team, led by Cristian Secouer, was to remain incountry and continue to gather intel and send in reports.

Once the orders had been issued, the admiral turned his attention back to Mr. Boulanger. "Thank you for bringing this to my attention."

"Of course, Sir." Boulanger said. "Pulling our men out is the right and ethical call. Tomorrow will be ugly. Admiral I am staying incountry as well. I want to observe the situation closely and if necessary, deal with the Warlord myself."

With that, the call ended, and the vice admiral was left to reflect on the gravity of the situation.

The rebel leader Aziza Samira's unpredictability had introduced a new layer of complexity to the mission.

"Bella Rosa" Italian fishing boat, off the coast of Italy

Anzor Mayrbek, the Chechen Mercenary Leader, stood on the deck of the fishing boat, the salty sea breeze tousling his hair. Beside him, one of his mercenaries, a skilled pilot, was steering the vessel towards Cavallo Island just south of Corsica. Anzor turned to the pilot and asked. "How long until we reach our destination?"

The pilot glanced at the navigation instruments and replied. "We should arrive at the island about 4 am local time Anzor. The winds are in our favor, and the boat is performing exceptionally well."

Anzor nodded in approval. "Good. We need to approach the island under the cover of darkness."

The pilot smiled, his admiration for the boat evident. "This boat is a true gem, Anzor, she is fast, quiet, and agile."

Anzor's eyes gleamed with satisfaction. The success of their mission relied on the element of surprise, and the boat's performance was essential for their plans to unfold smoothly. As they continued their journey towards the island, Anzor's mind was focused on the task at hand.

He knew that he was about to face some formidable resistance, but not much, and he was confident in his thirty well-trained and ruthless mercenaries. His plan was simple, deadly, and impossible to stop. Besides, he had an Ace in the hole, he had a spy on the island giving him eyes on everything.

Meanwhile, as the boat glided swiftly through the dark waters, the multinational collection men below rested and enjoyed the voyage. They were excited at the prospect of earning over a year's wages in one day and some even shared their dreams of what that money could do for their families.

As the night deepened, Anzor's crew remained calm and relaxed as the darkness shrouding their approach, silently moving them ever closer to their target. Anzor's heart pounded with anticipation and excitement, the moment of reckoning was drawing near, and he was ready to unleash chaos and earn his bonus.

* * *

2350 Hidden surveillance center, Cavallo Island

The weight of the impending battle bore heavily on his mind, Adélard found himself lying on top of his bed, eyes closed, but not quite asleep. His body felt tense, muscles slightly clenched, as if they were already preparing for action.

Thoughts and plans swirled in his mind, replaying the details of the briefing, the strategic positions, and the potential scenarios they might face. He tried to calm his racing thoughts, but the adrenaline coursing in his veins resisted.

Ring, ring.

"Adélard, it's time." The voice on the other end said.
"Graham?"
"What is it?
"What is going on?"

"We got eyes on the fishing boat Adélard."

"Good Work Graham. How far out?

Hold a minute, Adélard." Graham said, turning to Lieutenant Laurent, who was monitoring the drone's feed.

"What do you say Laurent?"

"Based on its current speed and course, I estimate about 4 hours." The lieutenant answered.

"Looks like 0330 Adélard." Graham repeated.

"And what about our peeping Tom? Where is he?" Adélard asked.

"Adélard, this is Dupont, I have had eyes on him most of the night. Currently he is in an empty house on the south side near the marina. He has not move in a couple of hours. Probably sleeping."

"Well done guys. Keep me informed." Adélard said.

"Master Philippe, get ready you are a go in 0100. Confirm?"

"Confirmed Adélard."

"Julio, it's on. Rolling at 0030. Confirm?

"Luigi. get your team ready and the Bugatti's up. Thanks to Graham we have additional time. You need to be rolling by 0030. Confirm?"

"Confirmed Adélard. Can the girls dress? It is cold outside."

"Yes, but do not be late. 0030 at the Defender" Adélard answered.

"Julio confirm?"

"I'm on it, Adélard, heading towards the truck now, I'll have it nice and toasty for the girls."

"Henri it's on. Suit up. 0100 at your position. Extra Ammo. Confirm?"

"Confirmed Adélard."

"Noel it's on. Suit up. 0100 at your position. Extra Ammo. Confirm?"

"Confirmed Adélard." Bringing a crate of ammo to the mansion as a fall back."

"Good thinking Noel."

"Adam, David it's on. ETA Cavallo 0400. Stay in connect with Dupont for site reps. Confirm?"

"Confirmed." Adam.
"Confirmed." David.

"Jojo it's on. Meet me in the mansion at 0130."

Bring two HK's and four extra Clips. Confirm?"

"Heard. Turn the pool heater on boss." Jojo answered.

* * *

"Graham, get Ross and Gaston on the horn and conference me in." Adélard Ordered.

"Heard. Give me ten." Graham answered.

* * *

Commandant Gaston picked up his phone quickly anticipating the call all night. As the line connected, Adélard wasted no time and immediately conveyed the news.

"Commandant, the fishing boat has been located enroute to Cavallo. Drone coverage is constant. Intel reports 30 Mercs aboard. ETA at Cavallo is 0400. Launching the Requin at 0100."

Gaston's voice came through the line, calm and composed. "Good work, Adélard. Have you informed Commander Ross?"

"I'm on the line Gaston." Ross answered.

"Graham. I will need location reports on the fishing boat every 30 minutes or so to move the sub into position. Doable?" Commander Ross asked.

"Yes Sir. Lieutenant Laurent is full time on the Toulon drone watching them. He will keep you updated." Graham Answered.

"Adélard, I will have my helo assault team loaded and ready by 0230. We are planning on a Bugatti compound LZ and we will be coming in Hot."

GHOST COMMANDO – Battle for Cavallo

"Much appreciated Commandant. Time you get here the party should be interesting." Adélard answered bravely.

"I know son, I know. Leave a few for me Adélard."

"Yes Sir."

* * *

"Dupont, Adam needs to know where the mercs are when they arrive so he can keep innocents where they are not. And I need to know if our peeping Tom moves an inch. Understood?"

"Loud and clear Adélard." Dupont answered.

"Graham, one favor?" Adélard asked.
"Anything mon ami."

"Try to keep Father Paulo safe. He might try to play the hero." Adélard said.

"I'll do my best." Graham answered sincerely.

"We are ready for this, Adélard." Graham said, trying to instill confidence in his friend and in himself. "We all know what to do and why we are doing it. God is with us!"

Adélard nodded to himself, his mind already running through the contingency plans he had in place in case things went south. "I know, Graham, I know. I tell you what, you point them out and I will shoot them down. Deal?"

"Heard."

In the early hours of the morning, as darkness still blanketed the island, Luigi gently knocked on the door of Isabella and Armand's bedroom. The soft tap was enough to stir Isabella from her slumber, and she quickly sat up, the worry already etched on her face. As she switched on the bedside lamp, the room was bathed in a warm glow.

"Armand, Isabella, wake up." Luigi called softly, stepping into the room. "We need to get ready. The mercenaries are getting close."

Isabella's heart skipped a beat as she looked at Luigi, her eyes wide with concern. "How close, Luigi? Are we in danger?"

Luigi offered a reassuring smile, though his eyes reflected the gravity of the situation. "We have a little extra time, if you want to dress the girls. It's very cold outside. Julio is already in the Defender; he has it warmed up and ready. We need to leave by 12:30. I will be outside with the security team to escort you downstairs."

Armand, who had been awakened by the conversation, got out of bed, and joined them. His face was tense as he asked.

"How much time do we have, Luigi?"

"Approximately four hours for the attack." Luigi replied, his voice steady. "Adélard wants Isabella and the girls off the island in an hour. Captain Philippe is ready at the cove and Julio is waiting downstairs to transport us."

"It is time Armand. We can't afford any delay."

GHOST COMMANDO – Battle for Cavallo

Isabella nodded, her mind racing with thoughts of their safety. "I'll start packing our bags immediately."

Armand gave wife a reassuring hug. "You have already done that my Isabella and the bags are already loaded in the defender." Everything is ready, we just need to get the girls up and dressed."

As they made their way to the twin daughters' room, Isabella couldn't help but feel a mix of fear and sadness. She gently woke Reine and Taber, who blinked sleepily at their mother.

"Mommy, what's happening?" Reine asked, her voice small and uncertain.

"We're going on a little adventure, my love." Isabella said, trying to keep her voice steady. "We need to leave the island for a little while, but don't worry, we will be safe."

Taber reached out to hold her father's hand. "Are we leaving because of the bad men, Daddy?"

Isabella's heart ached at her daughter's innocence. She knelt, hugging both girls tightly.

"Yes, my darlings. But we have Luigi and the brave men outside to protect us. We'll be okay."

Reine looked up at her father, her eyes filled with concern. "Daddy, will you be with us?"

Armand crouched down to meet his daughters' gaze, his emotions threatening to overwhelm him.

"I have to stay here for now, my angel, to make sure the island is safe. But I promise you, I'll be with you again soon."

Taber's eyes welled up with tears, and she hugged her father tightly. "I don't want to go, Daddy. I want to stay with you."

Armand swallowed hard, fighting back his own tears.
"I know, sweetheart, but sometimes we have to do things we don't want to do to keep the people we love safe."

As Isabella watched the emotional exchange between her husband and their daughters, tears streamed down her cheeks. She embraced Armand, seeking solace in his arms.

"You must promise me you'll be careful, Armand." Isabella whispered, her voice trembling. "Promise me!"

Armand held her close, his voice breaking with emotion. "I promise, Isabella. I promise I will do everything in my power, but right now I need you and the girls to go. We do not have that much time." The next few minutes passed in a blur of emotion as the family gathered their belongings and made their way to the waiting Defender.

As they prepared to leave the safety of their home, Isabella looked back at the mansion, her heart heavy with uncertainty. With one last embrace, Armand kissed his wife and daughters, his eyes filled with love and determination.

"I Love you. Take care of each other."

Isabella trembled, her emotions boiling over. "I Love you, my husband."

GHOST COMMANDO – Battle for Cavallo

As the Defender drove away, Isabella looked back at Armand one last time, holding desperately onto the belief that they would be reunited when the danger had passed.

* * *

As Isabella and the girls, accompanied by four Bugatti security men, arrived at the cove, Captain Philippe was there to graciously welcome them aboard the Requin boat. With a warm smile, he escorted the family below into the cabin, ensuring they were comfortable.

Inside the cabin, Isabella and the girls settled in, their nerves slightly eased by the reassuring presence of Captain Philippe.

The twins looked up at him with wide eyes, curious about this kind older man with a salt and pepper beard and a tattoo of a girl on his arm. Philippe knelt to their level, a big smile on his face, his voice gentle and kind.

"Bonjour, my little ones." Philippe said with a twinkle in his eyes. "Do you like fast boats?" He asked.

Reine and Taber both nodded their heads yes as their mother Isabella marveled at how attentive they were to Philippe.

"Oh . . . I see, the Bugatti racing blood is strong in you both." The girl's eyes grew wide at the mention of the family racing tradition.

"Well tonight my dears, you are on the fastest boat in all the oceans, and you two are going to get a fun ride out in the open sea. How does that sound?"

Reine and Taber exchanged excited glances before turning back to Philippe, nodding enthusiastically.
"Yes, please!" They chimed in unison.

Meanwhile, Captain Philippe had quietly spoken to Luigi, emphasizing the importance of keeping the family physically secure during the journey. "If we need to avoid an issue, things can get bumpy fast." Philippe warned Luigi. "Under no circumstance allow them to leave this cabin if I deploy the guns." Captain Philippe told Luigi firmly.

"Yes Captain." Luigi said between clinched teeth.

With everything in place, Captain Philippe returned to the deck, giving the order to prepare for launch. The four commandos who had been guarding the cove came down from the rocks and got on the boat, expertly securing the lines as the boat began to glide smoothly out of the cove.

From the hill above the cove, Julio watched the scene unfold. He waited patiently until the Requin boat was underway before he got into the Defender. "Fair winds, Master Philippe." He muttered driving away.

As the Requin boat started its journey, Philippe's keen eyes scanned the sky and sea. He yelled down the open hatch to the cabin below. "Are we ready to go fast girls?"
"Yes!" He heard Taber yell back loud and clear.

In an instant the Requin jumped out of the water onto a plane and was cruising at 60mph causing the cabin to be filled with giggles and Captain Philippe to smile.

Chapter 10: All Hell breaks Loose

Driving back from the hidden cove Julio picked up the two Requin boat Commandos that had been guarding the road and returned to the compound. Once inside the men moved swiftly to their assignments. Julio joined Henri on the east side of the entrance wall while the two Requin commandos joined Noel on the west.

"Good to have you and your big gun back Julio. I was getting lonely out here all by myself." Henri told him with a pat on the back, his eyes never ceasing to scan the surrounding area.

"I thought Adélard was with us?" Julio asked.

"Oh, he is, but first he had to hold Jojo's hand and walk him to the pool." Henri said chuckling.

Julio smiled at the joke, but inside his heart pounded with a mix of anxiety and determination.

* * *

Adélard with Jojo dressed in full dive gear walked to the rear of the mansion, their steps purposeful and focused.

"Listen I did agree to spend half the night in that freezing water for you Adélard, but I am wearing my shoes." Jojo told him, lifting one foot to demonstrate.

"White sneakers to go along with your black night dive gear. Jojo you are a fashion icon." Adélard told him smiling.

"Dress for Success, mon ami." Jojo stated grinning.

As they reached the pool area, Adélard pointed out the position he wanted Jojo to take. "Put the extra HK here on the coping by the deep end of the pool." Adélard instructed.

"I want you stationed at the shallow end."

"If that was a short joke, you need more practice, Adélard." Jojo told him while setting down the extra HK and 2 clips on the coping.

"Jojo." Adélard said in a muffled voice. "I don't know if they will try the back door, but if they do it will happen here with them coming up over the cliff."

"They will not expect Jojo the human popsicle hiding in the pool waiting for them." Adélard said patting his dear friend on the shoulder. "Serious Jojo, I need you to be in the pool, underwater, waiting for them."

"I understand. You can count on me." Jojo answered.

Jojo glanced at the extra rifle, then back at Adélard, a hint of curiosity in his eyes. "Is that second rifle for me?"

Adélard paused for a moment before answering, "It's for me, Jojo. If your dance party back here goes south, I plan on being in the pool with you."

"Understood. You don't mind if I pee in the pool, do you Adélard?" Jojo asked, forcing a smile on his face.

Before Adélard left, he instructed Jojo to get into the water to check his communication system with Graham.

GHOST COMMANDO – Battle for Cavallo

"Graham, make sure communications with Jojo are working perfectly." Adélard ordered, as Jojo submerged into the cold pool water, to conduct the check.

Adélard turned to walk back. Passing through the house Adélard saw Armand sitting in his office and gave him a reassuring nod, signaling that everything was under control.

Reaching the compound, he joined Julio and Henri at the wall, where they were keeping a watchful eye on the surrounding areas.

The six commandos sat in cold silence guarding both sides of the Bugatti compound entrance until Jojo keyed his mic.

"Hey Adélard, I found a six of Despérados beer at the bottom of the pool. Thanks."

"Save two for me." Henri chimed in.

* * *

Adélard, his mind abuzz with the need for a real-time update on the island reached up to key his mic.

"Graham. How is everything looking on the island?" Adélard asked, his voice calm but focused.

"Everything's quiet so far, Adélard." Graham replied. "No signs of any activity around the compound or the surrounding area."

Adélard nodded, relieved to hear the news.
"Good. What about the swarm drones?"

"The swarm drones are fully charged and ready for action." Graham answered with pride.

"Perfect. Let's launch them and assess their night vision swarm capabilities on the compound and areas we suspect the attack will come from. I want to know how much coverage we can have tonight."

"Will do." Graham answered.

"We have 36 micro drones, but how much flight time do we have before they need charging?" Adélard asked worried that he would lose that advantage during a battle.

"About 20 to 30 minutes." Graham replied. "The battery packs are replaceable, although we will need them to return to the grotto for that."

Adélard thought for a moment, then said. "Alright, let's launch twelve at a time. That way, we will maintain coverage."

"Agreed." Graham replied. "That will give us twelve in a swarm, twelve more ready in reserve, and twelve in the grotto getting new batteries."

"I'll get the first batch up and running right away and program one of monitors to show all twelve of the drone images at once." Graham answered enthusiastically.

"Good Graham, give me a site rep when they are up."
"Understood." Graham responded.

* * *

As Graham's voice came through the communication earpiece, he sounded pleased and excited. "Adélard, the first swarm of drones are up, and the images are sharp and clear at 50feet. With twelve up we have full coverage of the compound and the surrounding area."

"Great work, Graham." Adélard replied, a sense of relief evident in his voice. "You and your team have done an excellent job. I'm impressed."

"Thanks, Adélard." Graham responded with a hint of pride.

As Adélard was about to express further appreciation, Graham interrupted. "You might want to turn around, Adélard. Looks like you have a friendly visitor."

Quickly turning, Adélard was taken aback when he saw François strolling calmly across the compound, carrying a large thermos of coffee, a bag of freshly baked croissants, and paper cups. Adélard could not believe his eyes.

"François, are you out of your mind?" Adélard exclaimed, trying to keep his voice low. "We are about to be invaded by an overpowering force of 30 mercenaries, and you're here with coffee and pastries?"

François kept his face impassive, seemingly unfazed by Adélard's words or the impending danger.
"That is almost correct monsieur Adélard, these are croissants not pastries. It is my experience that a good cup of coffee and fresh croissants can work wonders." He replied with a nonchalant smile.

"The mercenaries can be here at any moment." Adélard persisted in trying to drive some rational thoughts into François's head.

"Yes monsieur, I do understand." François said calmly, pouring coffee into a paper cup for Henri, then Julio, and finally for Adélard.

Adélard sighed, realizing that François could not be persuaded. François placed a reassuring hand on Adélard's shoulder.

"As for the coffee." François continued with a playful glint in his eye. "I will not be serving any to the invaders."

Adélard chuckled, finally able to see the humor in the situation. "Fair enough. Thank you, François, for being here and for the coffee."

* * *

"Commander Ross?"
"Go ahead Dupont." The commander said.

Lieutenant Dupont's voice came through the communication system on the submarine. "Commander the fishing boat is now on a course towards the east coast of Cavallo. ETA 60 minutes."

Commander Ross acknowledged the report. "Roger that, Lieutenant. Any intel of the hostiles onboard?"

Dupont glanced at his screen reconfirming the previous data. "Yes, Commander. According to the Toulon thermal drone, there are 37 to 39 men on board the boat."

"Shit!" Commander Ross replied, his mind racing with the information. "Well done, Dupont. Keep on it."

Meanwhile, at the command center in the underground grotto, Graham was relaying the same information to Adélard.

"Adélard." That fishing boat is approximately an hour away, tracking clearly towards the eastside of the island. The thermal drone indicates 39 armed men on board."

Adélard's face grew tense as he absorbed the news. "That is a much larger force than anticipated." Shaking his head in frustration, Adélard set his jaw and started issuing orders.

"Alert all the commandos and the Americans on the Island. Find that damned priest and tie him down. Everyone needs to be aware of the situation."

"Have Dupont find Gaston and update him. I want that helo here as fast as possible."

"Contact Master Philippe yourself. Give him our intel and tell him to be on the lookout. The size of this force makes me think there maybe be another waiting to intercept him."

"Get the word out Graham, I want every innocent out of harm's way as of right now."

"Tell Laurent I want him on top of every camera, motion detector, and his eyes watching anything our island thermal drone sees. I want a constant location update for everyone on this island and that damn peeping Tom."

"On it, Adélard." Graham answered jumping into motion.

Graham swiftly got to work, sending out the urgent message to the squad and the reinforcements. "Attention all squads and operatives, this is a priority update. The fishing boat is less than an hour away from Cavallo's east coast, carrying 39 heavily armed men. Prepare for potential hostile activity. Be on high alert."

As the message spread through the network of commandos and operatives, the atmosphere in the underground grotto became more focused and determined. Graham. Dupont, and Laurent understood that the moment they had been preparing for was imminent.

Graham reached behind his back and pulled out his Beretta pistol, placing it on the desk in front of him dramatically.

Seeing the Bugatti emblem embossed on the grip caused Graham to nod a silent affirmation, his resolve more focused than ever before. Turning to the officers next to him, he placed his hand over the gun and spoke. "Dupont, Laurent, this is real, our mission is critical. If any of us are going to survive today. Nothing and no one must be allowed to stop us. Am I clear?"

"Clear, the men answered checking their sidearms."

* * *

Commander Ross stood at the edge of the submarine's control room, relaying the critical information privately to Captain Renault.

"Captain, we've just received an update from our team on the island. The fishing boat is approximately 60 minutes away from the east coast of Cavallo. There are 39 armed men on board."

Captain Renault listened intently, his face set in a serious expression. "More than we thought. Any change in plans Commander?

"No Captain, but our timing must be perfect if we are to help Adélard before it's too late."

"Commander, we can take out that boat right now. Both forward tubes are loaded. Just give the word and this will be over." The captain said fulling knowing the gravity of his suggestion.

Closing his eyes before answering, Commander Ross let out a slow exhale. "No Captain, that we will not do, for if we did, we would be murders and no better than the evil we are sworn to protect against. We must wait until that boat launches an assault on the island. Then and only then will we unleash our might. Am I perfectly clear Captain?"

"Yes commander. Perfectly." The captain answered.

Captain Renault walked back to the center of the control room and called his executive officer over. "Lieutenant, get our squads ready to deploy, we are 60 minutes out."

"Yes Sir." Lieutenant Patel responded sharply. "I will go below immediately. We will be ready upon your order."

Captain Renault quickly issued orders for his chief engineer. "Mr. Donato takes us down, level at 150 feet and continue current course until we have a radar lock on the fishing boat."

Lieutenant Donato acknowledged the order and quickly adjusted the submarine's depth. "Diving to 150 feet, Captain."

As the minutes ticked by, tension filled the control room. The entire crew of the submarine was on high alert, prepared to execute their mission with precision and speed. Captain Renault's voice broke through the tense atmosphere. "Keep me updated, Mr. Patel."

"Yes Sir." Lieutenant Patel responded from the dive deck of the submarine.

* * *

Graham quickly dialed the satellite phone number for Captain Philippe, hoping to reach him before the Requin boat was too far along its course to Toulon. After a few rings, the captain answered, his voice calm and steady. "This is Captain Philippe of the Requin. Go ahead."

"Captain Philippe, this is Graham from the island. We have an urgent update for you." Graham said, trying to keep his own voice steady. "Drone intel reports the fishing boat carrying the attackers is approximately an hour away from Cavallo. There are 39 men on board, heavily armed."

Captain Philippe's voice remained composed, but he clearly understood the gravity of the news. "Thank you, Graham."

Graham continued, relaying Adélard's concerns. "Adélard fears that we may have underestimated the size and capabilities of the mercenary force. He warns that there could be a secondary force waiting to intercept you and murder the Bugatti family. He is worried that if that force exists, that they might be coordinating with the fishing boat." Graham added.

Captain Philippe appreciated the warning and knew that he needed to assure Graham and in turn Adélard that he would protect the family. "Received and understood. Tell Adélard the family will remain safe in my care."

As the conversation ended, Captain Philippe relayed the information to his commandos, who quickly went into action, preparing for any potential threats. The atmosphere on the Requin instantly intensified.

Isabella and the girls were seated in the cabin, unaware of the imminent danger that surrounded them. The four-man security team, led by Luigi, was also on high alert, positioned strategically around the boat.

Captain Philippe joined the security team on deck, his eyes scanning the horizon for any sign of approaching boats. The wind was calm, and the sea was eerily quiet, adding to the tension in the air.

Suddenly, one of his commandos called out. "Captain Philippe, I have a small boat approaching from the north. It's about half a mile away."

The captain's heart flooded with adrenaline as he immediately issued orders to the commandos. "Deploy the gunwale guns, stand ready."

"Luigi get your men below and protect the family."

As the boat came closer, it became apparent that it was a small fishing vessel, seemingly innocent enough. However, Captain Philippe knew better than to let his guard down.

"Captain, the fishing boat is changing course and heading directly toward us." The commando reported watching the boat through his binoculars.

"I got them on radar as well." One of the commandos called out."

"What is going on?" Isabella asked, opening the cabin door.

"I will explain later Mrs. Bugatti. Please get below right now." Philippe told her, closing the cabin door in her face.

Captain Philippe's mind raced, considering the possibilities. Could this be a decoy to some unseen attack? A legitimate threat that was meant to deceive them.

As the two boats neared each other, the fishing boat slowed down and came to a stop near the Requin. Several men were visible on deck, their intentions unclear. But after seeing combat commandos with assault rifles on the Requin deck.

And the two 50mm machine guns pointed in their direction the men became animated and scurried about their boat.

GHOST COMMANDO – Battle for Cavallo

Captain Philippe picked up his bullhorn and called out to the innocent looking fishing boat.

"This is Captain Philippe of the ship Requin. Are you in need of assistance?"

Not receiving a response, he tried again.

"Are you in need of assistance?"

Suddenly, the fishing boat's engines roared to life, and it began to veer away from the Requin.

Captain Philippe and his crew watched as it sped off, disappearing into the distance.

"No guns aboard Captain, at least none that I could see, and the men were not armed." One of the commandos informed Philippe.

Feeling relieved, Captain Philippe turned to the commando. "Good to hear. It seems then, that we just scared the shit out of some poor fishermen."

"Not a bad night's work." The commando answered smiling.

Moments later, Captain Philippe stood with Mrs. Bugatti and Luigi in the cabin of the Requin boat, a sense of determination and concern etched on his face. He took a deep breath before addressing them both.

"Mrs. Bugatti, I have made a difficult decision.

"After receiving new information, I am deeply concerned for your safety." Captain Philippe began.

Isabella looked puzzled, her eyes searching his for answers.

"What is it, Captain?"
"Why the heavy guns?"
"Why the change of plans?"

Philippe hesitated for a moment before continuing. "We have learned that an overpowering force is about to land on your island. Visual reconnaissance confirms they are mercenaries, heavily armed and will attack within the hour." Isabella's eyes narrowed; she clenched his fists. "How many of them?"

Captain Philippe paused, weighing his words carefully. "We believe there are close to 40 men on the approaching boat. There is also a possibility that they may have a secondary force waiting to ambush us on our way to Toulon."

Isabella's eyes widened with fear, and she glanced at her twin daughters, who were playing nearby.
"What do we do now, Captain?"

"Isabella, your safety, and that of your daughters are my top priority. After careful consideration, I have decided to change our route. Instead of heading straight to Toulon, we will take a circular route to the Melusine base on Corsica."

"But why Corsica?" Isabella asked, still trying to process the sudden change.

GHOST COMMANDO – Battle for Cavallo

"Melusine is a highly secure naval facility designed to repel an armada of attackers from the sea and from the air. There are over 150 men currently on duty there. And most importantly no one anywhere, not even our own command would expect us to go there."

"You and the girls will be welcome and safe there, I promise." Captain Philippe added, trying to reassure her. Isabella took a deep breath, trying to compose herself.

"Thank you, Captain. I trust your judgment."

As the Requin boat set off on its new route towards the Melusine base on Corsica, Isabella clung tightly to her daughters, finding comfort in the thought of reaching a secure location and yet her mind filled with concern and fear for the danger her husband would be facing on cavallo.

The rest of the journey was tense, but they navigated through the sea with precision and caution, avoiding any suspicious boats or potential danger. Captain Philippe made sure to communicate regularly with Melusine, providing updates on their progress and ensuring a smooth arrival.

Finally, the Requin boat arrived at the base and glided gently into the converted submarine cave as the shielded doors opened, docking next to the 3 other requin boats.

A sense of relief and amazement washed over Isabella and the girls as they stepped out on the dock.
"This is cool, like some super-secret spy stuff." Taber said aloud to her sister who stood gazing in wonder.

Four commandos dressed in crisp white uniforms walked closer and welcomed them warmly to camp Melusine.

Isabella embraced Captain Philippe; her eyes filled with gratitude. "Thank you, Philippe, for protecting my girls and me." She said her voice full of emotions as tears flowed freely down her face.

At that same moment Isabella's daughter Reine came closer and pulled on Philippes trousers, interrupting her mother's emotional outburst. Kneeling to hear what the shy child had to say he asked.

"What it is little one."

"I like your boat Monsieur Philippe; can you take Taber and I for a ride again tomorrow please? Reine asked with the sweetest little voice any of the men listening had heard in a long. long time.

* * *

Adam and David moved quickly on foot going door to door trying to get the locals that had not responded to François' emergency text to move to the Musk estate. Recognizing the number of mercenaries coming was more than they had anticipated, Adam and David had changed their original plan to protect the locals and decided to gather everyone in the basement of the estate.

At the first house, Adam and David were met by an elderly couple. They opened the door with concern in their eyes as they saw the armed men standing outside.

Adam spoke gently. "I know this is alarming, but we need to evacuate you. The attack we were worried about is happening. Please come along, we have food and men at the Musk estate that will protect you."

The elderly woman looked hesitant. "Evacuate? No young man, I do not think so."

Her husband shook his head, stubbornly. "We're not leaving our home. We may be old, but we can take care of ourselves. Get along now, we don't need you."

Adam exchanged a worried glance with David, knowing they were running out of time. David tried again. "I understand that you want to protect your home, but it's not safe. We have a secure location with protection and communication devices. Please, let us take you there."

"No." The husband said slowly closing the door.

At the next house, they encountered a younger family that was receptive to their warnings, the wife was visibly scared.

"I heard others talking about this, but I didn't think it was actually going to happen. Not even when François texted." She. said tearfully. Her husband did not hesitate, he guided her out the door with his arm around her waist. "I know the way he told David."

As they continued Adam and David faced a mix of responses from the island residents. Some were fearful and willingly followed their instructions, while others were stubborn and adamant about staying put.

At the final house on their list, they encountered Mr. Forgeron, a large, stern, and resolute man. He refused to leave his home.

"I'm not going anywhere. Forget it!" He said with a scowl on his face. "Now get out of here. Next someone that comes to my door is going to get shot." Forgeron emphasized his words by holding up a double barrel shot gun.

Adam and David exchanged glances, knowing they could not force him to leave. "Very well Mr. Forgeron, good luck to you sir." Adam told him sincerely.

"That is one tough old bird Adam." David said chuckling. "True that brother, let's get back the estate." Adam answered breaking into a trot.

Adam clicked his mic. "Adélard this is Adam we have 29 locals in the basement of the Musk estate. They are scared, but we are doing our best to keep them calm. 3 couples and one nasty bastard that refused to come are still out there."

Graham broke into the conversation. "Adélard, the thermal drone has eyes on all 36 residents of the island, including the 29 in the Musk estate's basement, and those out in the community. I will inform you if any of those 7 are at any risk of being discovered.

Adélard frowned, worried about those who had chosen not to seek shelter. "We can't force them to come with us. Keep Adam and I in the loop Graham."

"Heard."

GHOST COMMANDO – Battle for Cavallo

"Wait . . . Graham, what about our peeping Tom?"

"Our cameras have eyes on him." Laurent reported. "He has a sidearm and has moved to the marina. Took up residence in the office and hasn't moved much recently.

* * *

Lieutenant Dupont stared intently at the feed from the Toulon drone, monitoring the movements of the mercenary boat. He had been keeping a close eye on it, and his heart raced as he noticed the boat slowing down and coming to a stop, roughly 200 meters off the beach on the east side of Cavallo.

Quickly, he grabbed his communication device and dialed Commander Ross aboard the submarine Liberté.

"Commander Ross, this is Dupont" He said urgently, trying to keep his voice steady. "The mercenary boat has just stopped. I repeat, they have come to a stop."

"We have them on our radar as well Lieutenant." Commander Ross informed him. "Is there any sign of activity?"

Lieutenant Dupont focused on the live video feed, his eyes darting across the screen. "Not at the moment, sir. It looks like they have come to a complete halt. No visible movements from the boat or the men on board."

Commander Ross considered the information carefully. "Keep a close eye on them Dupont. Let me know if there's any change in their status."

"Yes Sir. Understood!" Dupont answered with his attention fixed on the screen. "I'll keep you updated."

Commander Ross stood next to Captain Renault as they focused on the large map display showing the position of the mercenary boat and the sub.

"Captain, I want us to move under the mercenary boat, but for now, maintain our depth at 100 feet."

Captain Renault nodded. "Understood, Commander."

"Mr. Donato; move us in slow, maintain depth at 100. I want the Liberté directly under her keel."

"Yes, Sir Captain." Donato answered. "Captain, what if they have their fishing radar on? They will see us and try to attack the ship somehow."

"Yes Mr. Donato, that is a possibility.

"And then what do we do Sir?" The Lieutenant asked.

"Then Mr. Donato we will show them what the sons of Kraken and the Liberté can do."

"Maintain course and speed." Captain Renault called out to the helmsman.

The submarine glided smoothly under the water, its silent propulsion systems ensuring they remained undetected. The Liberté took position directly beneath the mercenary boat.

Captain Renault could feel the tension in his control room as they waited, the weight of the mission bearing down on them all. Minutes passed, and the mercenary boat remained stationary, with no report of activity.

* * *

The mercenary boat bobbed gently in the calm waters off the coast of Cavallo as Anzor Mayrbek, the Chechen Mercenary Leader, stood at the helm addressing his attack force. The group of heavily armed men, dressed in a mish-mosh assortment tactical gear, listened intently, their eyes fixed on their leader.

"Listen up." Anzor began, his voice commanding and authoritative. "Our fun night is about to begin. We have a billionaire to kill and a vulgar capitalist mansion to burn to the ground with everyone in it."

"No one on that island deserves our mercy. They are pigs, fat on the honey of the earth leaving nothing but scrapes for us and our families. We are the righteous, their redeemers."

A murmur of agreement rippled through the ranks of the mercenaries. They knew that mercy had little to do with their success or with the large bonuses they had been promised.

He pointed to the inflatable lifeboats lined up along the deck. "These lifeboats can only hold 14 men at a time. So, we'll need to launch in waves."

"I will lead the first wave." Anzor declared confidently. "We'll make our approach under the cover of darkness, and I expect absolute silence."

"When we reach the beach, we need to move according to plan and take control of the island."

He looked around at his men, they were eager, ready, their faces set with determination.

"Once the first lifeboat has dropped its men off, it will return to pick up the rest of you." Anzor continued. "With any luck, by the time the second wave gets to shore this will all be over."

One of the mercenaries raised his hand, seeking clarification. "What if we encounter resistance?"

Anzor smirked, his eyes flashing with confidence. "Resistance is unlikely." He replied. "Our intelligence indicates that the island's defenders are few in number, and they won't be expecting an attack of this scale."

"We will overwhelm them before they even have a chance to react." He gestured to the arsenal of weapons and ammunition piled nearby. "But just in case." Anzor added. "We brought enough firepower to take down any French bastard that gets in our way."

The mercenaries nodded, reassured by their leader's words. They had trained for this mission extensively, and they trusted Anzor's strategic expertise.

"Remember, once we kill the Bugatti's we will be in control of the island." Anzor said. "Our employer is paying top dollar for the Bugatti's. He doesn't give a damn what we do with the rest of the island or its people."

GHOST COMMANDO – Battle for Cavallo

The mercenaries let out a unified cheer, their adrenaline pumping as they prepared for the easy battle ahead. Anzor knew that they were hungry for glory and eager to earn their bonus no matter what it entailed.

"Let's get those lifeboats in the water. I need 27 men for the first wave. Line up and get ready for some fun." Anzor ordered.

* * *

In the dimly lit underground grotto beneath the church graveyard on Cavallo, Lieutenant Dupont's gaze was fixed on the bank of monitors in front of him. The air was tense as he monitored the thermal images displayed on the screens.

His eyes narrowed as he observed the mercenary boat, its signature appearing as a distinct heat source against the cool backdrop of the sea. Dupont's fingers tapped lightly on the keyboard, adjusting the focus and angle of the thermal cameras to get a clearer view.

As he watched, his heart rate seemed to quicken in response to the impending action. The boat remained steady on the water's surface, a sinister silhouette against the horizon. Dupont's trained eye caught a movement on the deck, and he zoomed in to see the details.

Two lifeboats were being lowered from the boat's side, their dark forms contrasting starkly against the thermal images. He counted the figures as they boarded the lifeboats, one by one. The heat signatures of their bodies stood out against the cooler sea.

Dupont's jaw tightened as he observed the cold efficiency with which they moved, each man taking their place in the lifeboats. In total, he counted 28 mercenaries boarding the lifeboats. The gravity of the situation settled heavily on his shoulders as he realized the sheer force they were about to unleash.

Dupont's hand hovered over his headset, ready to relay the information.

Not yet, he told himself, not yet.

The seconds ticked away like heartbeats in his chest. Each beat highlighted the full measure of the danger he was watching on the screen.

"Almost." He called out to Graham. "Any second now."

Chapter 11: Desperate Hour

Anzor Mayrbek stood at the edge of the deck on the fishing boat, his calculating eyes fixed on the operation unfolding before him.

The soft lapping of waves against the boat's hull created an eerie contrast to the impending violence about to erupt. He exuded an air of quiet confidence, his presence commanding the attention of the men around him.

As he watched, the mercenaries moved with practiced precision, passing down weapons and crates of ammunition to their comrades in the inflatable lifeboats.

Anzor's lips curled into a satisfied smile. He appreciated the discipline of his team, the way they operated as a well oiled machine, ready to unleash chaos at his command.

Anzor's keen eyes tracked every movement, his mind assessing the readiness of his men. The island was their prize, and he intended to claim it with brutal efficiency.

Anzor was the last to board the lifeboat, he moved to the front and took his place. Where else but at the point of the spear would a glorious leader be. Confident and eager for battle he turned facing the men in both lifeboats.

"Weapons free." Anzor declared, his words slicing through the silence like a blade. "I want Bugatti dead." His lips twisted with a sinister smile, and his voice rose in a fervent crescendo. "Glory and riches await us, my comrades. Let the island tremble and the women weep."

With that, he gave the signal, and the assault began. The engines of the inflatable lifeboats roared to life, propelling them forward with a determination that matched their leader's resolve.

Anzor smiled looking out towards the island. The night was alive with the promise of violence, and he was ready to seize his destiny with both hands, no matter the cost.

* * *

Lieutenant Dupont's eyes were fixed on the thermal images displayed on the screens before him. His heart raced as he watched the lifeboats launch from the mercenary fishing boat, the heat signatures of the motors and the men aboard clearly visible against the cold backdrop of the sea.

"Lifeboats launched." Dupont declared urgently, his voice cutting through the tense silence in the grotto.

Laurent and Graham, stationed nearby, immediately sprang into action. Laurent activated his communication device and swiftly relayed the information to Commandant Gaston at camp Melusine. "Gaston, this is Laurent. The attack is underway. lifeboats launched with 28 aboard."

At the same time, Graham was on another line, contacting Adélard who was positioned at the entrance of the Bugatti compound with the rest of the squad.

"Adélard, it's Graham. They are coming now, two lifeboats with 28 enroute to the beach."

GHOST COMMANDO – Battle for Cavallo

Dupont reached for his own communication device and contacted Commander Ross aboard the submarine.

"Commander, Dupont here. The attack has commenced. Two lifeboats are on their way to the island. 28 in transit, 11 more still on the fishing boat."

In a matter of seconds, the critical information flowed through the channels, connecting every defender of the island.

* * *

Commandant Gaston, hearing Laurent report, wasted no time. "Listen up, everyone, the mercenaries have launched their attack. The Adélard squad is outnumbered 6 to 1. I want us in the air in 5." He told the team that had assembled in the dark waiting for the word.

"Load up." The squad leader yelled.

The commandos immediately sprang into action, gathering their equipment and checking their weapons. Medics double-checked their medical supplies, and the sergeant strapped himself into the heavy door gun with a nod from the pilot, Captain Auclair.

Commandant Gaston climbed aboard last, pulling the straps on his bullet proof vest tighter and checking the clip in his pistol. He sat near the door next to sergeant Moreau, his mind focused on the mission ahead.
Within minutes, the deafening sound of the rotor blades filled the air over camp Melusine as the aircraft lifted off from the landing pad.

As the helicopter soared through the sky, Commandant Gaston's mind raced. He knew his men on the island were facing a far superior enemy in numbers and he was desperate to help them. He pulled out his communication device and dialed Lieutenant Laurent on the island.

"Laurent, this is Gaston." He yelled over the noise of the helicopter. "We are airborne eta 30 minutes. "I will need continuous situation reports."

"Yes Sir." Laurent answered.

As the helicopter reached its flight altitude, the Commandant could see Cavallo island in the distance. Gaston looked down at his hands sensing his body responding to the danger ahead. "This will be a hot LZ. Be prepared to come down shooting." He yelled to his men.

"Captain Auclair, can we sweep first. This gun might make the LZ cool off a bit before we drop the squad." Sergeant Moreau asked over the flight intercom. "Sure thing, gunny." The pilot answered.

* * *

As the words echoed through the air that the mercenaries had launched the lifeboats, tension tightened its grip on every man present at the compound. Graham's announcement resonated with gravity, and the urgency of the situation. Every member of the squad, along with Armand and François in the mansion, and the Americans Adam, and David, heard the report and mentally prepared for all hell to break loose.

"Confirm, how many hostiles aboard?" Adélard asked.

"28 Adélard, with 11 more on the fishing boat." Graham answered.

The news hit them like a jolt. Adélard's mind raced, quickly adapting to the new information.

"Graham get the swarm drones up. We need eyes on the beach."

"Heard."

"Noel, Julio, get more ammo for the Grenade Launcher, mix it up and when they come don't stop firing until the barrels melt."

"On it." Both men responded running to the mansion for additional ammunition.

Graham swiftly operated the drone controls to deploy the swarm drones into the air. The drones hummed to life, all twelve cameras linking back to the monitor in the grotto.

"Swarm drones deployed." Graham confirmed, his focus on the screen displaying the live footage capturing the scene on the beach below.

"Dupont patch me through to Commander Ross." Adélard ordered.

"You're in Adélard." Dupont responded almost immediately.

"Ross this Adélard."

"We are ready now Adélard." Commander Ross told him.

"Sir I would appreciate it if those 11 men never make it to the party Sir. Our dance card seems full at the moment."

Adélard told his commander with a bit of bravado.
"I hear you, son." Commander Ross answered.

* * *

"Boats are in the water; the attack is underway." Commander Ross told Captain Renault, standing next to him aboard the submarine Liberté.

Captain Renault instantly issued orders. "Mr. Donato, bring us up, level at 30 feet."

"Sir, yes Sir. Level to 30." Donato confirmed.

Keying the intercom, the captain called executive officer Patel on the dive deck.

"Mr. Patel change in plans we need double charges on that hull. Alert the squad and lieutenant Coop. I want the dive chamber flooded in 3 minutes."

"Sir, yes Sir. Double charges Sir." Patel confirmed.

Once the submarine reached the designated depth, the outer doors to the dive chamber opened. 7 Commandos swam out, each man carrying double explosives and prepared to fight along the way if necessary.

GHOST COMMANDO – Battle for Cavallo

Their training and experience guiding them up through the dark waters as they approached the vessel. Time was of the essence; each diver placed their two charges and dove back down to the safety of the submarine as quickly as possible.

Back on the submarine, the tension was obvious as everyone watched the clock, counting down the moments until the diver's returned.

"Mr. Patel report." The captain's voice echoed through the communication system.

"Charges placed, Captain." The executive officer reported. "Divers returning, 2 on board, 5 in the water."

Watching as the last diver reentered the chamber. "Close the outer door. Pump the chamber." Lieutenant Patel ordered.

"All aboard Captain." He reported.

"Helmsmen get us out of here. Get me closer to that beach. Mr. Donato, takes us to 100 feet." The captain ordered in quick succession.

"Sir radar showing small craft, likely one of the lifeboats returning to the fishing boat." Chief engineer Donato told his captain.

* * *

Lieutenant Dupont's voice came in clearly through the communication channel aboard the submarine Liberté.

"Commander Ross, this is Dupont. Two inflatable lifeboats have landed on the beach."

"One boat has unloaded its men and is returning to the fishing boat. The other boat is continuing north along the coast, carrying a small group of mercenaries."

Commander Ross, his tone focused and composed, replied. "Understood, Lieutenant. Maintain surveillance on both boats."

Ending the call, Commander Ross turned to Captain Renault. "Louis, we can't allow them to send another group to the island."

"I know Commander, but we are still too close."

* * *

As Dupont continued to monitor the situation, relaying information back to the submarine, Graham was already informing the Bugatti compound his voice urgent but controlled. "Adélard, 23 landed, 4 moving north over water."

"Night vision drones have eyes on the main force. They've left the beach and are in the village. They are advancing towards compound, coming up on both sides of the road, moving fast."

"Well done mon ami." Adélard told him his voice tinged with a cold determination.

"Noel, Julio, you ready?" Adélard asked.

"Locked and loaded." Noel answered.
"Same here." Julio added.

"Listen up, all you sons of Kraken. No one coming to our party without an invitation is leaving here alive. Don't wait for an order. You are free to fire at will."

* * *

Hearing Adélard lay down his verbal gauntlet Graham turned his attention back to the screens, closely monitoring the mercenaries' progress. Meanwhile, Lieutenant Laurent updated the Toulon1 team on the helicopter.

"Commandant, this is Laurent. Lifeboats have landed, 23 on the ground moving fast, 4 advancing north along the coast. Contact expected at any moment." Laurent reported.

"10 minutes out. Tell Adélard we're coming in hot." Gaston told him his voice steady but full of urgency.

Laurent adjusted the controls, ensuring that the thermal drone maintained a precise focus on the targeted zone.

"Thermal drone is locked on, Commandant. We'll continue to provide updates."

* * *

The three communication channels buzzed with a sense of urgency, Graham, Dupont, and Laurent working seamlessly to gather and relay critical information.

"The only edge our guys have before reinforcements arrive is us." Graham told his men.

Just then, the two church altar boys burst into the grotto, obviously scared and out of breath from running.

"We saw the mean men in the streets, there are so many. Father Paulo said we would be safe with you." One of the young boys said trembling.

* * *

In an instant, the tranquility of the island transformed into a living hell. The cold night air was shattered by the sudden eruption of chaos as the mercenary assault on the Bugatti compound began.

Explosions rang out almost simultaneously on both sides of the entrance, as unexpectedly rockets were fired towards the commando's defensive positions.

The ground quivered beneath the detonations, plumes of smoke. and flying debris filled the air as the mercenaries executed their coordinated battle plan designed to quickly overpower and breech the compound.

From behind the cover of rocks and buildings, the mercenaries unleashed a torrent of gunfire, creating a deadly crossfire that rained down on both sides of the entrance where the commandos were positioned. Adélard and his 5 valiant commandos were faced with a relentless onslaught, all their senses assaulted by the blinding flashes of gunfire and the deafening roar of rocket explosions.

Amidst the chaos, the commandos fought back with unwavering determination. Their training kicked in, and they moved with swift precision, returning fire with a ferocity that matched the intensity of the assault. Their assault rifles spat flames, sending round after round tearing through the night.

Noel and Julio emerged as the linchpins of defense. Their grenade launchers roared to life, sending a never-ending barrage of explosive, smoke, and personnel rounds hurtling towards the attackers.

Explosions blossomed everywhere in the night, enveloping the surrounding area in a haze of smoke, fire, and confusion. The sheer force of their counterattack forced the mercenaries to stop their advance momentarily, providing the crucial time the commandos needed.

Amid the turmoil, a rocket struck close to Henri, hitting the compound wall sending a slice of razor-sharp cement hurdling towards him. Henri momentarily fell to the ground, a spear of cement wedged into his thigh. Adélard jumped to his aid leaving only Julio to hold back the advancing horde.

Henri gritted his teeth as Adélard pulled the wedge from his leg and slapped a wound patch from his med kit on Henri's leg. Screaming in pain Henri reached for his assault rifle and stood up. Blood stained his pants and ran down his leg, but he refused to yield. His adrenaline surged and as if a man possessed Henri stood reloading and firing his assault rifle with accurate and deadly precision.

The stately Bugatti compound now became a battleground, the gallant commandos facing their adversaries head-on, fighting back with everything they had in a crucible of fire and lead, refusing to yield an inch of ground.

* * *

Laurent's urgent voice crackled over the communication device, breaking through the chaos of the ongoing battle.

"Adélard, we've got a situation. I've spotted four mercenaries near the cliffs on the shore, and the Peeping Tom is making his way into the marina area."

"Heard." Adélard responded.

Adélard's heart raced as he processed the information. The assault was already a warrior's nightmare, and now this new threat added another demon to the dream.

He responded swiftly, his voice firm and determined.

"Jojo you're getting company real soon. Be ready!"

"Laurent, keep thermals on Jojo's position. Any scum comes up over the cliff I want to know."

* * *

Dupont's voice came through the communication link, tense and urgent. "Commander Ross, the compound is under heavy assault. The mercenaries are using overwhelming firepower and tactics. Our team is holding up, but honestly Sir I don't know for how long."

Commander Ross's response was calm yet determined. "I read you loud and clear."

Dupont continued his voice reflecting an element of fear. "Commander Adélard squad will not back down. If we do not get there soon . . ."

"Understood. Ross out."

GHOST COMMANDO – Battle for Cavallo

* * *

Commander Ross stood on the control deck of the Liberté. The urgent report from the island had brought a no-win reality of the battle crashing down on him.

The heavy assault on Adélard's squad demanded his immediate action, they needed help, they desperately needed the commandos waiting below deck ready to reinforce Adélard before it was too late.

Looking up to the navigation map he could clearly see the submarine was still too close to the fishing boat to fire the demolition charges that the squad had placed on its hull.

He glanced at the console displaying the status of the demolition charges placed on the mercenary fishing boat, each one armed and ready flashing small green lights. The dilemma was stark: if he ordered the charges to explode too early, the shockwaves could potentially endanger the submarine itself, if he waited too long the Adélard squad might never see the sunrise.

"Commander, demolition charges ready." Lieutenant Patel, who had returned to the command deck informed him, knowing full well the danger they represented.

The Commander looked out across the control deck. Seeing the brave men whose lives he would risk with the wrong decision. Then he gave the order. "Captain Renault, fire the demolition charges."

The captain hesitated then replied. "Not yet, commander, we are still too close."

Commander Ross understood the risks but also knew the urgency and he was willing to take the risk.

"Louis, we don't have the time. Those men on the island are going to die if we don't help them."

"You think any of us don't know that." Captain Renault said then immediately turned to his crew spitting orders.

"Mr. Patel, set the timer for 60 seconds on those charges."

"Sound the emergency horn and blow ballast I want us topside in under a minute. Mr. Donato."

"Sir, Yes Sir." Donato answered, putting the orders into motion.

"Emergency main ballast tank blow! 10 seconds." Chief engineer Donato voice rang out through the submarine's intercom system.

"Lieutenant Nickalos, have Toulon3 squad ready to deploy in 2 minutes. We're going up fast, grab on to something." The captain ordered the assault squad waiting in the forward compartment.

"Yes Captain." Nickalos answered.

Hearing the warning, the rest of the crew swiftly prepared, their training and experience guiding their movements.

Donato looked at his captain, his hand hovering over the emergency button. "Do it." Captain Renault ordered.

GHOST COMMANDO – Battle for Cavallo

The submarine shook as the air rushed into its ballast pitching the boat nose up tossing anything loose to the deck and the crew grabbing something solid as it rose quickly to the surface.

"25 seconds to detonation." Lieutenant Patel announced.
"15."
"10."
"9."
"8."
"7."
The submarine jumped out of the water like a performing dolphin and quickly settled onto surface just as the explosion disintegrated the mercenary boat sending debris and waves across the surface at high speed.

The detonation was powerful, sending shockwaves through the water. The submarine shuddered from the force, and crew members stumbled as they held onto rails and fixtures. Alarms blared momentarily, and the lights flickered, casting a temporary eerie glow within the narrow confines of the vessel.

"Status report!" Captain Renault barked, his voice cutting through the aftermath of the explosion.

Lieutenant Patel assessed the situation and reported.
"No damage to the Liberté, Captain, a few crew members have minor injuries.

"Lieutenant Nickalos, launch the inflatable and deploy your squad immediately. Get your asses into this fight." The captain growled his orders.

"Mr. Patel get below and help Lieutenant Coeur get the dive squad ready to go to shore on the next boat double time."

"Sir. Yes Sir." Lieutenant Patel answered running to the hatch.

* * *

"That was some trick captain. Doing an emergency ascent to minimize the force of the shockwaves." Commander Ross said complimenting his fellow officer.

"Thanks, I just hope we are in time to save Adélard."

"I am sure we will." Commander Ross answered confidently.

"By the way commander if any of that shrapnel flying around from the fishing boat scratched my lovely Liberté, you will owe me a paint job."

"Agreed mon ami. Any color you want." Commander Ross answered smiling for the first time in days."

* * *

Lieutenant Laurent's focus was unwavering as he meticulously watched the thermal imaging feed from the Toulon drone. His fingers danced, adjusting angles, and zoom levels. Color coding the images helped him quickly differentiate between the mercenaries, the locals, and the squad defending the compound.

The images told a desperate story as dozens of red dots kept inching closer to the 6 blue dots of Adélard's squad. On the ground the mercenary assault was fierce, and well executed.

As his eyes darted across the screen, he spotted three heat signatures climbing the cliffside at the back of the Bugatti compound. Without hesitation, he tapped into his communication device, his fingers flying across the keys as he reached Adélard, who was entrenched in the fierce firefight at the gates to the compound.

"Adélard, 3 mercenaries climbing the cliff at the compound's rear. They're closing in fast."

Adélard's response crackled through the communication device, his voice commanding despite the chaos around him.

"Understood."

"Copy." Jojo added as he sank under the surface of the pool, hiding him from visual or any form of electronic eyes.

* * *

The firefight at the entrance raged, with bullets whizzing through the air and explosions echoing across the compound. Noel and Henri keyed into the same communication understood and assured Adélard with a nod and a hand signal that they would hold their ground.

They covered for Adélard's exit unleashing a barrage of bullets and grenades, fending off the attackers with their relentless determination. Adélard's heart pounded in his chest as he left them running hard maneuvered through the chaos that enveloped the compound. The mansion's grandeur seemed a distant memory as he darted through hallways, his mind solely focused on reaching the pool deck where Jojo was stationed alone.

Emerging onto the deck, Adélard sprinted towards the pool and dove headfirst into the water as gunfire erupted from the mercenaries that had breached the cliff's edge and were advancing on the mansion.

* * *

The inflatable boat glided toward the beach; the sound of the boat's motor masked by the intensity of the ongoing battle on the island. Toulon3 squad, led by Lieutenant Nickalos, held their weapons ready, their senses heightened as they prepared to join the fray.

The squad had barely made landfall when a hail of bullets suddenly erupted from the shadows, punctuating the night with lethal intent. One of the mercenaries, hidden behind a cluster of rocks, had been lying in wait, ready to ambush any reinforcements.

The squad immediately took cover, returning fire as they scrambled to find shelter from the unexpected assault. The darkness and chaos of the situation made it challenging to pinpoint the enemy's exact location.

"Take cover! Return fire!" Lieutenant Nickalos shouted over the cacophony of battle, his voice commanding as he rallied his men. Bullets ricocheted off the rocks, sending up showers of sparks, as the squad engaged in a fierce exchange of gunfire. The distant bursts of muzzle flashes illuminated the night, casting fleeting shadows on the beach.

"Graham, two wounded, one bad, we're pinned down." Nickalos called out.

* * *

GHOST COMMANDO – Battle for Cavallo

Laurent's communication device crackled to life, and he swiftly answered the call from Commandant Gaston aboard the helicopter.

"Two minutes out and coming in hot. I need mercenary locations for a sweep." Gaston ordered his voice intense.

"Both sides of the Bugatti entrance. Concentration at 20 to 25 meters and advancing." Graham reported instantly.

* * *

Hearing the submarine squad under fire and pinned down at the beach, Adam's instincts kicked in. He exchanged a determined glance with David, his fellow American security officer, before breaking away from the basement where they had been safeguarding the locals.

"David, stay here." Adam shouted his entire persona instantly changed from protector to hunter. "I'm going to help the squad at the beach."

David winked, understanding his partner all too well. "Go brother, do your voodoo. I got this."

With that, Adam dashed through the village, his heart pounding in his chest. Sprinting along the narrow streets, he kept his senses sharp, his eyes scanning for any signs of danger. He could hear the echoes of gunshots in the distance as he approached the beach, his gaze locked onto the scene before him.

One mercenary had the Toulon3 squad pinned down, his weapon trained on the stranded commandos who were taking cover behind whatever they could find.

Adam's jaw clenched as he assessed the situation. Without hesitation he ran up directly in front of the mercenary, taking three bullets in the chest and raised his weapon.

The mercenary fell limp on the ground with a double tap to the head as Adam stood rubbing his chest over his bullet proof vest muttering. "I'm getting too old for this shit."

"Nice work sir" The commando said appearing next to him. "My name is Nickalos."

"Thanks, they call me Adam. There is a shitstorm at the compound, any of your guys capable of moving?"

"One sidelined but he will live."

"Want to show us the way Mr. Adam?" Nickalos asked smiling.

"Just waiting for the invite. We need to double time, Adélard squad can't hold out long." Adam answered checking the clip in his weapon.

* * *

Without a word, Dupont pushed his chair back and stood up, his movements determined. "I'm going to the beach to help that wounded commando." Dupont announced, his voice laced with urgency. He turned to Graham.

"There is no more fishing boat or mercenaries coming, they are all here. That man needs my help. Graham, give me the keys to the Ducati in the graveyard. Please, I can save him!"

GHOST COMMANDO – Battle for Cavallo

Graham nodded, his face mirroring the resolve that emanated from Dupont. He pulled the keys from his pocket and handed them to Dupont.

"Be careful out there." Laurent added in acknowledgment, his eyes conveying both concern and determination.

With a swift nod, Dupont headed towards the exit of the grotto. The Ducati motorcycle sat waiting amidst the tombstones, with a quick glance back at the grotto, Dupont revved the engine, the roar breaking the stillness of the night as he tore through the graveyard, leaving behind a trail of dust and safety.

* * *

The two altar boys huddled in the corner of the grotto under a heavy blanket that Graham had given them against the cold. Both boys heard and understood everything going on, they feared for their new friend Dupont as he left the grotto.

"We will pray for him Monsieur Graham."

Chapter 12: Armageddon

Graham's eyes were fixed on the array of screens displaying live feeds from the night vision micro drones. Each screen held a fragment of the island's activity, a mosaic of images that painted a picture of the ongoing chaos.

Then something caught his eye sending a chill up his spine.

He saw the unidentified mercenary they had named "Peeping Tom" climb up and get behind the wheel of the marinas massive fuel truck. Graham continued watching closely hoping his fears would not come true.

"We got a big problem." He said aloud seeing the truck lurch forward leaving the marine and heading towards the island's central road directly to the compound.

Graham's fingers flew across the keyboard, he tapped into the squad's communication channel; his voice urgent as he addressed them all at once. "Listen up, everyone. We have a serious situation here. The Peeping Tom has hijacked a fuel truck, and he is driving it straight towards the compound. It looks like a suicide mission."

"Heard." Henri responded, for the squad.

"How do we stop him, Graham?" Julio asked.

"Short of a tank, or a missile, I don't know." Graham answered. The danger of that truck crashing into the mansion becoming very real.

Racing across the pool deck Adélard now faced a second battle at the rear of the mansion. He had feared that the mercenaries would try to use the all-out assault on the entrance of the compound to hide a covert assault up the cliff and had planned accordingly, leaving one lone commando Jojo to stop them.

Amidst the chaos of the attack at the rear of the house, the muzzle flashes from the three attacking mercenaries illuminated the night, peppering the mansion and the ground around him with deadly intent.

Adélard's survival instincts kicked in. With a swift and fluid motion, he dove headfirst into the deep end of the pool.

Adélard surfaced, wasting no time, he immediately reached for the assault rifle that had been strategically placed waiting for him on the pools coping.

His senses on high alert, Adélard scanned the field looking for targets. Curiously, finding none, he turned to look for his comrade, fearing the worst.

There at shallow end of the pool stood Jojo as if waiting for a trolley. His air tanks laying on the ground in front of him and his dive mask pulled up over his head, revealing the Jojo patented smile.

Jojo's voice was playful as he spoke. "You could have earned a solid 10 for that dive mon ami. It hurts me to tell you, it will not be today. The judges are all dead."

* * *

Graham's voice crackled over the communication devices. "The fuel truck is accelerating and nearing the compound. "

Julio's reaction was swift and resolute. Without a moment's hesitation, he left his position and sprinted towards the garage. Reaching the Defender, he yanked open the driver's door and leaped into the vehicle. The engine roared to life, the sound resonating in his ears like a battle cry. He had only one goal . . . to stop that fuel truck from reaching the compound at any cost.

The Defender surged forward leaving the compound through the automatic gates. Bullets ricocheted off its armored plating as he drove past the mercenaries attacking the compound. Ignoring the hail of bullets, Julio focused solely on the massive fuel truck barreling towards him.

With stubborn determination, Julio pressed his foot down on the accelerator driving nose to nose towards the fuel truck. At the very last moment before impact, he pulled the steering hard to the left causing the defender to drift sideways and be broadsided by the fuel truck.

The collision was a cataclysmic event that brought both vehicles to an abrupt and jarring stop. The impact reverberated through the air, a shockwave of force that sent echoes of the collision across the island.
Metal twisted and groaned as the two vehicles locked in a deadly embrace in the middle of the road. Crushed and mangled on the passenger side the Defender amazingly had stood its ground blocking the fuel truck from advancing.

GHOST COMMANDO – Battle for Cavallo

The force of the impact had been extreme. Julio's body was flung against the side of the vehicle, his arm taking the brunt of the impact and snapping with a sharp and agonizing pain.

His head struck the steering wheel with a sickening thud, leaving a deep laceration on his forehead that was bleeding profusely. The chaos of the collision seemed almost a dream, the world spun in a disorienting haze around Julio.

He fought to stay in the moment, but his vision blurred as the fog of unconsciousness descended upon him.

Inside the fuel truck, the driver's fate mirrored that of Julio's. The force of the impact had rendered him unconscious; blood splattered the cabin as his body slumped over the steering wheel.

* * *

The deafening impact of the fuel truck colliding with Julio's Defender reverberated through the air, a thunderous sound that cut through the chaos of the firefight. Every man on either side of the battle turned their attention towards the source of the sound.

Graham quickly redirected the drones' cameras towards the scene of the collision. The visual feed revealed the twisted wreckage of the fuel truck and the Defender. Searching frantically for his friend, relief washed over Graham as he spotted Julio still inside the vehicle.

"Julio is alive. Looks like he is unconscious, but he is alive I can see him breathing." Graham announced.

Running back towards the front of the compound Adélard made a split-second decision hearing the sound of a helicopter's rotor blades growing louder.

"Noel, get to Julio. Jojo and I will back up Henri."

Never responding, Noel sprinted through the open gate, his heart pounding as he ran towards the wreckage.

Commandant Gaston and the Toulon1 squad arrived not a moment too soon. His Commando helicopter swept over the compound, inspiring a silent cheer from the commandos below.

Meanwhile, within the twisted metal of the Defender, Julio's consciousness wavered in and out. The pain in his head and arm was sharp and pulsing, and the world around him seemed to blur and spin. Through the haze, he caught glimpses of movement, of figures approaching the wreckage. He vainly reached for his sidearm.
"Julio, Julio. Come on!" Noel yelled, pulling Julio's limp body from the wreckage. In a moment of clarity Julio saw his friend and smiled, passing out.

Seeing the rescue mission in progress, Mercenaries began targeting the wreckage. Noel manhandled open the two crushed armored doors of the Defender and pushed Julio up between them as bullets peppered their position. The sound of the helicopter overhead provided Noel with a glimmer of hope. "I could use a little help here." He shouted into his communication device.

"Heard." The familiar voice of sergeant Moreau answered.

GHOST COMMANDO – Battle for Cavallo

Instantly the unmistakable sounds of a Vulcan Gatling gun firing 6,000 rounds per minute filled the air driving back the mercenaries. The Helicopter circled the wreckage like a bird of prey defending the men below.

Jojo, still in his wetsuit who had never stopped running from the pool arrived and started helping Noel carry Julio back to the compound.

Julio was a big boy and none too helpful in his condition as Jojo and Noel began carrying him towards the compound amongst the violent battle happening in every direction.

When Noel looked up, unbelievably he noticed the fuel truck with the driver revived, again moving forward pushing the Defender still blocking its way like a snowplow.

"Is this a bad joke?" Jojo yelled.

"I got this, get Julio to safety." Noel yelled over the sound of the Vulcan overhead. Stepping out into the street, Noel raised his weapon disregarding the battle happening in every direction and fired six explosive grenades in rapid succession. The fuel truck loaded with 1000 gallons exploded instantly cause a burst of flames reaching up into the night sky and temporarily lighting the entrance to the compound.

* * *

As the chaos of the firefight raged on, the sudden appearance of Adam and the Toulon3 commandos from the submarine added a new front to the battle.

Their arrival injected a fresh surge of determination and firepower into the defense. Bullets flew and explosions rocked the air as the mercenaries were no longer the hunters, and now fought for their lives as the hunted.

Amidst the turmoil, Adélard spotted Adam running with the Toulon squad, his assault rifle blazing. The commandos swiftly took up positions, their disciplined training shining through as they engaged the mercenaries with precise gunfire. The compound's defenders now faced the attackers from two sides, their coordinated efforts creating a crossfire that pinned the mercenaries down.

* * *

With the helicopter's blades spinning and its engines still roaring, the helicopter descended with precision, its landing marked by a swirl of dust and debris.

"Move out!" Gaston's commanding voice echoed as the Toulon1 commandos disembarked ready for action. The squad swiftly advanced, their training and experience evident in their calculated movements. The helicopter's arrival had turned the tide of the battle, overwhelming the attackers with the combined force of 3 squads of commandos.

* * *

Laurent's eyes were glued to the thermal drone feed, his heart racing as he observed the intense battle unfolding. Suddenly, a blinding flash of light consumed the image. Laurent shielded his eyes instinctively, his heart pounding as he realized what had happened . . . the fuel truck had detonated.

GHOST COMMANDO – Battle for Cavallo

As the smoke and dust began to clear, the thermal imaging started to come back into focus. Laurent's heart sank as he saw no thermal images near the wreckage of the two vehicles.

Unwilling to accept the loss of his comrades, his eyes continued scanning the area, looking for anything to help Adélard and his men. Then he spotted something that sent a new surge of dread through him . . . a lone mercenary, moving cautiously through the mansion.

Laurent wasted no time. He reached for his communication device and quickly called Adélard. "This is Laurent. I've a thermal on a mercenary inside the mansion. Southeast corner, near the kitchen, moving slow."

Adélard's response was swift and determined. "On my way! Laurent, I need moment by moment."

"Heard."

Outside, the battle raged on, Graham kept all three squads well informed as his night vision drones followed the mercenaries running like rats on a sinking ship. Laurent's focus remained on his screen and the thermal drone that could see inside the mansion. He tracked the mercenary methodically moved from room to room. Reporting each new location and direction to Adélard.

Adélard sprinted across the compound and into the mansion. He knew that he had to reach Armand before the mercenary did.

"Mercenary nearing Armands office. Any moment now." Laurent reported his heart in his throat.

Dropping his assault rifle, Adélard burst through the side door to the office, his arms raised high as if in surrender.

"Don't shoot, don't shoot. I am unarmed." Adélard yelled seeing the mercenary and Armand 15 feet apart facing one another.

"It doesn't matter to me. I will kill you both." The mercenary responded with a Chechen accent.

Adélard slowly continued walking into the room, his arms held high until he was standing just in front of Armand.

"I am here to talk." Adélard said all the while backing up with imperceptible small steps.

"I am not here to talk my French poodle I am here . . . "

"You are here for the money, yes?" Adélard interrupted.

"For much more than just money." The mercenary said, raising his gun in both hands to end it.

"Nooooooooooooooooo . . ." Screamed François running into the room waving his arms.
Two shots sounded in that instant.

François screamed and hit the ground limp, spitting blood as a bullet pierced his lung.

GHOST COMMANDO – Battle for Cavallo

Anzor Mayrbek, the Chechen mercenary leader, lay dead on the floor a single bullet hole between his eyes.

Adélard screamed with blood gushing from his ear, turned around to face Armand still holding Adélard's Beretta. "You shot me in the ear Armand!"

"Forgive me mon ami." Armand said falling to one knee trembling in the aftermath of killing the mercenary.

"It's ok Armand, take deep breaths."

Leaving Armand, Adélard ran to François to check on his wounds.

"Gaston, I need a medic in Armands office asap. Armand is safe but the butler has been shot in the lung." Adélard said, his ear raining blood while he desperately worked to stop François's bleeding with his hands.

"On the way." Gaston replied relieved it was not Armand that was shot.

* * *

Submarine Liberté's, Cavallo Island
Captain Renault's voice crackled through the communication system aboard the submarine Liberté. "Commander Ross, Toulon2 squad is loaded and ready to deploy on the inflatable.

Commander Ross considered the situation for a moment before responding. "Hold the squad, Captain. I'll be going to shore with them."

Acknowledging the order, Captain Renault relayed it to Toulon2 squad as Commander Ross made his way to the submarine's deck. He was met by Lieutenant Patel, the executive officer, who stepped forward and handed him an assault rifle. "Stay safe, Commander."

"Thank you, Patel." Ross replied, his expression determined. He knew that he needed to be on the ground with his men, leading by example.

The atmosphere on the deck was tense as Commander Ross prepared to disembark. The inflatable was ready, the commandos poised for action. The rope ladder hung over the side of the submarine, swaying gently in the sea breeze. Ross glanced back at the submarine for a moment, then turned his attention to the mission ahead.

As he started his descent down the rope ladder, Lieutenant Patel's voice reached his ears. "Commander, take this." Patel handed him a headset, ensuring that he could maintain communication with both the submarine and the commandos on shore.

Ross nodded his gratitude, securing the headset and adjusting the straps of his assault rifle. He continued down the rope ladder, the sea spray misting his face as he descended. With every rung, his determination solidified. He was joining his men in the fight, standing shoulder to shoulder with them against the mercenary threat.
As the inflatable moved towards shore, commander Ross activated his headset and contacted Graham in the grotto. "Graham, this is Ross. I need a situation and location report on the mercenaries."

GHOST COMMANDO – Battle for Cavallo

Graham's voice crackled through the headset. "Commander, the situation on the ground is still intense. Mercenaries have abandoned their assault on the compound and are spread out across the island in small pockets of resistance."

"Understood, Graham." Ross replied. "We're on our way."

* * *

"Commander Ross, Adélard and Toulon3 squad are not at full strength. I am ordering those squads to fall back to the compound. My Toulon1 squad and yours will conduct search and destroy for the remaining mercenaries." Commandant Gaston ordered.

"Yes Sir." Ross answered.

"Graham, Laurent, I want the location of every piece of scum on this island. Send coordinates to Toulon1 and 3 for immediate action." Gaston ordered.

"Yes Sir." They answered in unison.

Commandant Gaston's voice echoed through the communication device as he addressed Adélard and Lieutenant Nickalos. "Adélard, Nickalos, I need you both to fall back to the compound. Establish a defensive perimeter with the commandos that are capable and work with the medical team to set up a field location for the wounded."

Adélard and Jojo who had been in the thick of a running battle with the retreating mercenaries, acknowledged the order. "Understood, Commandant. We're on our way." Adélard responded.

"Engaged with three. Will comply when finished." Nickalos answered the sound of intense gunfire in the background.

As the two squads began to execute the command, Adélard relayed the orders to his team. "Alright, everyone, fall back to the compound. We are setting up a defensive perimeter."

The commandos moved with purpose, adjusting their tactics from the frontlines to securing their home base. Explosions and gunfire still rang out in the distance, a reminder of the ongoing battle.

Nickalos's squad followed suit, providing covering fire as they withdrew toward the compound. They moved methodically, ensuring that no one was left behind and maintaining constant communication with each other.

As they arrived back at the compound, Adélard and Nickalos immediately set to work. Adélard addressed his squad, "Secure the compound perimeter. Set up defensive positions. Jojo, take Julio's heavy gun and establish a crossfire with Noel if needed."

Meanwhile, Nickalos coordinated with the medical team. "We need to establish a field treatment location. Find a suitable area within the mansion and set up a temporary medical station. We need to provide care for our wounded. Let's move commandos." Lieutenant Nickalos ordered.

The compound quickly transformed from a battleground to a fortified haven. The wounded began to arrive at the field treatment location, Nickalos oversaw the operation, ensuring that the wounded were being cared for.

GHOST COMMANDO – Battle for Cavallo

* * *

Amidst the aftermath of the battle, Adam arrived at the compound with the Toulon3 squad. He sought out Adélard, his eyes reflecting the intensity of the situation as he approached his leader. "Got a minute Adélard?"

Adélard turned toward Adam, his expression a mix of exhaustion and determination. "Sure, what's on your mind?"

Adam's voice was low but resolute. "That attack was better planned and more brutal than we anticipated. Those mercenaries were the real thing."

Adélard nodded in agreement. "Yes, they were."

"You did well young blood for your first time out." Adam added patting him on the shoulder.

"You didn't do so bad yourself, old man. By the way, how many bullets are in that vest your wearing?" Adélard asked smirking.

"Hell, at my age you lose count after five or six." Adam answered laughing.

Adam's gazed passed the gate to the compound. "I am worried about those locals who refused to take shelter. With the fighting happening all over the island they could be in danger."

"Agreed, but at the moment all we can do is ask Graham to keep an eye on them." Adélard added. his voice somber.

Adam's fist clenched as he made a decision. "I'm going back out, alone. I need to check on those locals and make sure they are okay. I could use a few more clips, Adélard."

Adélard squinted his eyes looking hard at the elder warrior. "Take as many as you need." He answered, pointing to the mansion.

"Thanks."

"Adam, don't play the Hero, ok?" Adélard told him.

"Seems I am a creature of habit Adélard. I don't know any other way." Adam yelled over his shoulder walking towards the mansion.

* * *

The early morning darkness still blanketed Cavallo as the hunt and destroy orders were conducted, with the assistance of Graham and Laurent providing real-time updates and locations. One by one, the commandos methodically eliminated the remaining mercenary force that had infiltrated the island.

Toulon1 squad, having arrived in the helicopter, moved swiftly through the island hunting their prey. Each encounter played out with a sense of purpose as they engaged the remaining pockets of resistance.

The roar of the helicopter and the sound of gunfire highlighted each of their encounters.

Toulon2 squad, which had emerged from the submarine with Commander Ross in command, followed a similar path of engagement. Their movements were calculated, guided by the detailed information provided by Graham and Laurent.

The mercenaries, their ranks now diminished and disoriented, found themselves facing a determined force that left no room for escape. Some skirmishes ended in quick, decisive victories, while others resulted in tense standoffs, resolved only when the remaining mercenaries realized the futility of their resistance and surrendered or died.

* * *

As the sun began to rise on the horizon, both squads converged back at the compound. The distant sounds of gunfire had been replaced by an eerie calm. The mercenary force apart from three prisoners no longer existed.

Commander Ross approached Adélard, his expression a blend of weariness and satisfaction. "The Island is secure Mr. Adélard." He reported, his voice reflecting the struggle of the past few hours.

Adélard nodded, his eyes reflecting his gratitude. "Thank you, Commander."

Commander Ross stood proudly next to Adélard as they both looked around at compound, noting the four squads that now occupied the Bugatti estate.

"Those are all good men, Adélard. You have earned your place among them. I would be proud to have anyone of them and you next to me in a fight." Commander Ross told him.

"Would it be ok if we wait a few days for that next fight Commander. I think my guys would appreciate a break." Adélard told his commander smiling.

"I think that can be arranged Adélard. Still days like this and those men we are watching are special, make no mistake."

"Commander, those are all men you trained to be Kraken commandos. To be the absolute best at what they do." Adélard told him.

"As are you, Mr. Adélard. As are you!"

* * *

Chapter 13: Blessings and Heros

Sunrise March 15th, Bugatti Compound

As the first rays of the sun broke through the horizon, a sense of calm and relief settled over the Island of Cavallo. The early morning light cast a warm glow over the cold landscape, illuminating the aftermath of the fierce battle that had unfolded overnight. The sounds of gunfire and explosions giving way to the distant lapping of waves against the shore.

The Bugatti compound, which had been the epicenter of the conflict, now stood as a testament to the resilience and determination of its defenders. The cement walls bore scars from rocket impacts, windows were shattered, and debris was scattered across the grounds.

Yet, amidst the destruction, there was a palpable sense of unity and purpose as the remaining commandos and island locals worked side by side to clean up and restore order.

Adélard, flanked by his loyal commandos, surveyed the scene with a mixture of exhaustion and satisfaction. The battle had been hard-fought, against overwhelming odds and now it was over.

The sound of approaching footsteps caught his attention, and he turned to see some of the island locals walking into the compound, armed with brooms, shovels, and grateful smiles.

An elderly woman with a weathered face approached Adélard with a tray of steaming cups. "Coffee, monsieur?"

Adélard gratefully accepted the cup, taking a sip of the hot beverage. "Thank you, Madame. Your kindness means a great deal to all of us."

She smiled pulling back the scarf she wore against the cold, her eyes filled with gratitude. "We are all part of this island, monsieur. It is our home, we will do what we can to help."

As the cleanup efforts continued, a familiar figure emerged from the crowd. Father Paulo, the island's devoted priest, walked with a purposeful stride, his brown robes with a white collar flowing gently in the breeze with his two altar boys at his heels carrying baskets of fresh bread.

Adélard, Jojo, with Henri now on crutches greeted the priest with respect, their fatigue momentarily forgotten in the presence of the spiritual leader.

"Father Paulo!" Jojo called out his voice carrying a note of reverence.

"Oh, my sons." The priest replied, his eyes filled with a mixture of concern and relief. "I have been praying fervently for your safety."

Graham joined them reaching down to ruffle both boys' hair. "I see you brought your midget spies with you this morning Father."

"Monsieur they are not my spies. They are simply two curious lads that would rather chase unicorns and firefly's than study." Father Paulo answered smiling as both boys tucked behind his robes.

GHOST COMMANDO – Battle for Cavallo

Father Paulo raised his hands, his expression becoming solemn, his voice booming in the cold morning air.

"Let us gather, my children. Let us offer our thanks to the Almighty for his protection and the blessing he has bestowed on us with these fine young men."

A makeshift circle formed, commandos and locals alike coming together with bowed heads and clasped hands. Father Paulo's voice, steady and soothing, carried his prayer of gratitude and humility. Father Paulo spoke of walking with the shield of God's grace, of the island's resilience, the courage of its defenders, and the blessings of unity in the face of adversity.

As the prayer concluded, the island locals offered quiet amens, their faces uplifted by a renewed sense of hope.

Father Paulo turned to Adélard and all the commandos, including Commandant Gaston, Commander Ross, and Armand Bugatti who had joined in the prayer. He raised his arms skyward towards the heavens, his gaze filled with appreciation and love.

"You, our gallant guardians, sent by providence, empowered by the sword of divine justice, and protected by the holy mother are our champions. We are forever in your debt."

"We are honored to have stood by your side Father." Adélard said humbly.

The day continued to unfold, the sun rising higher in the sky, casting its warm light over the island's rejuvenation.

Debris was cleared, windows were boarded up, and wounded commandos were tended to with care.

The local women prepared meals, bringing sustenance to the defenders who had given their all. As the island began to return to a semblance of normalcy, a sense of unity and gratitude permeated all the people.

* * *

The morning light filtered through the windows as Adélard walked into the makeshift medical area within the mansion where Julio lay, still recovering from his injuries. Graham, Jojo, Noel, and Henri followed closely behind, their expressions a mix of concern and camaraderie.

"There he is . . . the boy hero. Had you lost your mind or were you just trying to get some attention running into that big ass truck Julio?" Adélard quipped as they approached his bedside.

Julio managed a weak smile, propped up on pillows, with his arm in a sling and his head wrapped in gauze and still suffering the aftereffects of his concussion. "It seemed like a good idea at the time Adélard."

Laughter filled the room as his friends exchanged amused glances. Graham chimed in. "Next time you decide to take on a fuel truck three time your size, can you at least let us know in advance?"

Jojo nodded in agreement. "Yeah, send up some fireworks or even just a text . . . dumb shit about to happen, stay tuned."

GHOST COMMANDO – Battle for Cavallo

"I bet you did it, thinking we would hold a parade in your honor?" Noel added with a grin.

"Yes, Yes, a parade." Henri joined in. "Complete with a marching band."

Amidst the good-natured ribbing, the room was filled with a sense of friendship and gratitude. As the banter continued, the door swung open, and Armand, Ross, and Gaston entered. Their presence carried a weight of respect and admiration.

The squad instantly came to attention and saluted their officers.

"As you were." Commandant Gaston ordered.

Armand approached Julio's bedside, his eyes filled with a mixture of concern and pride. "Julio, my boy, you've certainly given us all quite a scare."

Julio offered a faint smile. "I am sorry Mr. Bugatti for ruining your new Defender."

"He only got his driver's license last month Armand." Jojo interrupted, standing next to Julio's bed. "Some leniencies would be appreciated." Which caused everyone to laugh, including Julio who complained it made him hurt.

Ross, his usual stoic demeanor softened by a rare smile, extended a hand to Julio. "You demonstrated exceptional courage, Mr. Julio. You saved countless lives last night."

Gaston, his expression serious, stepped forward. "Julio, your actions were nothing short of heroic. You put your life on the line to protect your comrades, this island, and its people. I'm recommending you for the highest medal honor in France, the Légion d'honneur."

The room fell momentarily silent, the weight of Gaston's words sinking in. Julio's eyes widened in surprise, his voice barely a whisper. "I... I don't know what to say."

Armand placed a reassuring hand on Julio's shoulder. "You don't have to say anything, mon ami. Your actions have already spoken for you."

Graham, who had been quietly observing, spoke up. "You may have started as a mason Julio, but today and forever more you will be recognized as a true hero of France."

"Stop already." Jojo blurted out slapping at Julio's toes sticking out from under the sheets. "You guy are filling his head so big it won't fit into a green beret. We are getting our green berets are we not sir?" Jojo asked, turning to Commander Ross.

"Yes Jojo, you all are, and maybe even a medal." Commander Ross answered.
"Better make it a small medal commander. Jojo doesn't have much of a chest." Noel added grinning.

"Don't worry about the truck Julio." Armand spoke up interrupting the laughter. "I will order a new one with your name and the Légion d'honneur embossed next to the Bugatti logo."

GHOST COMMANDO – Battle for Cavallo

"Here we go again." Jojo said picking on Armand. "Couldn't you just give us the keys to your wine cellar instead Armand."

"That might be a bridge too far Jojo." Commandant Gaston told him smiling.

* * *

Amidst the laughter and heartfelt words, Julio's eyes shone with a mix of humility and pride. He had faced down danger, not seeking recognition, but simply doing what he believed was right.

As his friends and comrades celebrated his bravery, they also celebrated the spirit that had brought them together . . . a spirit of unity, courage, and an unyielding determination to protect the ones they held dear.

* * *

Amidst the recovery efforts, Commandant Gaston was coordinating various tasks to ensure the safety and well-being of the wounded and the island's residents. As he stood near the helicopter, assessing the damage, Captain Auclair approached him, a concerned expression on his face.

"Commandant." Captain Auclair began. "I regret to inform you that the helicopter sustained significant damage during the attack. The tail rotor took a direct hit. That helicopter is not safe for us to fly in this condition."

Gaston paused, his gaze shifting to the helicopter as he processed the information. "I appreciate your candor, Captain. Suggestions?"

Captain Auclair nodded. "My main concern right now is the wounded. We can't risk their safety or ours on this bird. I have already called for a repair team, and I took the liberty to request a replacement helicopter to be sent over as soon as possible."

Gaston's shoulders relaxed slightly at the prospect of a solution. "Good thinking, Captain. Restrict transport to medical evacuations before any personnel transport." The commandant ordered.

"Sir. Yes Sir." Captain Auclair answered saluting his Commandant.

* * *

"Gaston, what do you want us to do with the prisoners?" Commander Ross asked walking up.

"How many are there?" He asked.
"There are three, Sir. All with minor wounds and all have been treated. We have them housed in the garage with two commandos guarding them."

"Well done commander. I will order prisoner transport to Toulon where they can be held and tried for their crimes."

* * *

Sitting in his home office, Armand Bugatti took a deep breath before dialing the satellite phone. The seconds felt like hours as he waited, finally, the line clicked, and he heard Isabella's voice on the other end.

"ARMAND?" Isabella asked, her voice full of worry and emotion.

GHOST COMMANDO – Battle for Cavallo

"Isabella, my love." Armand replied. "It's me, I'm safe."

Tears welled up in Isabella's eyes as she clutched the phone tighter. "Armand, thank God you're okay. We were so worried. The people here knew some of what was going on, but they didn't tell me much. Only that the island was under heavy attack."

Armand's voice held a mixture of relief and tenderness. "I know, my love. I've been worried about you and the children as well."

Isabella let out a shaky breath. "We're all right, Armand. The boat ride was terrifying, but we made it to the camp safely."

Armand nodded, his eyes closing briefly as he absorbed her words. "I'm so glad to hear that. How are the girls holding up?"

Isabella's voice warmed with affection. "They were a little shaken, but they're fine now. Captain Philippe was wonderful, he changed plans and brought us here to protect us when he heard you were under attack. He comes by twice a day even now to check on us and takes the girls down to the little beach they have to pick shells."

Armand smiled, grateful for the protection offered by Captain Philippe. "He's a good man. I am relieved to know you are in capable hands."

Isabella's tone turned more serious. "And what about you, Armand? How are you doing? What is the situation there?"

Armand took a deep breath, his mind replaying the events of the battle, none of which he wanted to share with his wife at the moment. "The battle is over, my love, the mercenaries are gone, Cavallo is at peace once again."

Relief flooded Isabella's voice. "Thank God. Are you hurt?"

Armand hesitated for a moment before answering. "I'm fine, Isabella. A few scrapes and bruises, but nothing serious."

"Our butler, François, was badly injured trying to protect me, but he is stable now, they are going to evacuate him to the medical facility where you are, but the doctors here assure me he will make a full recovery."

Isabella answered her concern real. "Oh, my poor François."

Armand's voice softened. "He was very brave, Isabella. He did everything he could to keep me safe, even risking his own life."

Isabella's tone shifted, a mixture of hope and longing. "When can we come home, Armand?"

Armand's heart ached at her words. "I wish I could give you a definite answer, my love. The mansion and the compound took quite a beating. We need to make repairs before it's safe for you and the children to return."

Isabella's sigh was audible.

"I understand, Armand. Just know that we're thinking of you and waiting for the moment we can be together again."

GHOST COMMANDO – Battle for Cavallo

Armand's voice held a promise. "Cavallo might not be ready to host your smile my wife, but I am free to do as I please. I am coming to Corsica to be with you as soon as I can. We are restricting transport currently to medical evacuations. I miss you and the girls terribly."

Isabella's voice trembled with emotion. "We miss you too, Armand." She said with tears flowing down her face.

"You aren't hiding something from me Armand, are you?"

"Are you hurt? Ten fingers, ten toes, one silly nose?"

"Are the people, ok?

"Are those nice boys, ok?

"No Isabella. I am not hiding anything of importance. And yes, all my fingers and toes are still in place. It is an unimaginable miracle, but all the people of the Island and all the commandos are alive and well."

"That makes me happy, Armand." Isabella answered relieved yet still sobbing softly.

"I have a lovely underground room with 24 beds all to myself. Come visit soon my husband. I miss you." Isabella told him quickly, changing her demeanor.

* * *

By the middle of the day the natural beauty of Cavallo and the usually tranquil Bugatti compound stood in stark contrast to the events that had unfolded just hours before.

Two Naval NH90 Caiman Helicopters descended gracefully, their rotors cutting through the cold winter air.

The rear of the compound at the cliffs edge with direct access to the mansion and relative lack of destruction from the assault made it the logical choice as a landing zone.

As the helicopters touched down, their powerful engines gradually quieted, and the dust stirred by their arrival began to settle. The rear of the elegant mansion providing a surreal backdrop to the events unfolding.

Under the still moving blades of one of the helicopters a figure in a military police uniform approached Commandant Gaston with purposeful strides.

"Commandant Gaston." The officer saluted, his voice carrying the weight of authority. "I've been assigned to oversee the transportation of the prisoners to Toulon for processing and further investigation."

Gaston acknowledged the salute, his respect for protocol evident in his demeanor. "Understood Lieutenant. They are under guard and ready for transport.

The military police officer's gaze swept over the rear of the mansion, his trained eyes assessing the aftermath of the battle. "It seems you had an easy go of it, Commandant."

"Yes Lieutenant, it does seem that way from here." Commandant Gaston told him, with a small smile on his face. "Dismissed."

From the lead helicopter emerged a figure in crisp military attire, her posture exuding authority and determination.

Commander Audry Brielle, a seasoned officer from the Toulon naval base, stepped onto the firm ground with purpose. Her eyes scanned the surroundings, taking in the signs of the recent battle and the figures of the commandos and medical personnel moving with about.

Commandant Gaston stood waiting for her to approach. "Good to see you, Commander Brielle."

Commander Brielle offered a crisp salute before engaging in conversation. "Commandant Gaston." She replied, her tone composed. "We received your orders and arrived as swiftly as we could. Our helicopters are equipped to transport the wounded and provide secure transport for the prisoners."

"Walk with me Commander." Commandant Gaston ordered. "I want you to see what we are dealing with."

As they walked through the Bugatti mansion Commander Brielle noticed the elegant yet simple and clean modern design of the décor and furniture. Her perceptions soon changed as they walked out the front door seeing the destruction and debris in every direction.

Commander Brielle gaze swept over the compound, taking in the evidence of the intense battle that had raged there just hours before. "It looks like you put up quite a fight Sir." "We did, but my Toulon squad was primarily clean up.

The real heroes were a single squad of recruits. The Adélard squad." Gaston told her proudly.

"Only six men Sir, against how many?"

Reaching the now open gates to the compound the burned remains of the Bugatti Defender and the marina fuel truck were clearly visible.

"27 made landfall, 12 more were eliminated at sea by Commander Ross." Gaston told her. "That brings us to the other reason I wanted to talk to you in private."

The commander stopped searching the compound with her eyes and looked directly at Gaston. "Yes Sir?"

"The military security team you brought are taking three prisoners to Toulon for justice. The rest we have collected and stored in the basement of one of the local mansions as a temporary morgue. Fortunately, with the weather being as cold as it is, we have not had any problems, but we need to transport them to Toulon."

"Then admiral Vacheron can decide what he wants done." Stretching his neck, the commandant paused a moment then added. "Commander what happened here last night is not a secret and I for one have no intention of making it one. At the same time seeing 22 body bags caused by French Commandos all over social media is not something I want to deal with. I want those bodies respectfully tagged, bagged, and discreetly transported to Toulon."

"Understood Sir." Commander Brielle answered.

GHOST COMMANDO – Battle for Cavallo

"Good. Then my orders are for you to return to Toulon on the security helicopter with the prisoners, assemble a team and return tonight to accomplish this mission. Am I clear commander?"

"Sir. Yes Sir. I estimate I can have a team on the ground by 1930 tonight."

* * *

Walking back from the gate Commandant Gaston and Commander Brielle neared the damaged Helicopter in the center of the compound. Captain Auclair and the transport pilot emerged from the cockpit talking until seeing the commandant.

The pilot stepped forward with a determined look in his eyes. "Commandant Gaston." He greeted him with a salute.

"I have brought a crew for the damaged helicopter. They are already at work on the repairs." The pilot said, turning to show the Commandant the men working diligently on the damaged helicopter before turning back to Gaston.

"Once we have the repairs done, we'll start transporting the wounded. The medical facility at Melusine has been altered and is prepared to receive them."
"Not soon enough young man! Some of our men need urgent attention. I want my wounded off this island in 30 minutes. Am I clear?"

"Sir. Yes Sir. My bird is good to go. I will begin transport to the Melusine medical facility immediately."

The pilot saluted and turned quickly to get things underway, leaving Captain Auclair with the Gaston and Commander Brielle.

"I think you scared him, Gaston." Captain Auclair said smiling.

"This is a commando mission, not a tea party for officers and their wives, Mr. Auclair. I need men that can think on their feet." He growled.

"He is just young, Commandant. Still 1 2 3 by the book, but a damn fine pilot Sir." Commander Brielle added.

"I still say, you scared him with that *'not soon enough young man'* line Gaston." Captain Auclair added laughing as the three of them walked back into the mansion.

* * *

The aftermath of the battle for the Bugatti compound was evident in the scorch marks on the walls and the debris littering the ground. Amidst this scene, the medical commando staff worked with precision and urgency, their white coats standing out against the backdrop of the compound.

François, the butler, lay on a stretcher near the waiting NH90 Caiman helicopter. His usually composed demeanor had given way to a pale expression of pain, as the medical team checked his injuries. His bloodied butler's coat at his side bore witness to the sacrifice he had made to protect Armand Bugatti and the compound.

Julio, his arm in a splint, his face bruised, and his head wrapped in gauze stood nearby, his eyes fixed on the helicopter. Unwilling and unhappy despite his injuries to leave his squad.

The commando from the Toulon3 squad, his face grimacing with pain, was carefully carried on a stretcher towards the helicopter. His fellow commandos stood by, offering support and solidarity. The air was heavy with tension, the squad's collective acknowledgement of the life threatening wounds their comrade was suffering through.

* * *

The chief medical officer, a seasoned professional with a demeanor that exuded both authority and compassion, approached Commandant Gaston.

"Commandant. We need to accompany these severely wounded patients on the helicopter. Their condition requires constant monitoring. This will ensure they receive the care they need during the flight and upon arrival at the medical facilities at Melusine. We will return on the next flight available to continue caring for the minor wounds here on the island."

Gaston regarded the chief medical officer with a nod, recognizing the logic of his statement. "Do what is necessary Doctor." He replied, his voice carrying a mixture of gratitude and concern.

With a coordinated effort, the medical team carefully lifted François onto the helicopter's interior, securing the stretcher in place, his condition serious yet stable at the moment.

Julio followed under his own power with the aid of Adélard and Noel even as his steps were shaky and measured.

The commando from the Toulon3 squad was carried in next, his injuries internal and varied requiring constant monitoring to stabilize him before any surgery could be performed.

Once the rest of the patients, including Henri walking with crutches, were situated, the medical team secured themselves in their seats, their expressions focused on the task at hand as the helicopter's rotor blades began to spin.

Adélard and his remaining men stood by. They had been by Julio's and Henri's side the entire time until the medical staff had sent them away.

The four commandos stood watching the helicopter take off, giving their comrades their silent support.

"Don't be such sour faces." Jojo said. "Julio will be fine. I am more worried about Henri's dance moves."

"Can I sit on him please Adélard?" Noel asked grinning.

* * *

Commandant Gaston watched as the helicopter ascended, a mixture of relief and concern washing over him. The chief medical officer's assurances echoed in his mind, a reminder that the wounded were in capable hands.

As the helicopter gained altitude and disappeared from view. Commandant Gaston and the commandos turned their attention back to the compound.

GHOST COMMANDO – Battle for Cavallo

* * *

Standing alone at the side of the compound, Commandant Gaston listened intently to his cell phone. A look of sadness was on his face as the call ended.

Looking up at the clear winter sky the Commandant shoulders slumped, his entire body took on the aspects of a tired, weary man. Looking back down he nodded his head slowly from side to side.

Then the Commandant picked up his phone and dialed.

"Commander Ross, I want all senior officers, Armand, and the Adélard squad assembled for a briefing at 1800."

"Sir, the mansion is not suitable, I recommend the Rousseau guest house basement." Commander Ross advised.

"Fine, make it happen Commander." Gaston said, ending the call.

Chapter 14: The price of Victory

Commander Ross walked towards Bugatti garage where the mercenary prisoners were being held, his expression one of determination curiosity. Reaching the entrance, he noticed a commando standing guard outside.

"At ease." He said as the commando snapped a salute. "Is Sergeant Moreau inside?"

"Yes Sir."

"Please tell him Commander Ross would like to speak with him."

Moments later the two men slowly walked around the mansion seeking privacy for their conversation.

"Nice to have you on the island Sergeant Moreau. I understand you made quite an entrance." Ross told him smiling. "Just like Mali, Commander." The sergeant answered him. "That seems like a lifetime ago, we were both much younger men then mon ami." Ross commented.

"Sir." Moreau stopped walking and looked at his commander. "How can I help you?"

Ross glanced towards the garage before focusing back on Moreau. "Any developments with the prisoners?"
The sergeant shifted his stance, his gaze slightly thoughtful.
"Some."
"What have you found out?" Ross asked speaking his word deliberately.

Moreau cleared his throat, his voice measured as he began to share what he had learned.

"Most of the prisoners are from Pakistan. They've been quite tight-lipped about their mission or who hired them, except for one."

Ross raised an eyebrow, his curiosity growing. "And who's the exception?"

Moreau hesitated for a moment before continuing. "There's one among them who's been unwilling to disclose where he's from. He's been defiant, hostile towards the other prisoners and refuses to give us any information."

Ross's lips tightened. "Probably part of their command structure. Have you learned anything from the others?"

Sergeant Moreau's tone turned more animated. "We did manage to get some details about how they were hired. They were paid 2000 Euro upfront and promised 25000 more once their mission was completed."

Ross's eyes narrowed slightly as he processed the information. "That's a lot of money in Pakistan.

Moreau nodded in agreement. "Indeed, sir. It also raises questions about how the Warlord could provide such a large amount of money for this attack."

The commander's gaze shifted to the garage once again before returning to Moreau.

"Good work, Sergeant. Keep pressing for more information. We need to know if there is more here than just one psychopathic Warlord."

Moreau saluted. "Sir. Yes Sir."

* * *

Commandant Gaston walked up to the Adélard squad sitting on the steps of the mansion eating sandwiches that a sweet older lady had made for them, the stress and weariness of the past hours etched on their faces.

'I don't know about your squad Mr. Adélard, but I could use a hot shower and a beer." The commandant said in a friendly voice walking up.

"Sir. Yes Sir." Jojo answered "Unfortunately commander Ross didn't supply any beer for this mission. Obviously, an oversight you should correct Sir."

Gaston joined the men in laughing at Jojo then he sat down next to Adélard and began to address the men.

"We're all tired, and I know you've been through a lot. But we need to start thinking about the next steps. How long do you think it'll take to pack up your gear and get ready to head back to Melusine?"

Graham, always quick to respond, started.
"Given the complexity of our surveillance setup and the underground grotto, I'd say it will take about a day to ensure everything is properly packed and the grotto is returned to its original state."

GHOST COMMANDO – Battle for Cavallo

Commandant Gaston nodded, taking in the information. "Understood, a day for you Graham. What else?"

"Adélard what do you need help with? Is there anything the other squads can do to help expedite the process?"

Adélard, his eyes showing a mixture of exhaustion and determination, spoke up. "Actually, Commander, there's something you could help us with."

"The road outside the compound is cluttered with wrecked vehicles from the battle. It would be great if we could clear that up before we leave. The good people of this island have enough to do as it is."

Commandant Gaston considered the request, a faint smile tugging at the corner of his lips. "Clearing the road, you say?" He mused. "Well, I can't say our men are much in the realm of mechanics, but I will see how many I can lend you."

The lieutenants exchanged amused glances, and Lieutenant Laurent stood up to speak, his tone playful. "Gaston, I know you love your teams to be in constant motion, but honestly sir, Dupont and Graham could use a little shut eye. Matter of fact if you all stop talking, I could take a nap right here."

Commandant Gaston clapped Laurent on the shoulder, a sense of camaraderie between them. "Understood. I will schedule shut eye as soon as possible."

* * *

As the squad members started to get up, Commandant Gaston paused for a moment then added one last comment.

"Well done gentlemen, your courage and valor are the only reason anyone on this island can continue their lives.

Adélard and his squad exchanged appreciative looks, a shared acknowledgment of the challenges they had faced and overcome. "Thank you, Commandant." Adélard replied.

Commandant Gaston nodded, a sense of mutual respect passing between them. "Let's get to work then. We will clear that road, and then we go home."

* * *

1800 Bugatti Guest House, Cavallo Island

Armand joined Adélard and Commander Ross as they walked side by side across the compound, heading towards the Rousseau guest house for a briefing called by Commandant Gaston.

As they reached the entrance of the guest house, Armand turned to Commander Ross and Adélard. "Before we go down to the basement, I just want to thank you both again. I will not forget what happened here, and your friendship."

'France does not abandon her friends Armand." Commander Ross told him.

Together, they descended the steps to the basement, their footsteps echoing softly against the walls.

The room, which had once been the heart of the Adélard squad operations, still retained an air of purpose. Maps and charts adorned the walls, weapons and diving equipment were neatly arranged.

Inside the room, Lieutenant Dupont, Lieutenant Laurent, and Graham were already present, engaged in conversation. Commander Ross greeted the men and sat down scanning the room for the first time.

"This is one hell of a basement Armand."

Armand smiled. "It is one of my little pleasures."

"Commander, Mr. Bugatti is not telling you the half of it. This basement has a modern two lane gun range, a weapons locker, and a tunnel which leads to the main house." Graham added.

* * *

Lieutenant Laurent leaned back in his chair. "I wonder what Commandant Gaston has in store for us this time."

Lieutenant Dupont, who had been busy examining a set of surveillance logs from the battle chimed in. "Whatever it is, I am just happy we are all here to hear it."

Just as the conversation began to settle, the sound of footsteps approached from the hallway outside. The door swung open, revealing Commandant Gaston, his presence commanding the room's attention.

"At ease, gentlemen." Commandant Gaston said as the commandos all rose to their feet, offering salutes.

Commandant Gaston gestured for them to be seated as he took his place at the front of the table. "I've called this briefing to discuss the state of the mission and the ongoing threat to Mr. Bugatti and his family."

"First, as to the state of the mission. The defense of Cavallo and the Bugatti compound has been accomplished with no loss of life by either the military or local residence."

"As you are all aware, there is significant damage to buildings and property near and on the compound, with some assorted minor damage throughout the island."

With a nod from Gaston, Armand stood up to address the group. "My offices in Marseille are assembling supplies and craftsmen to make repairs. They assure me that the work will begin in four days' time."

"Thank you, Armand." Commandant Gaston told him before continuing.

"As to the continued military presence on this island. I have decided to leave my Toulon1 squad on the island as an insurance policy against unforeseen threats and to serve primarily as a liaison for me to help Armand and the people of the island during this rebuilding. Armand has generously offered the use of this guesthouse during their stay."

"Commander Ross, please outline your evacuation plan."

"Commandant." Commander Ross acknowledged standing up. "Captain Renault of the submarine Liberté is preparing to depart Cavallo for camp Melusine at 1900 tomorrow."

"Recommendations from medical staff is that the wounded should not be transported by the Liberté."
"Therefore, she will carry the Toulon2 and 3 squads as well Lieutenants Dupont, Laurent and myself."

"The Adélard squad and their two replacement commandos will depart the following day. With Captain Philippe aboard one of the Requin Gun boats."

"Mr. Bugatti will depart tomorrow morning on the first Helicopter transport available for camp Melusine to rejoin his wife and children."

* * *

"Commandant you mentioned the ongoing threat to Mr. Bugatti and his family." Can you brief us on that Sir?" Adélard asked.

"Yes. Please Gaston. What about the Warlord? Is my family safe?" Armand blurted out his voice full of concern and uncharacteristically loud.

Commandant Gaston's demeanor remained composed as he addressed the questions.

"Armand let me start by telling you the Warlord is dead and no longer a threat to you or your family."

"As to the how gentlemen, that is a longer story that gives me no pleasure in sharing with you."

Commandant Gaston cleared his throat before continuing.

"Through our French intelligence operative Mr. Boulanger, we contacted a Burundian self-proclaimed rebel leader one Aziza Samira. She had the same desire to eliminate the Congo Warlord although she lacked resources, her people were suffering, and she needed weapons and money."

"Using our influence, her refugee camps began receiving international aid in the manner of food, medical supplies, and temporary housing. Various Russian weapons were also supplied via our Polish friends."

"Gérard Constantin, our Senior Operations Officer infiltrated in country with two combat commando squads to assist the rebels with the assault."

"Timing for the assault was critical to our mission of protecting Armand and his family from the mercenaries. Our trigger was the 10 million euro she demanded for her assistance."

"72 hours ago, the money was transferred, her reaction at that time deeply concerned Mr. Boulanger. He feared Aziza was unstable and recommended to the admiral to retract our commandos and not be involved in any combat operations."

"It is important to understand that at no point was Frances's involvement known to her or to anyone within the Congo."

The room was filled with a mixture of curiosity and anticipation as the commandant continued.

"After sunrise yesterday the rebel forces, led by Aziza Samira, executed simultaneous attack on seventeen of the Warlord's facilities in the town and his main headquarters."

Commandant Gaston's tone remained steady as he answered. "The attack from the rebel's perspective was a resounding success."

"To that regard, the rebel forces overwhelmed the Warlord's defenses. The main battle lasted a little over an hour."

Commandant Gaston's next words were delivered with a measured weight. "The battle resulted in the deaths of hundreds, if not thousands, of the Warlord's forces as well as innocents. Those that surrendered were slaughtered publicly and those that escaped the initial battle are now in hiding avoiding the roaming assignation teams."

The room fell silent, each man absorbing the gruesome facts.

"Although our purpose was honorable, even our limited involvement in this bloodbath sickens me and makes me question my and commands judgement. I am relieved that Mr. Boulanger had the good sense to advise the Admiral to stop any plans for our direct involvement and that no commando actively participated in this inhuman slaughter."

After a long pause Adélard spoke up. "Sir, forgive me, but do we have confirmation of the Warlords death? I am concerned of a continued threat to the Bugatti's."

"Understood Mr. Adélard. After what has happened here, I would be asking the same question if I were you."

The answer is yes Mr. Adélard, we most certainly do. As it turns out the Congo warlord was captured alive by the rebel forces. Then in a public display the rebel leader Aziza Samira video recorded herself beheading him in front of her army and as an added warning to any wishing to reclaim his territory she stuck his head on a pole and placed in front of rubble that was once his headquarters.

1930 Catholic Church, Cavallo Island

The small island church stood as a sanctuary of calm amidst the turmoil that had recently gripped the island of Cavallo. Armand Bugatti stepped in his heart heavy with the weight of recent events. He had sought solace within these walls before, but today was quite different.

Father Paulo welcomed him with a warm smile.
"Armand, my son, it is always a pleasure when you visit." He said, his voice carrying a soothing cadence.

Armand weakly returned the smile. "Father Paulo, I've been struggling with something heavy on my conscience."

The priest motioned for Armand to take a seat. "Tell me, Armand. Speak from your heart."

Armand gaze fixed on the centuries old cross. "Father, I killed a man during the attack on the compound."

"Yes, Armand I know."

"And because of me a great deal of death and suffering happened in the Congo."

"I understand Armand, Go on."

"Paulo, I can't help but feel a tremendous guilt."

Father Paulo listened attentively. "Armand, the human heart is a complex vessel. Guilt is a heavy burden, but it is also a sign of the divine spirit within you. It shows that you possess a conscience, a moral compass that guides you."

GHOST COMMANDO – Battle for Cavallo

Armand lowered his head in shame, his fingers tracing idle patterns on the wooden pew. "But how can I find peace when my hands are stained with so much blood."

Father Paulo's response was gentle, yet firm.
"Consider this Armand, evil thrives when good people do nothing. The Congo Warlord caused unspeakable harm, and while the means to stop him were undoubtedly violent, they were necessary to prevent further suffering."

"Your actions may have caused death, but they also prevented even greater evil from being done."

Armand absorbed the priest's words, a mixture of contemplation and relief filling his heart. "Father, are you trying to say that my guilt is a testament to my humanity?"

Father Paulo nodded. "Exactly. Embrace your guilt, for it's a sign that you're attuned to the moral fabric of God."

As the sunset cast its last rays through the stained-glass windows, Armand sighed deeply.
"Father, I would like to believe that."

Father Paulo placed a reassuring hand on Armand's shoulder. "Armand, let us pray together. Let us pray for the strength to use your experiences to be a force for good."

The two men bowed their heads, their words a whispered communion between them and the divine. Armand's burdens felt lighter as he spoke aloud his regrets, his hopes, and his desire to do good. And when their prayer concluded, Father Paulo smiled warmly.

"Armand, the path to peace is not always easy. But remember, my son, that you are not alone on this journey."

"God's love is boundless, and He sees the intentions of your heart. The lives that have been spared because of your actions are a testament to your commitment to justice."

Armand's eyes glistened as he met Father Paulo's gaze. "Thank you, Father. Your words bring comfort and solace to my soul."

Father Paulo stood, extending his hand in a gesture of blessing. "Go in peace, Armand. Embrace your journey, and let your heart be your guide."

As Armand left the church the burden of guilt had not disappeared, but it had found a place of understanding within him. And as he looked out at the island's peaceful landscape, he carried with him the knowledge that his actions, both painful and necessary, were part of a larger tapestry guided by the divine hand to do good not harm.

* * *

Camp Melusine, Corsica
In the quiet and orderly medical facility at Camp Melusine, Isabella Bugatti walked with a sense of purpose.

Her heart carried a mix of gratitude and concern as she approached the bedside of the man who had risked his life to save her husband.

Francoise lay in a clean and comfortable room, his form illuminated by the soft light filtering through the curtains.

The attending doctor met Isabella with a gentle smile. "Madame Bugatti, I'm glad you could visit.

Isabella nodded appreciatively, her gaze drifting toward Francoise's prone figure. "Thank you, doctor. Please tell me how he's doing."

"Francoise is stable now, thanks to the efforts of the medics on Cavallo and the care he has received with us."

The doctor's voice carried a reassuring tone. "Francoise was shot through his right lung during the attack on your home."

"It was a critical injury, but the medics on the island were able to stabilize him, reinflate his lung, and stop the bleeding. He's still in the process of recovery, but he's out of immediate danger."

Isabella's eyes softened as she regarded the unconscious man before her. She turned back to the doctor. "Thank you for everything you and your team have done."

Isabella approached Francoise's bedside and took a seat beside him. She watched his peaceful face for a moment, then with a sense of compassion, she leaned closer and gently placed her hand on his.

"Francoise." She began softly, her voice carrying a mixture of gratitude and sincerity. "I don't even know where to start. "You saved my husband's life, Francoise. You protected him when danger was all around. Your actions showed the depth of your love and loyalty to Armand and to the family."

As if in response to her words, Francoise's fingers twitched slightly, a faint indication of his presence. Isabella smiled gently, her gratitude flowing from the depths of her heart. "I promise you, Francoise, we will never forget what you have done. You are our hero."

* * *

Bugatti Compound, Cavallo Island

Commander Ross found Adélard overseeing the final stages of packing up the equipment. He approached with a purposeful stride and a warm smile. "Adélard." He greeted, his tone a mix of camaraderie and professionalism.

"Commander Ross." Adélard acknowledged, straightening up from his task. "Is there something I can do for you?"

Commander Ross leaned closer; his voice lowered to a conversational tone. "Actually, I wanted to talk to you privately." He glanced around to make sure they had a modicum of privacy amidst the bustling activity.

Adélard answered his expression curious. "Go on Sir."

The commander's eyes met Adélard's, his gaze steady. "First I want to officially congratulate you and your squad on your promotion to active commandos. Regardless of how or why it occurred your squad has proven beyond question that you all deserved it.

A sense of pride swelled within Adélard, his features breaking into a pleased smile. "Thank you, Commander. That is an honor coming from you."

Commander Ross reached out putting a hand on Adélard's shoulder. "Typically, the Commando ceremony is held on Toulon. However, I've decided to make an exception for your squad."

Adélard raised an eyebrow, curiosity evident in his eyes. "An exception? How so Commander?"

The commander's smile held a touch of warmth. "I have arranged for the ceremony to take place at Camp Melusine with full honors. The Admiral has already approved the idea and is planning on coming himself for the ceremony."

A mixture of surprise and appreciation crossed Adélard's face. "That is . . . unexpected, Commander. Thank You."

"I thought it fitting, especially since Julio and Henri are restricted to the medical facility and would not be allowed to travel to Toulon."

Commander Ross clasped Adélard's shoulder in a gesture of solidarity. "I had thought of giving you the option, but then I realized you would demand for the entire squad to be together when you are awarded your medals. So, I pulled a few strings and made it happen."

Adélard nodded in agreement. "You are correct Sir."

The commander laughed and then continued. "And on a similar note, I have been giving some thought to your future assignments." Adélard's gaze sharpened, his senses alert. "Where did that thinking take you Sir?"

Commander Ross took a moment, as if gathering his thoughts. "I believe keeping your squad at Camp Melusine for a while is the right move."

"Once your squad is at full strength, we'll confer with Commandant Gaston to determine the most suitable direction for your continued training and missions."

Commander Ross nodded, a sense of respect underlining his words. "You've all proven your capabilities, Adélard. For now, focus on your men recuperating and preparing for the ceremony. Once that's done, I'll be ordering a well-deserved 30-day leave for your squad."

Adélard's eyes gleamed with gratitude. "30 days? Thank you, Commander. That would be most welcome."

* * *

Late that night, the Rousseau guest house was draped in a serene stillness, a stark contrast to the chaos of the night before. Armand Bugatti, his thoughts heavy with the weight of recent events, stood outside Adélard's door. With a gentle knock, he roused the sleeping commando leader.

Adélard groggily opened the door, blinking against the sudden intrusion of light. "Armand? What's going on?"

Armand offered a small smile and a nod towards the hallway. "I couldn't sleep, and I thought maybe we could talk."

Adélard rubbed his eyes, his fatigue evident, but he nodded in agreement. "Sure, come on in."

GHOST COMMANDO – Battle for Cavallo

As Armand entered, he carried with him a tray holding two baguette sandwiches and a bottle of rich red French wine.

"I brought us a late-night snack. I thought we could go to the basement and enjoy some good food and conversation."

Adélard's curiosity piqued as he glanced at the tray. "You're full of surprises tonight, Armand."

The two men made their way to the basement, where a dim light cast a cozy atmosphere. They settled around the table, with Armand opening the bottle of wine and setting the sandwiches out.

Armand sighed as he unwrapped one of the baguette sandwiches. "I've been thinking a lot about what happened yesterday, Adélard."

"Which part Armand?" Adélard asked.

"The part when we were in my office . . . about me killing that mercenary leader." Armand blurted out.

"Oh, and I am truly sorry about shooting your ear."

Adélard took a bite of his sandwich, his expression thoughtful. "Don't worry about my ear, Armand, but I understand what you mean. Taking a life is never easy, even when it's in defense of others."

Armand nodded in agreement. "It's just... it weighs on me. I never imagined I'd have to do something like that."

Adélard's gaze was sympathetic as he spoke. "Armand, you're not alone in feeling that way. Every life taken leaves a mark on all of us. Killing is not something to be enjoyed."

Armand leaned back in his chair, his fingers tracing the rim of his wine glass. "I suppose you're right. It's the price we pay to maintain a civilized society. To prevent the rise of warlords and chaos like we saw in the Congo."

Adélard's expression turned somber, his eyes reflecting the weight of his own experiences. "Exactly. We do what we must to prevent that darkness from spreading."

Armand looked at Adélard with admiration in his eyes.
"I can't express how grateful I am for you and your squad. Facing overwhelming odds, standing up in an impossible situation. You were all incredibly brave."

Adélard's gaze met his, a hint of a smile on his lips. "I am just happy we can sit here and talk about it, Armand."

* * *

Armand's tone turned earnest as he set down his wine glass. "Well, I want to show my appreciation. I've thought about it, and I want to offer financial compensation for your squad's bravery."

Adélard's response was immediate and firm. "Armand, we can't accept money for doing our duty. For protecting a citizen of France from a foreign hostile. For protecting a friend and his family from harm. NO Armand."

Armand responded frustration in his expression. "But I want to show my gratitude."

Adélard reached across the table, resting his hand on Armand's. "You already have, Armand. Your gratitude means a lot to us. Knowing that you, your family and the good people of this island are safe is reward enough."

Armand sighed, his initial frustration giving way to understanding. "I suppose you're right. But still, I need to do something. I'll find another way to express my appreciation."

"My father use to say, 'Don't be so dramatic Adélard.' Maybe I should tell you the same thing Armand?"

"Isabella would probably agree with you." Armand answered smiling causing both men to laugh.

As the two men sat in the quiet basement, the simple act of sharing a meal and a bottle of wine reflected the permanent friendship they had formed.

Chapter 15: Next to the End

The distinct sound of rotor blades cut through the air of the Bugatti compound, heralding the arrival of the helicopter from Melusine returning the medical personnel.

The sleek NH90 Caiman descended gracefully, its powerful blades creating a small windstorm as it settled at the rear of the mansion.

Adélard and Armand Bugatti stood together by the landing area waiting.

"Mr. Bugatti." Captain Auclair called out with a warm smile from the open door. "Ready when you are sir."

Adélard helped Armand step up into the helicopter then handed him his bag. Armand reached out putting a key in Adélard's hand.

"What's this Armand?" Adélard asked.

"The keys to the wine cellar . . . just in case." Armand answered smiling.

As they spoke, the engines became louder, and the blades of the helicopter began to spin faster overhead. Adélard stepped forward, extending a hand to Armand. "It has been an honor, Armand."

Armand shook Adélard's hand firmly. "Thank you, mon ami."

With the helicopter's engines roaring, Captain Auclair motioned towards the straps. "Buckle up Mr. Bugatti, your wife and children are waiting for you."

Adélard stepped back, shielding his eyes from the swirling dust as the door closed. He watched with a sense of happiness as the helicopter lifted off, carrying Armand Bugatti to his loved ones.

* * *

Brazzaville, the Republic of the Congo
Government spokesperson confirms international news reports that another turf war has broken out between rival factions within refugee camps that has left thousands injured and hundreds dead.

With an emergency resolution the UN has condemned this lawlessness, and vows to increase material support to help stabilize the Republic of the Congo government.

* * *

Rousseau guest house, Bugatti Compound
The morning sunlight filtered into Julio's room in the guest house. Inside, Noel and Jojo worked together, methodically packing up Julio's personal belongings and equipment. The room was filled with a mix of camaraderie and reflection as they went about their task.

"Man, Julio really did a number on that fuel truck." Jojo remarked, shaking his head in amazement.

Noel chuckled, folding a shirt with care. "Yeah, he sure did. I mean, who would drive head on into a fuel truck like that?"

"Only one crazy commando." Jojo answered grinning. "The youngest member of our Ghost Squad. A natural born knuckle dragging Kraken named Julio D'Parma."

"True that. I'm just happy the silly bastard is ok." Noel said.

"Well, he wouldn't be if we hadn't dragged him out of the Defender." Jojo added for once being serious.

Amidst the seriousness, Jojo's sense of humor shone through. "Hey, speaking of crazy moves, how about you, standing in the middle of the road like some Cowboy out of an Italian movie shooting the fuel truck over and over until the explosion shook the entire island? Even Graham said the blast was so bright it blinded his drones for a while."

Noel grinned sheepishly. "Yeah, well, I had to do something after that damn truck started moving again."

"So, two crazy commandos." Jojo quipped.

"Better make that three, I seem to remember your skinny ass dragging Julio across the road with bullet flying in every direction, mostly aimed at you."

As they continued to pack, their conversation turned more serious. "You know, if Julio hadn't stopped that truck, who knows what kind of disaster it would have caused." Noel mused.

Jojo nodded in agreement. "Seriously, that thing was a 1000 gallon bomb on wheels racing straight for the mansion."

GHOST COMMANDO – Battle for Cavallo

Noel's gaze turned distant as he considered the implications. "Man, it's heavy when you think about it. We were up against some ruthless sons of bitches and a lot of them. I think Julio turned the tide and made all the difference."

"Between Julio spoiling their plan to suicide bomb the mansion and the helicopter showing up with Sergeant Moreau blasting that Vulcan gun at them nonstop. I think it broke their backs. They had lost, there just wasn't enough of them dead yet to realize it." Jojo added.

With Julio's personal items carefully packed, Noel and Jojo left the room, heading down to the basement of the guest house. The atmosphere shifted slightly as they approached the basement, knowing they were about to pack up the squad's diving gear and weapons.

As they began sorting through the equipment, Noel broke the silence. "It's been one hell of a ride, hasn't it Jojo?"

Jojo nodded, his expression a mix of nostalgia and camaraderie. "Definitely mon ami. A month ago, we were playing hide and seek with dummies in a pool and now we be Kraken with the scars to prove it."

Noel picked up a piece of diving gear, his fingers tracing the familiar contours. "We saved this place Jojo. I feel proud I was part of that."

Jojo looked at him, a grin tugging at his lips. "Yeah, Noel we did, and we made one hell of a mess doing it."

"Ready for Melusine?" Noel asked, zipping up the last bag.

Jojo nodded, a sense of anticipation in his eyes. "Yeah, but I'll miss this place. Sort of like your first kiss from a girl. Not something you will ever forget."

"I remember my first kiss." Noel added smiling. "She bit my bottom lip."

* * *

Surveillance Grotto, Church Graveyard

In the dimly lit grotto, Graham and the lieutenants worked meticulously, organizing, and packing the surveillance equipment that had been crucial in monitoring the island's security. The monitors, wires, and delicate technology were handled with care as they prepared to move everything to the guest house.

"Careful with those power cables, Laurent." Graham called out, his tone a blend of instruction and camaraderie. "Somehow, one of them shocked me earlier."

Laurent nodded in concentration as he carefully coiled a cable and secured it. "I know, it got me as well."

As they worked, their peaceful atmosphere was interrupted by the two altar boys they had protected during the attack.

The boys approached the men, their eyes curious and innocent. Graham looked up with a warm smile.

"Well, if it isn't our brave altar boys." He greeted them, setting down a monitor.

One of the boys, Alex, spoke up. "Um, Monsieur Graham, we were wondering . . . could we see the flying bug drones work?"

The other boy, Lucas, nodded eagerly. "Please! We thought they were really cool, but we couldn't see much from under the blanket you gave us."

"Well, you might as well. Neither of you two can say no to them. I will pack up the rest of this stuff." Lieutenant Laurent told Graham and Dupont while winking at the boys.

Graham exchanged a glance with Dupont, who was equally unable to deny the two urchin's request.

"Well, you two, we were in the middle of packing up, but I think we can spare a few minutes for a quick demonstration." Lieutenant Dupont told them.

With excited expressions, the boys watched as Graham and Dupont set up the drones and prepared to launch them. They huddled around the monitors, their eyes wide with anticipation.

"Alright, Lucas, you're in charge of this one." Graham said, guiding the boy's hand to the controls. "Just move the joystick gently."

Lucas carefully maneuvered the drone, a grin spreading across his face as he watched the live feed on the screen.

"This is so cool!"

Dupont gave a similar demonstration to Alex, who was equally enthralled by the experience. As they explored the island from the drones' perspective, the boys' wonder and excitement was infectious.

"Look at that, Alex! You can see the commandos dragging the burnt trucks off the road." Dupont pointed out, reaching out to zoom the picture in.

Alex's eyes sparkled with fascination. "Wow, I can see everything."

For a while, they continued to explore, guiding the drones over the island, flying in and around the buildings and up and over the cliffs to the ocean and back.

The boys learned quickly, and, in a few minutes, they were operating the drones by themselves watching all the island activities unfold.

The innocence and joy in the boys' faces was in stark contrast to the fear they had experienced hiding in the grotto during the battle.

Eventually, Graham glanced at his watch. "Alright, boys, we would love to keep flying, we've got a lot of work to finish."

Reluctantly, the boys handed back the controls, their smiles still radiant. "Thank you, Monsieur Graham, Monsieur Dupont! That was fun!"

"Thank you, Monsieur Laurent." Alex said winking at the Lieutenant.

GHOST COMMANDO – Battle for Cavallo

Graham ruffled Lucas's hair with a chuckle. "Anytime, kiddo."

As the men continued to work packing up the grotto, Graham couldn't help but smile to himself. Sometimes, it was the simplest interactions that left the most lasting impressions.

* * *

Bugatti Compound, Cavallo

Adélard made his way back from the road outside the gates towards the mansion to meet with Commandant Gaston. His steps were purposeful, his mind already processing the tasks that needed to be completed. As he approached the mansion, he saw Commandant Gaston standing near the entrance, an undeniable figure of authority.

"Commandant." Adélard saluted, coming to attention.

"At ease, Adélard." Gaston replied. "Report."

Adélard shifted his weight slightly and began his briefing. "We tried to disassemble the burnt fire truck and the defender, but the damage was too extensive. Some progress was made, but the main carcasses are still blocking the road."

Gaston nodded, understanding the challenges they faced. "I see. We'll need to get those vehicles cleared before the road can be fully functional again."

Adélard nodded in agreement. "Yes, sir. We're working on finding a truck that we can use to drag them away."

Gaston studied him for a moment before speaking again. "Good. Once you have the truck, I want you to move those vehicles to the marina. I'll arrange for a disposal team to come from Toulon and take care of them."

Adélard absorbed the orders, his mind already calculating the logistics. "Understood, sir. We'll get it done."

Gaston's gaze held a mixture of approval and confidence. "Adélard, I've been impressed with your leadership and the way you've handled this mission. It's not easy to face such challenges, especially as a young commando.

Adélard felt a surge of pride at the commandant's words. "Thank you, sir."

Gaston's expression softened. "Adélard, you have proven yourself as a skilled commando and as a man of integrity. There's a situation brewing in the Pacific that might be of interest to you once your squad is back up to full strength."

Adélard's curiosity was piqued. "Sir?" Gaston offered a small smile. "I'll provide you with more details when the time is right. But for now, focus on completing the tasks at hand."

"Of course, Sir." Adélard replied with a determined nod.

Gaston's gaze held Adélard's for a moment, conveying a sense of shared understanding.

"Adélard, make no mistake I am proud of you and your squad, but all of you are still wet behind the ears baby Krakens." He told Adélard smiling.

GHOST COMMANDO – Battle for Cavallo

"What I want and what the core needs, is fire breathing, knuckle dragging full grown Krakens. Therefore, I am ordering Commander Ross to accelerate your squad's training to the highest level."

The commandant paused, smiling at Adélard. "The one thing the commandos cannot do Mr. Adélard, is to train desire into a man. You, it seems have a chest full."

Adélard, unable to resist, smiled from ear to ear.
"Thank you, Sir."

Gaston offered a final nod of approval. "Dismissed, Adélard. Carry on."

With another salute, Adélard turned and made his way back towards his squad. The weight of the commandant's words, rather than increasing the burden to be carried, added an additional spring, and resolve to his footsteps.

* * *

Surveillance Grotto, Church Graveyard
Father Paulo's footsteps echoed softly in the underground grotto as he entered. Graham, Dupont, and Laurent turned to face him, each offering a respectful nod of greeting.

"Father Paulo." Graham spoke first, his voice filled with joy. "It is good to see you again."

The priest smiled warmly, his eyes reflecting the sincerity of his words. "And it is good to see all of you. I wanted to come visit before you left and express my deepest thanks once again for what you've done for this island."

Graham inclined his head slightly smiling. "We were just doing our duty, Father."

Father Paulo's gaze moved to Dupont, who also offered a nod of acknowledgment. "Your presence and your actions went beyond duty. You protected this island and its people, and for that, we are truly grateful."

Dupont 's expression softened. "It was a team effort. We couldn't have done it without the support of the island."

The priest's smile grew, his appreciation evident. "Humility is a noble trait. But do not underestimate the impact of your actions. You've shown the island what true bravery and sacrifice look like."

Lieutenant Laurent stepped forward, his voice carrying genuine curiosity. "Father, may I ask about the two altar boys, Alex and Lucas?"

Father Paulo's eyes held a mixture of fondness and compassion. "Of course. Alex and Lucas are both orphans. I have taken them in, they live with me here in the church." Father Paulo nodded solemnly. "Unfortunately, their families were lost in a boating accident a few years ago. Since then, they have been under my care."

Father Paulo's expression brightened a bit. "They have their challenges, mostly because they are stubborn, willful children. which I must admit is partially my fault for indulging them, but they are smart and resilient. The island people have somewhat adopted them as all our children."

"Which I might add only makes raising them more difficult as they have 40 uncles and aunts spoiling them at every turn." Father Paulo added chuckling.

Laurent looked genuinely touched by the priest's words. "That's wonderful to hear, Father."

Father Paulo's eyes met each of theirs in turn. "You see, your actions not only protected the physical safety of this island but also nurtured the spirit of the people that call it home, including the boys."

Graham smiled warmly. "We were happy to do so Father."

The priest offered a gentle smile turning to leave. "May you find peace knowing that your actions have made a lasting impact. Thie island will always welcome you as its heroes."

* * *

1800 Beach loading zone, Cavallo

Commander Ross stood at the overlook; his gaze fixed on the inflatable boats bobbed gently in the icy water, their dark forms a stark contrast against the azure sea.

Down on the beach the members of Toulon squads were diligently loading their gear into the waiting inflatable boats.

The teams led by Lieutenants Coop and Nickalos, worked with an air of purpose, despite their exhaustion, there was a resilience in their demeanor, a determination to complete their tasks efficiently and to the best of their abilities.

The sun was beginning its descent, casting long shadows along the beach of Cavallo, as Adélard made his way to the overlook where Commander Ross stood. The waves gently brushed against the shore, the rhythmic sound serving as a backdrop to the conversation that was about to take place.

"Commander Ross." Adélard said as he approached.
The commander turned to face Adélard, his expression both attentive and thoughtful. "Mr. Adélard." Ross said, acknowledging him with a nod. "I trust you are as ready as I am, to get back to Corsica."

Adélard nodded in response, a sense of weariness and accomplishment etched on his face. "Yes, Sir. This island is beautiful, but our job is done. Time to go home Sir."

Ross looked out at the sea for a moment, as if contemplating the significance of their victories. "Indeed." He said softly. "Time now for a new chapter to begin."

The commander turned his attention back to Adélard, his gaze steady. "Commandant Gaston has given me direct orders regarding the continued training for your squad."

Adélard's interest deepened. "What type of training, Sir?"

"After you return to camp Melusine, the four capable members of your squad will undergo specialized training." "Specialized training?" Adélard repeated, intrigued.

Commander Ross smiled and paused, allowing the words to sink in. "Your squad will be trained in both HALO jumps and Helo-rappelling."

GHOST COMMANDO – Battle for Cavallo

Adélard's eyes widened in surprise. "HALO jumps and Helo-rappelling, sir?"

"Yes, Adélard." Ross affirmed chuckling. "High-altitude, low-opening jumps into the sea with full dive gear and when you get tired of falling out of perfectly good airplanes, you will learn Helicopter rappelling . . . rapid descends on a rope without using harnesses."

Adélard's mind raced with possibilities, envisioning the challenges and the skills that such training would require. "That sounds like extreme training, Sir."

Ross smiled faintly. "It is, but it's also essential. You and your squad have proven your capabilities, but there is always room for growth. These skills will prove invaluable in future missions."

Adélard nodded, his thoughts a mixture of anticipation and concern. "Understood, Sir."

Ross clapped a hand on Adélard's shoulder. "The only difficult part is the landing. I promise you after this week, it will seem like a walk in the park."

Commander Ross looked at Adélard with a reassuring smile. "I have more news for you. The promotion ceremony for your squad will take place at Camp Melusine in three weeks' time. This will allow Julio and Henri to fully participate, and it will coincide with the beginning of your 30 days of leave."

Adélard's eyes brightened with a mixture of surprise and gratitude. "That's sooner than I expected, thank you, Sir."

Commander Ross nodded. "Your squad has earned it, make sure they continue to do so Mr. Adélard." Ross said with a hint of pride in his voice. "Dismissed."

"Yes, Sir." Adélard replied with a crisp salute.

With a final nod, Commander Ross turned back to the overlook, his gaze fixed on the horizon. Adélard turned and walked away with a sense of pride for his team and the journey they had undertaken together.

As the last of the gear was stowed away, Commander Ross took a deep breath, inhaling the salty scent of the sea. The inflatable boats were now ready with the commandos prepared to depart for the waiting submarine Liberté.

With a final look at the distant homes and the people he had come to admire and respect, Commander Ross began walking down to the waiting boats.

* * *

Camp Melusine, Corsica
As the NH90 Caiman helicopter touched down at Camp Melusine, the rotor blades slowly came to a halt.
The rear door of the helicopter opened, and Armand Bugatti stepped out onto the landing pad, his heart pounded with joy as he took in the sight of his wife Isabella and their daughters Reine and Taber waiting for him with open arms.

"Armand!" Isabella's voice carried over the tarmac as she rushed forward, tears of happiness in her eyes. Their two girls followed suit, running to embrace their father with a mixture of happiness and exhilaration.

"Isabella, Reine, Taber." Armand murmured; his voice choked with emotion as he held them close. "I love you so much."

Isabella's arms tightened around him, and she looked up at him, her eyes shimmering with tears.
"We missed you, my Armand."

As the family embraced, the weight of the past days seemed to lift, replaced by a profound sense of togetherness and gratitude. After a few moments, Isabella pulled back slightly, a warm smile on her face. "Let's go visit François darling, he has been slow to recover."

Together, they made their way to the medical facility where François had been recovering. Inside, they found him awake and alert, propped up in bed. His eyes brightened as he saw them enter.

" Monsieur Bugatti." François said softly with a weak smile. "I am happy to see you sir."

Armand approached the bed, his voice filled with genuine appreciation. "François, you saved my life."

François' smile grew wide causing him to cough and hold a tissue to his lips. "I did what any good butler would do sir." François told him, regaining some of his haute attitude.

The medical staff stepped in advising the Bugatti's that unfortunately François should rest now if he is to recover fully. "Soon as you are able François you are coming to Paris, I promise you." Armand told him, grasping his hand.

* * *

"Captain Philippe." Armand said aloud seeing him walk across the compound. "I don't know how to express my gratitude for your protection and care of my family." He told him with a warm smile, extending his hand.

Captain Philippe shook his hand firmly, his expression serious yet kind. "It was my pleasure, Armand."

"And thank you for being so kind to the girls." Isabella added. Philippe's demeanor instantly softened. "Reine and Taber are special, they made every minute for this old man worthwhile. You tell them to call me anytime they want to go for another fast boat ride."

* * *

Two hours later, the Bugatti corporate helicopter landed at Camp Melusine, ready to transport the family and their chief of security, Luigi, to the Bugatti estate outside of Paris.

As the Bugatti corporate helicopter soared above the azure waters of the Mediterranean Sea, Armand Bugatti found himself gazing out of the window, watching the island of Corsica slowly recede into the distance. Beside him, Isabella sat, her hand gently resting in his, offering silent comfort. Turning his gaze to Isabella, he gave her hand a reassuring squeeze. "We're finally on our way home, my love."

Isabella smiled back at him, her eyes reflecting the same mixture of relief and contentment. "Yes, and we have so much to be thankful for."

Armand nodded, his thoughts momentarily carried back to the bravery and selflessness of the commandos.

GHOST COMMANDO – Battle for Cavallo

"Those men, Isabella. They risked their lives to protect us." Armand's grip on Isabella's hand tightened as he reflected on the enormity of what the squad had done. "We owe them more than we can ever repay."

Lost in his thoughts, Armand stared out of the window once more, his mind abuzz with plans and possibilities. The shimmering sea below mirrored his reflective mood, offering a serene backdrop to the whirlwind of emotions and thoughts that stirred within him.

Chapter 16: Odds and Ends

Bugatti Compound, Cavallo

Night had fallen over the island of Cavallo, casting a tranquil blanket of darkness over the battleground. The Adélard squad, weary but victorious, gathered around a makeshift campfire they built out in the compound.

As the squad members sat around the fire, sharing stories and laughter, the sound of footsteps approached. Adam and David, the American security officers, emerged from the shadows, carrying a bottle of fine American bourbon and glasses. The sight brought a grin to Adélard's face.

"Looks like our friends have come bearing gifts." Graham remarked with a chuckle.

Adam held out the bottle of bourbon. "Figured we'd share a drink to celebrate the end of a wild ride."

Glasses were poured, and the men raised them in unison. "To victory." They chorused before clinking their glasses and downing the fiery liquid.

David leaned back, looking at Adélard. "You know, kid, you've got that rare mix of leadership and guts."

Adélard's expression turned thoughtful. "I couldn't have done it without the incredible men in this squad."

Adam nodded in agreement. "True leaders recognize the value of their team. And you've got a hell of a team." He added lifting his glass.

GHOST COMMANDO – Battle for Cavallo

David leaned forward. "Remember this, Adélard, you might not always have the luxury of a perfect plan. But if you lead with your instincts, you won't go wrong."

Adam chimed in. "And never underestimate your opponent or the power of trust. Trust in your training, trust in your squad, trust in your gut."

Jojo, always the one to add some levity, raised an eyebrow. "Let's not forget trust in your bulletproof vest. Speaking of which Adam did you bring a second bottle for this old fart wisdom circle you got going on? "

Laughing, Adam raised his glass draining it in one swallow. "Nah just one. Besides, are you even old enough to drink Jojo?"

* * *

Camp Melusine, Corsica
Commander Ross stood on the deck, taking in the familiar sight of his base as the submarine Liberté gracefully glided into its hidden cave.

With the submarine safely docked, Commander Ross wasted no time. He quickly made his way to his office, the headquarters of camp Melusine and the place where he had made and set a hundred plans into motion.

As he settled into his chair, he picked up the phone and called for a meeting of the senior officers. It was time to gather and hear the reports on how the training had gone in his absence.

"Good morning, everyone." Ross began as he looked around the table. "Let's get down to it."

"Yes, Sir." One of the officers began. "Commander, we continued the training sessions as planned, with no injuries or reassignments."

"The recruits have completed all their training and are now prepared to ship out to Toulon for their team assignment." Another added.

"We've also seen promising leadership qualities in some of the squad leaders. It's a good batch commander." Captain DuPlessis second in command of the base added."

Ross leaned back in his chair, his gaze shifting around the room. "Good to see that our efforts are paying off. As you know, our responsibility goes far beyond just training these recruits Captain DuPlessis, we are shaping the future of the Marine Commandos." Commander Ross leaned forward, his gaze sweeping across his officers.

"Before we conclude, I have one piece of important news to share. The Adélard Squad has completed their mission with exceptional valor and skill. Prior to the mercenary assault on the island, their squad was given a field promotion by the Commandant and are now an active commando squad."

"Toulon command has decided that their medal and promotion ceremony will not be with the other recruits that have completed their training. It will be conducted here at Melusine in three weeks' time."

GHOST COMMANDO – Battle for Cavallo

"They will receive their medals as will all the commandos that fought on Cavallo."

"That is a rare honor." Captain DuPlessis interjected. "We have never hosted a medal ceremony at Mesuline."

"You are correct Captain on both counts. It is a rare honor and a first for our camp. I expect that we will be hosting some of the most distinguished individuals in the Navy, possibly the vice-admiral, therefore, I want every inch of this camp to be ship shape, and all the bright work polished. Am I clear?"

"Sir. Yes Sir." The officers responded vigorously.

Commander Ross cleared his throat, then continued. "This ceremony is not only a recognition of the Adélard Squad's achievements, or of the brave commandos that reinforced them. This ceremony will also serve as a testament to the quality of training we provide here at Camp Melusine."

"Captain DuPlessis, I want you to prepare a duty roster for all the officers and nco's on the base for that event. Everything from a reception gala for the dignitaries to which men are assigned to remove the trash. Nothing will be by chance. Understood?"

"Understood Commander."

As the meeting concluded, the officers left the room, returning to their various responsibilities. Ross sat back in his chair looking out of his office window at the bustling activity of the base . . . he couldn't help but smile.

* * *

Bugatti Cove, Cavallo

The Requin boat approached Cavallo, the rugged cliffs and lush vegetation that concealed the cove came into view. The three Bugatti compound security guards returning home exchanged glances, their familiarity with this terrain making them feel at once excited and nervous.

Captain Philippe expertly navigated the narrow channel, the boat's engines throttled down to a low rumble as the powerful boat gracefully entered the calm waters of the cove.

With a gentle thud, the hull kissed the wooden dock, and the Requin combat boat came to a rest. The Bugatti guards wasted no time as they quickly thanked Captain Philippe and disembarked. Their boots thudding softly on the wooden planks as they moved in unison towards the waiting Defender on the hill above.

* * *

Adélard helped secure the boat then jumped on approaching Captain Philippe, with his hand extended in gratitude. "Good to see you, Captain. I can't thank you enough for coming to pick us up."

Philippe offered a warm smile, firmly shaking Adélard's hand. "Commander Ross told me you boys were getting a little homesick."

Graham, Jojo, and Noel followed suit, expressing their appreciation to Captain Philippe while loading their gear aboard. The squad had formed a strong bond with him earlier, they respected his old-school, no-nonsense manner.

GHOST COMMANDO – Battle for Cavallo

"Enough of this touchy feely shit my baby Krakens, my wife expects me for an early dinner, and I intend to be there on time." Captain Philippe told them smiling."

The Requin boat idled slowly leaving the hidden cove and ventured into the open sea.

"Was it worth it?" Captain Phillipe asked Adélard as he steered the boat through the channel.

"Yes Captain, I believe it was." Adélard answered thoughtfully.

"Well then, good job Mr. Adélard, now let's get you home." With that he pushed the Requin throttles hard, the Requin jumping out of the water in response, the boat accelerating faster and faster until the occasional blast of cold sea water hitting the commandos stung like needles.

The roar of the Requin gunboat's twin engines reverberated through the air as it sliced through the water, carrying Adélard, Graham, Noel, and Jojo back to Camp Melusine from their mission on Cavallo island.

Captain Philippe stood at the helm, his skilled hands maneuvering the boat with precision. His experienced gaze shifted between the horizon and the boat's controls, a testament to his familiarity with these waters and the Requins remarkable speed. To the east the beautiful coastline of Corsica with its towering cliffs and lush greenery flew by. As they approached Camp Melusine, the pier jutting out into the sea and the camps' fortified submarine caves came into view, a welcoming sight after the squad's time away.

Camp Melusine, Corsica

Adélard leaned against the gunwale, his eyes fixed on the approaching submarine cave entrance. "Always impressive how you keep these boats hidden, Captain."

Captain Philippe chuckled, his grip on the wheel steady. "Adds a little spice to things, wouldn't you say Mr. Adélard? No better way to arrive at camp Melusine than on a disguised gun ship into a secret submarine cave, protected by live gun towers."

"I love it." Jojo blurted out interrupting the conversation.

Graham joined Adélard at the edge of the boat, a grin on his face. "Even if someone could find these boats, no one would ever guess how lethal they are."

"True that, they look like just some rich guy's toys." Adélard commented.

Jojo and Noel exchanged playful glances from their seats further back. "Do you think we could speed this along Captain. You bounced my kidneys all over the ocean for 3 hours, I need to pee." Jojo quipped, earning a chuckle from Noel.

As the boat entered the cave, the cement wall acoustics magnified the sound of the water lapping against the hull. The Requin slid gracefully through the entrance, and Adélard marveled at the precision as Captain Philippe docked the boat only using the thrusters.

With a deft maneuver, Captain Philippe guided the Requin to a stop next to the other three gunboats parked on either side of the submarine cave.

As the engine rumbled to a halt, the men exchanged appreciative glances, their gratitude evident. "Captain, we can't thank you enough for the ride." Adélard said, lifting his bag over his shoulder."

Captain Philippe's smile was warm and genuine. "No problem, Adélard. The sea is my playground, and it is my pleasure to share it with you from time to time."

Jojo and Noel approached, both wearing cheeky grins. "So, any time we want to take a couple of girls for a boat ride we just call you Captain?" Jojo asked.

Noel nodded in agreement. "We will bring our own snacks Captain."

Captain Philippe chuckled, his eyes crinkling with amusement. "You two are always welcome. Just promise to behave yourselves."

The banter brought a lighthearted atmosphere to the boat, a reminder that even amid intense missions, moments of camaraderie could be found. As the men disembarked and the Requin gunboat nestled among its companions, the sense of accomplishment from their mission mingled with the anticipation of the upcoming celebration.

"Until next time, Captain." Adélard said, extending his hand.

Captain Philippe grasped it firmly, his gaze steady. "Fair winds and following seas, Mr. Adélard."

The men quickly shouldered their bags and started up the ladder to the camp, each step taken with a sense of purpose as they moved toward their barracks.

As they walked across the camp, they were intercepted by the men of the Matis and Gilles squads with warm smiles and outstretched hands. Matis clasped hands with Adélard. "Good to have you back, Adélard, been too quiet without your squad around."

Adélard smiled in return. "It's good to be back."

"Couple of us have been visiting Julio and Henri. They are doing fine. The doctor told me they will be back at full strength in no time." Gilles told him.

* * *

Medical Facility, Camp Melusine
Still carrying their bags, the four men walked down the corridor of the medical facility, their footsteps echoing in the quiet hallways. Adélard led the way, his expression a mix of concern and relief as he approached the rooms where his comrades were recovering.

Stopping at the entrance of the room where Julio and Henri were, Adélard pushed the door open gently. The two men were seated on their beds, their conditions visibly improved from the last time Adélard had seen them. A wave of relief washed over him as he entered.

"Hey, you two." Adélard called out with a warm smile. "Sorry we're late to your party. We had some stuff to do." Noel said seeing his friends looking so well.

Henri chuckled, though a hint of fatigue lingered in his features. "Yeah, the commander said you guys were lost without us."

"Well, we did need to pack up all your stuff." Jojo added. "By the way Henri, I had to throw away some of your shorts. They were beyond washing."

"I thought I saw those in the bonfire last night, but I could swear they were Noels as big as they were." Grham added laughing.

Adélard walked over, giving each a pat on the shoulder. "I'm glad to see you both on the mend. "

Julio looked up, his own smile mirroring Adélard's. "Boss! Look who's up and walking around. They got Henri doing hall laps on crutches."

"Good to hear. You guys chat a bit I want to check on François and the Toulon commando."

Julio's expression softened. "He's in a separate room down the hall. Number 107, the doctors are good to him."

Adélard left his men and started down the hall, just then, the door to François's room opened, and a nurse emerged. Adélard nodded at her and entered the room, finding François awake and propped up in bed.

"François, it is good to see you. How are you feeling?"

François managed a weak smile. "Better, monsieur Adélard. Thank you for coming and your concern."

Adélard nodded. "You, maybe a stuffy old butler François, but you are a hero, a man of honor and valor."

François chuckled softly. "I would rather be a hero than a fool, although I think monsieur, I was a bit of both."

Smiling at François's moment of honesty Adélard asked. "How is the recovery coming along?"

"Everything has been repaired. The doctors wish to keep me restricted until my strength has fully returned."

* * *

After spending a few more minutes with François, Adélard made his way down the hallway to the room where Antoine, the wounded commando from the Toulon3 squad, was recovering. The door was ajar, and Adélard knocked gently before entering.

"Antoine?" Adélard called out as he stepped in.

Antoine looked up from his bed, his expression a mixture of fatigue and curiosity. "Adélard, right?"

Adélard nodded and pulled up a chair.

"That's right. I wanted to come and personally thank you for your squad's reinforcement."

GHOST COMMANDO – Battle for Cavallo

Antoine winced slightly as he shifted in the bed. "We arrived late. Missed the action."

Adélard sighed, his tone somber. "No, Antoine your squad arrived in the middle of it all. It was fierce, brutal, even with your squad we were outnumbered two to one."

Antoine's eyes widened, a mix of surprise and relief. "Really? They only told me that the mercenaries were defeated not the how. Did we lose any men?"

Adélard nodded, a hint of pride in his voice. "Yes, they were and no we did not lose one commando or civilian. But no lie it was tight until right at the end. When your submarine squad and the helicopter squad arrived, the tide turned in our favor. It was all over for that Congo scum."

Antoine let out a breath, his features relaxing. "Understood. Still your squad held them off, rockets blasting you and way outnumbered. You guys never gave up an inch of the island."

"It all happened in the moment Antoine, and standing our ground is what we know and what we did. You did your part, Antoine. You came running fearless into the face of battle. You and your squad are hero's."

Antoine managed a small smile. "I just wish I could have been there next to you in that shitstorm."

*　*　*

Headquarters, Camp Melusine

Adélard stepped into Commander Ross's office at Camp Melusine, saluting as he entered.
"Sir, you wanted to see me?"

Commander Ross looked up from his desk, offering Adélard a warm smile. "Adélard, welcome back. Please, have a seat."

Adélard nodded and took a seat in front of the commander's desk, his eyes attentive as he waited.

"I hope your return journey went smoothly." Commander Ross began. "Philippe does so enjoy showing off his boats."

Adélard nodded. "Yes, sir."

Commander Ross leaned back in his chair. "Good to hear. I wanted to let you know that you and your squad deserve a break after the recent mission.

Tomorrow, I've arranged for one of our ensigns to drive your squad to the airfield for jump training."

Adélard's eyebrows raised in curiosity. "Jump training, Sir?"

Commander Ross nodded. "Yes. High-altitude, low-opening jumps into the sea. It's an essential skill for our commandos."

"Sir that doesn't sound like a break Sir?" Adélard asked.

GHOST COMMANDO – Battle for Cavallo

"Relative to 30 lunatics shooting at you with rockets, I would say it would be a welcomed break, Adélard." Commander Ross answered grinning.

Adélard nodded in understanding. "Good point Sir."

Commander Ross leaned forward, his expression earnest. "I also wanted to personally welcome you back. The squad did a remarkable job on Cavallo Island."

Adélard's chest swelled with pride. "Thank you, Sir. If it wasn't for what we learned here, truthfully commander we wouldn't have lasted more than 5 minutes."

Commander Ross smiled. "Indeed."

"Now, for the jump training, I have specific instructions that I want followed. Julio and Henri will accompany your squad to the airfield. They will participate in the classroom training and the flights, but I want to emphasize that under no circumstances are they to actually jump."

Adélard nodded, understanding the plan and the concern for his men. "Of course, Sir."

Commander Ross leaned forward. "Adélard, you need to understand that this type of training usually takes around four to five weeks to complete. However, Commandant Gaston has ordered your squad to complete it in half the time."

Adélard's eyes widened slightly. "Half the time, sir? Two weeks Sir?"

"Actually 10 days is what the training schedule looks like. It will be a rigorous training schedule, with little time other than eating and sleeping between jumps. After Cavallo I have no doubt, your squad is up to the challenge."

Adélard nodded, his determination evident. "Yes Sir."

* * *

Adélard joined his squad for dinner in the mess hall. The atmosphere was relaxed and jovial, a stark contrast to the tense moments he faced moments ago with the commander.

Adélard slid into his seat, greeted by the familiar faces of his comrades. "Hey, Adélard, how was your meeting with the commander?" Graham asked from across the table.

Adélard smiled as he picked up his fork. "Good. He welcomed us back and told us about the jump training we'll be starting tomorrow."

"Tomorrow?" Graham asked.

"Tomorrow." Adélard answered, taking his first bite of food.

"Jumping out of a perfectly good airplane, always seemed stupid to me." Noel blurted out.

Jojo chuckled. "Jumping out of planes above the clouds, flying like a bird without wings. Sounds like a good time."

Noel raised an eyebrow. "Yeah, if you're a lunatic with a death wish or too ignorant to know humans can't fly. We are Marine Commandos, part fish, not part bird."

Laughter echoed around the table as they all exchanged playful banter.

"Seriously, though." Henri chimed in, "I don't think I'll be jumping out of airplanes anytime soon."

Julio, who was seated next to Henri, patted him on the back with his one good arm. "Don't worry, Henri I will keep you company."

Adélard grinned at the friendly teasing. "Actually, you both are going with us."

"What?" Both men said together.

"Orders mon ami's." You both will go to class training with the squad and on every jump flight. The only thing you will not do is jump."

"Oh great, now we get two grumpy chaperones." Jojo added grinning.

The conversation flowed naturally as they made light of the challenges they would face and shared stories from their time on Cavallo.

After dinner, the squad made their way to the medical facility, where Julio and Henri were ordered to stay during their recuperation. Adélard walked beside them, a supportive hand on their shoulders. "Ready for another night in the hospital guys?"

Julio smirked. "It's becoming a regular thing for us."

Henri chuckled. "Yeah, but I wish the nurses were more friendly."

As they entered the medical facility, the staff greeted them warmly. The mood was lighthearted as the squad engaged in friendly banter with the nurses and doctors who had taken care of their teammates.

Julio and Henri settled back into their rooms. Last man to leave, Adélard looked at them with a reassuring smile. "Get some rest, you two. We'll be back to pick you up at 0600."

Henri grinned. "No more sleeping in for us, Julio."

Chapter 17: Falling to Earth

The cold morning air was crisp as the Adélard Squad gathered in front of the base hospital. A military truck stood waiting, its engine rumbling softly as the squad members got on board, the moment highlighted with their usual banter and lighthearted jokes.

Adélard glanced around at his team, his gaze resting on Julio and Henri smiling and obviously happy to be back with the squad even with their injuries.

The squad burst into laughter, as Julio accidentally hit Adélard with his arm cast as the squad piled onto the truck. Julio winced adjusting his arm cast and mumbled an apology as Adélard rubbed his head.

"Maybe we should take a course in ducking instead of jumping Adélard." Jojo blurted out laughing.

* * *

The truck rumbled to life, and they set off for the small airfield. The journey was filled with light chatter and shared excitement. Adélard looked out of the window, a mixture of pride and determination welling up within him.

"Adélard, is it true that the fatter you are, the faster your fall?" Jojo asked shoving his shoulder against Noel sitting next to him.

"All objects free fall at the same rate regardless of their mass. Because the gravitational field at Earth's surface causes constant acceleration of any object." Graham added trying to explain the science.

"You mean this skinny runt of a commando and I will hit the ground at the same time?" Noel asked pushing back against Jojo.

"Correct." Graham answered.

"Not Correct Graham." Jojo blurted out.

"I don't believe that science Graham. If I jump last and land on top of Noel, it would be like a mosquito, he would barely notice. If Noel lands on top of me, I will be as flat as a crepe. No way you are jumping after me big fella." Jojo said pushing back at Noel with both arms.

"Stop it you two." Adélard told them laughing. "The only jumps any of us have done was 5 meters from a helicopter and if I remember correctly most of us thought that was extreme."

"Yes, Sir Mr. Adélard." Julio spoke up. "The way I remember it we all pooped our pants."

Jojo grinned, his eyes sparkling. "Ok, Ok, I'll be good. Skydiving, here we come!"

Graham chuckled. "Just remember, Jojo, no pushing anyone out of the plane, not even Noel."

* * *

Upon arriving at the airfield, the squad disembarked the truck a bit confused, as their eyes were drawn to the WW2 era hangar that looked more like an ancient relic rather than an active facility.

GHOST COMMANDO – Battle for Cavallo

As the squad members gathered, they found themselves face-to-face with the instructor, Captain Margo Solitaire. She stood confidently, her athletic build and spirited demeanor giving her a presence that belied her petite stature. Adélard and his team exchanged glances, a mixture of curiosity and readiness in their eyes as they approached her.

"Adélard squad reporting as ordered." Adélard said snapping a perfect salute.

"Good morning, as you were gentlemen." Captain Margo greeted them with a warm smile. "You must be the Adélard Squad. I've heard a lot about you. Seems that Commandant Gaston has a special interest in your squad."

Adélard stepped forward, extending his hand. "Yes, I am Adélard. These are my men, Graham, Jojo, Noel, and that is Julio in the cast and Henri on the crutches."

Captain Margo shook his hand firmly, her grip exuding confidence. "It's a pleasure to have you all here. I am Captain Margo Solitaire, your instructor for the jump training."

The squad exchanged nods and greetings with Captain Margo as they introduced themselves. Her energy and enthusiasm was contagious, and they could tell that this training was going to be intense yet rewarding.

Without wasting any time, Captain Margo led them to the rear of the hangar where a table and chairs that had been set up earlier. She motioned for them to sit down, her tone taking on a more focused demeanor. "Alright, gentlemen, let's dive right into it. We have a tight schedule ahead."

As they settled into their seats, Captain Margo began the classroom instruction. She spoke with authority; her words clear and concise as she covered the essentials of HALO jumps. The video screen behind her displayed detailed diagrams and graphics, illustrating the various phases of the jump process.

"You're about to undertake an accelerated jump training program that usually takes five weeks." Captain Margo explained. "Under orders, we have ten days to master every phase. The good news is that during this training your only other responsibility is eating and sleeping. We are going to cover everything from HALO jumps day and night as well as off target deployment, and Helicopter rappelling."

Her lecture continued, her words interspersed with real-life anecdotes, as she shared her own experiences as well as those of other experienced jumpers.

Adélard and his team listened intently, fully absorbed in the training material. Captain Solitaire's dynamic teaching style kept them engaged, even as the subject matter became more technical.

Captain Margo paused as the initial classroom instruction ended. "Remember, gentlemen, this is no small feat. HALO jumps require physical and mental endurance. Make no mistake, the sky is far less forgiving than the ocean."

After the classroom session concluded, Captain Margo led the squad out to an open area on the airfield. The sun was high in the sky, casting a warm glow over the tarmac as they gathered around her.

"Time to get it on men." Captain Margo began, her voice projecting a sense of authority. "As you know, HALO stands for High Altitude-Low Opening. This is not skydiving or something for mass movement of troops. HALO jumps are designed specifically for small covert teams. It is a technique used to insert a limited number of personnel and equipment with minimal detection by enemy forces."

"Ohhhhh, flying Ghost." Jojo whispered to Adélard.

Captain Margo walked among the squad members, making eye contact with each one as she continued. "The idea is simple: you jump from a high altitude, usually from an airplane either outside of radar range or of a type uninteresting to anyone watching. You will jump, freefall thousands of feet at a high rate of speed making it virtually impossible for enemy radar to detect your presence. Then, at the minimum safe height you will open your parachute and direct your path, landing at your mission target area."

Adélard and his squad members listened intently as Captain Margo emphasized that this technique was ideal for small teams like theirs, enabling them to insert into remote or hostile areas undetected, where larger aircraft might be spotted more easily. This would give the squad a tactical advantage and the element of surprise.

"But let's be clear," Captain Solitaire's tone became more serious. "HALO jumps are not without risks. The high altitudes mean you're exposed to extreme cold and low oxygen levels, which can lead to altitude sickness and other health issues, like freezing to death."

"The freefall phase demands precision and control, as any mistake you or your jump partner experience could lead to disastrous consequences during deployment. And then there is the landing, which is more lethal than any enemy."

Adélard and his team nodded, absorbing every word.

"Over the next ten days, we will cover every aspect of HALO jumps." Captain Margo concluded. "You'll undergo simulations, hands-on practice, and a series of jumps with parachutes. By the time this training is done, you will be proficient or wash out of the Marine Commandos."

* * *

For the next three days, the Adélard squad immersed themselves in an intense routine of their accelerated training, honing their skills with HALO jumps over and over specifically designed for water landings.

As the squad gathered on the tarmac, their faces set in determination, Captain Margo approached with a firm but encouraging smile. "Good morning, gentlemen. Today, we're going to focus on water landings. This is a critical skill, especially for coastal and amphibious operations."

They suited up in their specialized gear, which included oxygen masks for the third day's high-altitude jump.

Adélard glanced at Julio and Henri, who sat nearby, observing the preparations with interest. Sidelined due to their injuries, their presence added a sense of camaraderie to the proceedings.

The plane took off, ascending to 5,000 feet before the jump. The air was crisp, the sky wide open above them. One by one, the squad members leapt from the plane, their bodies arching gracefully in freefall before deploying their parachutes. The splashes into the water were met with cheers from the men already in the inflatable boat waiting below.

As the days progressed, the altitude increased, the challenges becoming more complex. At 10,000 feet, the jumps demanded more precision and control during the freefall, as well as careful navigation to land safely in the designated water area.

The third day brought a different level of intensity. The plane reached an altitude of 15,000 feet, and the squad members donned oxygen masks before jumping. The air was thin, the sensation of floating more surreal than before. Adélard felt the biting cold as he exited the plane, a stark reminder of the challenges posed by high altitudes. The rapid descent felt both exhilarating and daunting, a rush of adrenaline mixing with a fair amount of fear.

In the evenings, as the sun dipped below the horizon, the squad members would gather to discuss the day's training.

"Man, those jumps are something else." Graham said, his face still flushed with excitement. "You've got to be so focused, every second counts."

Noel chuckled, shaking his head. "Yeah and hitting that water . . . it's like a slap in the face. But damn, it's fun!"
"Next time we go up let's talk Captain Margo into some acrobatic stuff, add a little fun to it." Jojo offered smiling.

On the fourth day of their intense training, the Adélard squad assembled in the aircraft hangar, their eagerness and anticipation clearly visible. Captain Margo Solitaire, in her tactical gear, met them with a confident smile.

"Good morning, gentlemen. Today, I'll be joining you for the jumps. It's time to take things up a notch."

The men exchanged glances, a mixture of surprise and determination in their eyes. Having their instructor participate alongside them was a new wrinkle, one that signaled a shift towards a higher more dangerous level.

"You have all done well with the basics." Captain Margo continued, her voice steady. "Falling out of an airplane isn't easy, but now it's time for real precision work. We'll be practicing target jumps, where you must direct your descent to within 3 meters of a specific target. And you'll have a limited window of time to do so."

As they boarded the airplane, the tension in the cabin was real. The adrenaline rush mixed with a sense of determination, a desire to prove their skills. The plane ascended to 20,000 feet, the engine's drone filling the air around them. Captain Solitaire's calm presence was reassuring, a reminder that they were in capable hands.

As they reached the designated altitude, the cabin door opened, and the rush of cold air and the sound of wind enveloped them. Captain Margo turned to the squad.

GHOST COMMANDO – Battle for Cavallo

"Today, I will jump first. Watch closely and pay attention to my descent and aiming."

With those words, she stepped towards the open door and leaped into the sky. Adélard watched her silhouette against the backdrop of the sky, impressed by the grace and precision of her movements. She maneuvered her body skillfully, guiding her descent with a level of control that was nothing short of impressive even for a bird.

Jojo, standing beside Adélard, leaned over, and muttered. "I can't even see those targets, let alone aim for them."

Adélard chuckled quietly watching Margo during her jump.

As Captain Solitaire's parachute deployed, she turned and guided her descent, landing smoothly on the target below. The rest of the squad watched with a sense of awe. It was evident that she had mastered this to a remarkable degree.

"Alright, guys." Adélard yelled over the wind. "Let's go!"
One by one, the squad members jumped from the airplane, their determination evident in their movements. Adélard felt a surge of exhilaration as he descended, his focus zeroed in on the target area below. The ground rushed up to meet him, and he adjusted his body subtly to direct his descent.

After their jumps, they regrouped near the target area, adrenaline still coursing through their veins. Captain Margo joined them with a satisfied smile.

"You're all making great progress. Precision jumps are no easy feat, but you are well on your way. Let's go again."

After a grueling fifth day of jump training, the members of the Adélard squad returned to Camp Melusine, their exhaustion mingling with a sense of accomplishment. Adélard took a moment to catch his breath as he entered the barracks, the day's training still fresh in his mind.

As they began to change out of their gear, the topic of conversation shifted from jumps to the delicious meal that awaited them. Humor and laughter filled the air, a stark contrast to the physical demands they had endured.

Just as they were about to head towards the mess hall, an ensign entered the barracks, his expression urgent. "Adélard, the commander wants to see you in his office right away."

Adélard exchanged a quick glance with his squad mates. He nodded to the ensign, indicating that he understood, and quickly headed towards Commander Ross's office.

What could be so urgent that the commander needed to see him immediately? He reached the office and knocked briskly on the door.

"Enter." came the firm voice of Commander Ross.

Adélard stepped into the office, saluting the commander before he even had a chance to fully take in his surroundings. "You wanted to see me, sir?"

Commander Ross motioned for Adélard to take a seat. His expression serious. "At ease, Adélard. I've just received some news that I believe concerns you and your squad."

GHOST COMMANDO – Battle for Cavallo

Adélard's curiosity deepened, and he leaned forward slightly, his attention fully focused on the commander's words. "Sir, what's going on?"

The commander leaned back in his chair, his gaze steady. "We've received an urgent request from Commandant Gaston. It seems there's an escalating situation in the Pacific, and he's requested that your squad be deployed."

Adélard felt a mixture of surprise and determination wash over him. Deployed to the Pacific? It was a stark reminder of the unpredictable nature of their work as commandos.

"Sir, what's the nature of the situation?"

Commander Ross sighed, his expression grave. "Details are limited at this point, but it seems there is a regional threat near New Caledonian that may require our intervention."

Adélard nodded, absorbing the information. This sudden change in plans caught him off guard.

"You will be briefed further when needed." Commander Ross continued. "In the meantime, your schedule is unchanged for your medal ceremony and your vacations.

"Hold a moment, Adélard." Commander Ross said answering the phone.

The commander motioned for Adélard to stay seated, his expression still focused on his call. Adélard observed as the commander finished his conversation, his tone changed to professional yet relaxed.

Finally, Commander Ross ended the call and turned his attention fully to Adélard. "Sorry about that, Adélard."
Adélard nodded, understanding the demands of command.

"Of course, sir."

The commander reached for his phone again and handed it to Adélard. "This call is for you." He said smiling.

Surprised, Adélard took the phone and brought it to his ear. "Hello?"

A familiar voice came through the line, filling him with a mixture of warmth and curiosity.
"Adélard, it's Armand Bugatti."

Adélard's eyes widened slightly, his mind racing to comprehend the unexpected call. "Mr. Bugatti? It's good to hear from you."

Armand's tone held a genuine warmth. "Are we not past Mr. Bugatti Adélard? Please, call me Armand."

"Yes Armand." Adélard told him smiling.

"Good." Armand replied. "I wanted to personally extend an invitation to you and your squad. I am going to host a party in your honor on my yacht 'Isabella,' docked in Marseille."

"It is the least I can do to show my gratitude."

Adélard's surprise deepened at the generous offer. "Thank you, Armand. That's incredibly generous of you."

GHOST COMMANDO – Battle for Cavallo

Armand continued, his enthusiasm evident. "I understand you're all about to start a well-deserved vacation, and I thought this could be a great way to kick it off. I have arranged everything. Your squad will come to Marseille immediately after your medal ceremony."

Adélard hesitated, his thoughts racing. "That sounds amazing, really. But the men might have already made plans for their time off."

Armand's tone remained determined. "I insist, Adélard. Consider it a gesture of appreciation. I'll ensure you're all transported from the yacht to wherever the men want to go after the party. Your men will not lose a day of vacation. It will be much faster than any military transport.

Adélard's heart swelled with gratitude at Armand's generosity. "On behalf of the squad, I accept your invitation, Armand. Thank you."

Armand's voice held a satisfied note. "Excellent. I look forward to seeing you soon. Have a good evening, Adélard."

* * *

As Adélard hung up the phone, Commander Ross offered a nod of approval.

"You knew about this commander?" Adélard asked.

"Of course." Ross answered grinning.

"Seems like you've made a wise decision, Adélard. I couldn't agree more about your squad attending that party.

The commander leaned back in his chair, his tone light. "I've been to a few Armand parties in my time, and they are never ones to miss. Isabella knows how to host an event."

Adélard asked surprised. "You have?"

Commander Ross chuckled. "Yes, a few. Armand and Isabella's gatherings are legendary. You will find yourself surrounded by people from all walks of life, the food is amazing, and the atmosphere is always electric."

Commander Ross's gaze turned contemplative. "You know, Adélard, the fact that Armand is dedicating this party to your squad says a lot. It's a testament to the bravery and dedication you all displayed on Cavallo Island. I would hate to miss any Armand party, especially one honoring my men."

"What about New Caledonian?" Adélard asked.

"It seems that the Pacific can wait Adélard."

* * *

As the clock struck 2200, the dimly lit hangar was filled with the anticipation of the Adélard squad. They had become familiar with the routine of their training, but the introduction of night jumping introduced a new level of intrigue and challenge.

The quiet hum of conversations among the men was interrupted by the entrance of Captain Margo Solitaire.
The squad stood at attention, as she approached, their eyes fixed on her with a mixture of respect and curiosity.

"Good evening, gentlemen. At ease." She greeted them with a firm nod. "I hope you're ready for a unique experience."

Margo's lips curved into a reassuring smile. "Night jumps can be both exhilarating and challenging. It's a crucial skill for covert missions, and it requires not just individual skill but also impeccable teamwork."

Margo's gaze shifted across the faces of the men before her, her tone even. "Night jumping presents its own set of dangers. Darkness necessitates clear communication, split-second decision-making, and the ability to adapt to unforeseen circumstances."

"It also means that your visual cues will be limited to the moonlight and your night-vision goggles."

Jojo couldn't resist adding with a wry grin. "Sounds like a lovely midnight walk in the park, Captain."

Margo's gaze locked onto Jojo, her eyes sparkling with a challenge. "Oh, don't you worry, Jojo. I'll make sure your 'walk in the park' is both exciting and unforgettable."

Chuckling, Adélard stepped forward. "We are ready for whatever challenges you throw our way, Captain."

Margo's smile was infectious as she clapped her hands together. "That's the spirit. Now, let's get started. We have some briefing to do before we take to the skies."

The squad gathered around as Margo outlined the night's training mission, jumping procedures, and goals.

Captain Solitaire used a large screen to display the GPS coordinates they would be using to locate their landing zones. The men listened intently, their focus acute.

With Captain Margo leading the way, the night jumps began starting with lower altitudes at 5000 feet then moving higher. The Adélard squad embraced the nighttime jumps, growing ever more confident with each jump into the darkness.

* * *

The mess hall buzzed with the camaraderie of the Adélard squad as they gathered for dinner on the eve of their last day of Halo training. Their conversations were animated, a mix of excitement for their upcoming graduation and vacation plans. Plates clinked, and laughter filled the air as they settled into their seats.

"Can you believe we're almost done with jump training?" Noel remarked, a sense of accomplishment in his eyes.

"It's been a challenge, that's for sure." Graham chimed in, spearing a piece of chicken with his fork.

Adélard nodded, his gaze sweeping across his squad members. "Tomorrow, begins helicopter rappelling."

Henri, his eyes gleaming, leaned forward. "I will like that a lot more. If you screw up, the worst that happens is your break a leg."

"That HALO stuff made my butt hurt. Falling out of a Helicopter will be fun." Jojo said between bites.

Graham chuckled. "Leave it to Jojo to think falling out of a helicopter will be fun."

Julio, his arm still in a cast, grinned. "Well, it's better than being bored, right?"

Henri, his crutches resting against the table, chimed in. "Boredom has never been a problem in this squad."

As the laughter and chatter continued, Henri cleared his throat to get everyone's attention. "Hey, guys." He began, a grin spreading across his face. "I wanted to give you an update on my leg. The surgery went well, and they managed to remove the last bits of those pesky cement slivers from my thigh muscles."

Adélard's eyes lit up. "That's great. How are you feeling?"

Henri leaned back in his chair, his smile widening. "Honestly, much better than I expected. The doctor said my recovery is going faster than anticipated. I might need a cane for support, but I'll be able to attend the graduation ceremony."

Julio, leaning against the back of his chair, chimed in, "Well, I'll still be rocking this cast for a couple more weeks." He gestured with a wry grin.

Jojo, always quick with a joke, chimed in. "Ohhhhhh the Hero of Cavallo all dressed up with a cast to prove it. You will be a big hit at the yacht party."

"Shut up Jojo." The squad said laughing in unison.

Julio chuckled. "I think you will need to be my press agent Jojo. Maybe you can tell them a wild story about me fighting off a shark and 20 mercenaries single handed before I even met the fuel truck."

Laughter erupted even louder among the men, a testament to their bond, as they savored their meal, talk turned to the topic that had been most on their minds. Their vacations.

* * *

The sun had barely begun to illuminate the horizon as the Adélard squad assembled at the helo pad, the promise of a new day heavy in the air. Captain Margo Solitaire, with her unwavering determination and no-nonsense attitude, stood at the forefront. The helicopter that would soon take them on their next training journey loomed behind her, its blades cutting through the cold morning air.

"Good morning, gentlemen." Captain Margo called out, her voice carrying across the open space. "Today, we're moving on to helicopter rappelling, a crucial skill for fast and efficient insertion and extraction during mission scenarios."

The squad's members gathered around her, their eyes reflecting a mix of anticipation and excitement. "We will start with the basics." Captain Margo gestured toward the helicopter. "Let's get started." The captain said as she led them through the intricacies, benefits, and dangers of the helicopter rappelling.

"Better than the last time we jumped from a helo." Noel murmured. "You mean when we fell holding our bag of rocks like water wings." Jojo commented grinning.

GHOST COMMANDO – Battle for Cavallo

"Alright, gear up." Captain Margo instructed as she motioned for them to retrieve their equipment. "We'll start with ground drills to ensure you're comfortable with the gear and movements before taking to the air."

The next hours were a mixture of focused practice and hands-on training. The squad members meticulously went through the motions, rehearsing their actions until they became second nature. Captain Margo offered guidance, corrections, and encouragement along the way, her expertise shining through in her every move.

As the sun climbed higher in the sky, the helicopter roared to life. The moment had arrived for the squad's first helicopter rappelling exercise. The tension was palpable as each man prepared to put their training to the test.

"Remember everything we've practiced." Captain Margo reminded them, her voice steady and reassuring. "Trust your gear, trust your training, and trust each other."

One by one, the squad members stepped up to the helicopter's open door. Adélard watched as his comrades descended with practiced precision, their movements confident. It was a sight that made him immensely proud.

By the afternoon, the squad quickly advanced to the next level. Captain Margo's gaze held each man's attention. "In multiple target rappelling, we'll be taking a different approach. You will be deployed in two-man teams, each team landing at various locations around a series of targets. The goal is to quickly neutralize these targets and then regroup for extraction."

Captain Margo's tone grew even more focused as she continued to lay out their training agenda. "From now on, your helicopter training will take place in various locations and environments across Corsica. You will experience drops into open fields, dense woods, and rugged terrain. Each drop will present its own set of challenges, requiring you to adapt your techniques and tactics accordingly."

"Be prepared for the unexpected." Captain Margo continued, her words a rallying cry. "These exercises are designed to push your limits, enhance your skills, and test your ability to operate effectively in diverse conditions."

* * *

The rhythmic thumping of helicopter blades slowly faded as the Adélard squad returned to the airplane hangar, their last helicopter rappelling exercise completed. The squad members quickly organized themselves, gathering their gear and equipment. The atmosphere was a mix of satisfaction and weariness, a testament to the intense training they had undergone. The truck that would take them back to camp Melusine was waiting nearby, its engine humming softly.

Just as they were about to climb into the truck, a firm voice rang out. "Hold it right there!"

Adélard turned, snapping to attention along with his squad, as Captain Margo approached them. The squad lined up neatly, their fatigue momentarily ignored.

Captain Margo's demeanor softened slightly, and a faint smile tugged at the corner of her lips. "At ease, gentlemen."

GHOST COMMANDO – Battle for Cavallo

The squad members relaxed their posture, but their respect for Captain Margo remained evident.

"The Commandant was right about you men. We have been through a lot together in a very short period of time." Captain Margo continued, her voice a blend of warmth and pride. "It has been an honor to train each of you."

Adélard exchanged glances with his squad mates, a sense of unity and shared accomplishment binding them.

"In a few days, you will be honored at your medal ceremony." Captain Margo said, her gaze steady. "I for one will welcome each of you into the Commando family. Whatever you do, wherever you go . . . make us proud."

With a final salute, the squad members and Captain Margo exchanged nods of respect before the squad climbed onto the waiting truck. As the engine roared to life and the truck pulled away from the hangar, Adélard couldn't help but feel a sense of readiness for whatever lay ahead.

Chapter 18: Bérets Verts

The squad gathered in the dining hall for a relaxed late breakfast, a most welcome change from the rigorous jump training they had just finished. Adélard, taking a sip of his coffee, smiled. "Feels good to have a bit of downtime."

Jojo, ever the jovial spirit of the group, chimed in with a playful grin. "Yeah, my body was getting used to jumping out of planes, but I'm not sure it's ever going to be okay with waking up at the crack of dawn."

Adélard chuckled, giving Jojo a playful nudge. "Only thing that gets you out bed Jojo is breakfast."

Just then, the entrance doors swung open, and Julio walked in, his arm in a sling and a bright smile on his face. Adélard's eyes lit up as he saw his friend's improved condition.

"Julio!" Adélard called out, rising from his seat. The others followed suit, all smiles as they welcomed their injured comrade. Julio's grin widened as he approached the table.

"Hey, guys! Look." He gently moved his arm in the sling, his enthusiasm contagious.
"Congratulations Julio." Noel happily yelled at him.

"I am sure Adélard is just as happy as you, since you won't be hitting him in the head with your cast again." Jojo said standing up and playfully elbowing Julio. "You're just in time. Would you like a nice big breakfast buddy."
Julio chuckled. "Absolutely. You didn't think I came here for you, did you Jojo?"

GHOST COMMANDO – Battle for Cavallo

As the squad members exchanged more laughs and friendly banter, Henri entered the dining hall, leaning on a cane and walking with a slight limp.

"Henri, over here!" Adélard called out.

Henri made his way over, his expression a mix of determination and satisfaction. "Hey, everyone. This is only for show. I thought it might get me some attention from a sweet mademoiselle or three." He said twirling the cane.

Noel grinned and raised his cup. "To sweet mademoiselles." Henri smiled enjoying being with his squad mates.
"Thanks. Seriously, the doctors say I should be fully recovered in another couple of weeks. Then some PT to get back up to full strength."

Jojo chimed in with his trademark humor. "Well, just make sure you don't steal my spotlight with your . . . oh, look at poor me wounded in combat bullshit during the ceremony, Henri."

Noel rolled his eyes playfully. "Oh please, Jojo. You're always the center of attention, whether you like it or not."

"Who, me?" Jojo said with his most innocent face.

The squad members laughed aloud.

Adélard raised his coffee cup in a toast. "To us, the newest Green Berets of the Navy."

"And the best." Jojo couldn't resist adding.

Henri glanced around the dining hall, a nostalgic smile on his face. "Look at all these fresh faces. Hard to believe that not too long ago, we were in their shoes, ready to take on the world, without a clue how to tread water."

Adélard leaned forward, his elbows resting on the table. "I remember our first day here like it was yesterday." Jojo, always quick with a quip, grinned. "Yeah, and remember how green we all looked? Like a bunch of lost sheep."

"Not sheep Jojo. We were tadpoles. Remember the sergeant calling us that over and over." Julio added grinning.

Noel chuckled. "Speak for yourself, Jojo. I had everything under control from day one."

Graham joined in the laughter. "Oh please, Noel. I seem to recall you getting hot shells down your pants in the gun range and you jumping around like a 5-year-old on an Ant pile."

Adélard's gaze drifted towards the group of recruits who were energetically chatting. "We were lucky to have each other." He said thoughtfully. "I can't imagine going through all of this without you guys."

Jojo smiled, adding a serious note. "Most likely some of us would not have made it Adélard. Not through camp, and absolutely not out of Cavallo alive."

Henri nodded in agreement. "True words Adélard!"

Graham looked out at all the new recruits. "And now, it's their turn to see if they have the right stuff to be a Kraken."

GHOST COMMANDO – Battle for Cavallo

"You know, looking back." Adélard said looking at his men. "It's been quite a journey for us."

Graham nodded, his eyes shining with agreement. "Absolutely. From our first days of training to being dropped into that shitstorm with Armand, we've come a long way."

Jojo grinned and leaned forward. "Remember that time we were learning how to dismantle the pistols and I accidentally sent a spring flying across the room. Then everyone got on their hands and knees helping me look for it?"

Laughter erupted around the table, and Noel chuckled. "Yeah, and then it took us hours to find that tiny spring."

Henri raised an eyebrow. "Or that night we were on guard duty during survival training and that raccoon managed to steal half our rations?"

"That was not just a sneaky raccoon. He was a well-trained communist operative intent on disrupting our training." Julio chimed in, a playful glint in his eye.

Adélard smiled warmly, relishing the camaraderie of the moment. "And let's not forget Cavallo . . . Nothing could have prepared us for that and yet here we are."

"One of my favorites is when Commander Ross got mad when Henri's girlfriend gave us a ride." Jojo laughed.

Graham raised his cup. "To the Ghost Commando."
"Here, here." The men said in unison.

Adélard clapped his hands together. "We made it, so let's make the most of it. We have the medal ceremony to look forward to, and then 30 days of leave." Adélard leaned back smiling. "30 days without jumping, swimming, or getting out of bed in the dark with some grumpy officer growling.

* * *

As the Adélard squad continued reminiscing, the familiar figures of Lieutenants Dupont and Laurent approached their table, their smiles bright and greetings warm.

"Morning." Dupont said patting Graham on the back.
Laurent chuckled as he settled in a chair. "You all seem to be in good spirits. Must be the upcoming ceremony."

Graham nodded. "Absolutely. It's a big day for us."

Lieutenant Dupont leaned forward, his eyes reflecting a sense of shared excitement. "You know, we were with the first batch of commandos from Toulon to arrive. All the commandos who fought on Cavallo will be here."

Lieutenant Laurent nodded. "Yes, that's right. Including the submarine crew and Captain Renault."

Jojo's eyebrows shot up. "Captain Renault will be here too?"
Dupont nodded. "Yes, and Captain Philippe as well."

"All the commandos who fought on Cavallo, including Captain Auclair and Sergeant Moreau, will be receiving combat medals." Laurent told them with a knowing smile.

Julio's eyes widened. "Combat medals? For all of us?"

GHOST COMMANDO – Battle for Cavallo

Adélard grinned. "We get our Green Berets and a medal on the same day. Not too shabby."

Jojo chuckled, nudging Noel playfully. "Maybe we should practice some acceptance speeches."

Noel laughed. "Oh, God . . . somebody gag Jojo now please."

* * *

As the Adélard squad finished their breakfast and started to walk out of the dining hall, a fresh-faced young recruit approached with excitement and respect in his eyes.

"Hey there." The recruit said with a warm smile. "I'm Aigle Monter, from Réunion Island."

Adélard extended his hand. "Nice to meet you."

Aigle continued his voice excited. "Sorry, but I just had to come over, the stories about Cavallo are everywhere. You guys are already Legends."

Graham chuckled. "Legends might be a bit of a stretch."
Jojo grinned, giving Aigle a playful nudge. "Don't listen to Graham. I am good with Legend. Go on Aigle."

Aigle's eyes sparkled. "I've heard stories from the others, about your training, about Cavallo. Is it true they call you Ghost Commandos?"

"Well actually, Adélard here is the Ghost Commando and the rest of us are his amazing highly skilled squad." Jojo said grinning. "Basically, we make him look good."

"Ignore Jojo, he had too much orange juice this morning." Noel interrupted.

Julio, his arm in a sling, nodded. "We are just a squad that trained hard and stuck together when it mattered most."

Adélard clapped him on the shoulder. "Good luck Aigle. Sorry, but we need to get going."

"Right, you know all this Legend stuff takes a lot of time." Jojo whispered to Aigle as he walked past.

* * *

Walking towards the barracks, Sergeant Moreau caught Adélard's attention. "Adélard." Sergeant Moreau called out. "Commander Ross wants to see you. He's in his office."

"Alright, I'll head there now. Thanks, Sergeant."

Adélard turned to head in the direction of Commander Ross's office, but Sergeant Moreau's pressed something into his hand. Looking down, Adélard found himself holding a worn leg harness, and within it, a large 10" knife.

Moreau's stern expression softened ever so slightly. "Adélard, this was a gift from my sergeant to me, when I became a Kraken."
"He had it custom made in Japan and carried it for 35 years. I have carried in peace and combat for over 30 years."
"I think it's time for me to pass it on to someone who will take care of her with honor."

Adélard's eyes widened in surprise. "Sergeant?"

GHOST COMMANDO – Battle for Cavallo

Carefully Sergeant Moreau unclipped the harness and withdrew the knife. Far larger than any combat or tactical knife . . . the sergeant held her in his hand gently and passed it to Adélard. "Her name is Sorci."

The large blade gleamed with a razor-sharp edge and exquisite craftsmanship. Adélard couldn't help but be impressed. Moreau's eyes met Adélard's. "Sorci is hand folded of the finest steel and beyond sharp, I expect you to keep her that way."

Adélard marveled at the feel of it in his hand, its perfect balance and undeniable lethal beauty. "I still don't know what to say Sergeant, other than thank you."

Moreau's grizzled features softened into a rare smile. "You are welcome Mr. Adélard. Now, go on, move your ass, the commander is waiting."

* * *

Adélard entered Commander Ross's office. The room was neat and organized as always, at the center of the room, behind a large wooden desk, sat Commander Ross.

"Adélard, come in." Commander Ross said looking up. "Have a seat." He gestured towards the chair.

"Adélard." Commander Ross began, leaning forward slightly, "I wanted to discuss the next phase for you and your men. For the foreseeable future, your squad will be stationed here at camp Melusine." Commander Ross announced. "The Commandant and I believe having your squad here at Melusine is in the best interest of the Navy."

"Yes Sir. Understood." Adélard told him.

"Your squad cannot continue to stay in the recruit barracks forever, so you are going to move to more suitable quarters today." Commander Ross continued.

"Thank you, Commander." Adélard said. "To where Sir?"

The Commander leaned back in his chair crossing his hands. "On the north side of the camp, there's a cluster of smaller officers' barracks." Commander Ross explained.

"Each barracks contains eight separate rooms, and a command office. In addition, there is also a large common area which will serve as a central hub for your squad, a place where you can plan, strategize, and hold meetings."

Adélard's face clearly showed his surprise.

"Adélard." Commander Ross said, leaning forward, "I want you, your men and all your equipment in that barracks today in the next 2 hours long before the ceremony. Understood?"

"Yes Sir. Now Sir." Adélard answered, his mind already processing the logistics involved in relocating the squad.

"I'm assigning your squad to officer barracks 3." Commander Ross continued. "It's the one closest to the submarine caves, which might be a plus if speed is required."

"The command office is the most secure room in the barracks. Your weapons and equipment will be stored there when you're not actively preparing for a mission."

GHOST COMMANDO – Battle for Cavallo

"Sir, does that mean we will be keeping all our weapons?" Adélard asked.

"Yes, and more." Commander Ross assured him.

"Adélard." Commander Ross said, a hint of a smile touching his lips. "There is another matter I want to discuss with you."

"I've just received word that Admiral Vacheron himself will be attending the medal ceremony."

Adélard's eyes widened in surprise. "Wow."

"Wow is right Adélard." Commander Ross continued; his voice tinged with pride. "He's coming to present Julio with his medal the Légion d'honneur, Chevalier Distinction for his outstanding and selfless courage on Cavallo Island. However." Commander Ross added, his tone becoming more serious. "I want you to keep this information to yourself. I don't want Julio to know about it beforehand."

"Of course, Commander." Adélard replied with a firm nod. Adélard, sensing the meeting was over began to stand up, but was stopped by the commander.

"One more thing, Adélard." Commander Ross said with a knowing smile, leaning back in his chair.

"The Bugatti corporate helicopter will arrive here after the ceremony at 1800." Commander Ross continued. "It will take you and your squad to Marseille, to the yacht 'Isabella' where the party will be held."

"The party is scheduled for tomorrow afternoon." Commander Ross added. "Arrangements have been made for your squad to stay aboard the 'Isabella' for two nights."

"Now it's time for you to get out of here. 2 hours to move your shit Mr. Adélard. Dismissed."

"Yes Sir. On my way Sir." Adélard answered smiling.

* * *

Moara Beach, Lifou Island. New Caledonia

The warm breeze swept in from the turquoise waters, carrying with it the sweet scent of the ocean. Thérèse stood on the veranda of her charming bed and breakfast, gazing out at the breathtaking view of Moara beach on the east coast of the island.

Two weeks ago, Thérèse had welcomed a new paying guest to her home. A pleasant, although somewhat reclusive and shy young Korean woman named Mina, had checked in.

Thérèse's smiled listening to the soothing sounds of waves crashing against the rocky shore and the seagulls chirping as they scavenged the beach for mollusk.

Thérèse's smile faltered as she saw Mina approaching quickly, her footsteps deliberate yet eerily silent.

The distance between them seemed to shrink as Mina closed in, her eyes cold and calculating.

Thérèse's heart raced, sensing this unsettling and seemingly dangerous change in her houseguest demeanor.

"What are you doing?" Thérèse's voice trembled, her eyes flickering towards the small 25-caliber pistol that Mina had instantly slipped beneath her chin.

Fear clawed at the edges of her consciousness, and she struggled to comprehend the sudden turn of events.

Mina's lips curved into a chilling smile, her voice low and menacing dripping with ice.

"I know who you are, Thérèse."
"I know your past."
"I know what you do."

Thérèse's eyes widened, her mind racing to keep up with Mina's cryptic words. "I don't know what you're talking about. I'm just a divorced woman who owns this house, trying to get by renting rooms to rich visitors Mina."

Mina's grip on the pistol tightened as she pushed the barrel up into Thérèse's chin a little harder. "Stop it. Don't lie to me. I've seen through your façade."

Thérèse's denial was swift and desperate. "You're mistaken, Mina. Please don't hurt me. I am just a middle-aged woman living at the edge of the world."

Mina's expression hardened, her finger hovering over the trigger. "Do you want those lies to be the last words you say before you die?"

Thérèse's defiance burned brightly, her voice resolute. "No. I want those to be the last words you hear."

In a swift motion, Thérèse reached out, her fingers curling around the pistol's cold metal. The room echoed with a gunshot that shattered the tense silence. Mina's body collapsed to the floor, her eyes wide open and lifeless.

* * *

Hours later, the local police arrived on the scene, the crimson sunset casting a melancholic glow over the tranquil beach. Thérèse sat composed, recounting most of the events that had transpired. The evidence before them seemed to align with her story: Mina's lifeless body, the gun in her hand, and the undeniable self-defense claim.

The lead investigator looked at Thérèse, his expression a mix of curiosity and disbelief. "Ms. Thérèse, are you sure you didn't know this woman from somewhere else?"

Thérèse's gaze remained steady. "I am positive. I had never seen or heard of Mina before she checked in."

"Do you have any idea why she wanted to harm you?" The detective asked once again, still uncomfortable the facts, but mostly uncomfortable with how relaxed and composed Thérèse was since just killing a person.

"No. Not a clue."

The investigator exchanged a glance with his team before sighing. "Well, the evidence seems to corroborate your story. We'll wrap up the investigation and take the body. There will be the required autopsy. I will let you know what we find."

As the police left, the house settled into an eerie quiet.

GHOST COMMANDO – Battle for Cavallo

Thérèse gazed out at the sunset, her heart at peace now that all the strangers had left her home. Men can be so sloppy; they leave dirt everywhere they walk she thought. Tomorrow I will need to have the house cleaned again.

Her toy poodle sauntered up to her enjoying a glass of wine watching the sunset. "Oh, my sweet Pierre, what shall we do for dinner tonight?"

* * *

Camp Melusine, Corsica

Adélard's was smiling ear to ear after his meeting with Commander Ross. Walking quickly to the recruit barracks, he entered clearing his throat, catching the attention of the men who were chatting and lounging around.

"Listen up, everyone." Adélard announced with a grin.

"Oh Shit! Last time Adélard said that we ended up fighting an invading horde carrying rockets." Jojo whined too loud.

"No, no Jojo. This is all good news. Starting with the fact that Melusine is our permanent duty station as commandos."

Graham and Henri exchanged intrigued glances and perked up with interest. "As instructors?" Graham asked.

"No, as active-duty commandos."

"But we need to move out of this barracks on the double. Start packing boys. We have orders to be out of here and into our new quarters in 2 hours. They need this barracks for the new tadpoles." Adélard added.

"Please don't tell us we are moving into the underground bomb shelters." Jojo continued his fake whining.

Adélard paused, smiling. "We're moving to officer barracks on the north side of the camp, immediately, as in the moment I am done telling you." Adélard continued. "The entire barracks is exclusively for us. It has eight separate rooms, and an office to store our gear and weapons in."

"You mean I won't have to listen to Noel snoring anymore?" Graham quipped, earning a playful shove from Noel.

"Adélard, tell Graham, I don't snore. Do we get to keep our guns?" Noel asked.

"Yes. We keep all our stuff from Cavallo. The new dive gear, guns, ammo, even the med kits. We keep it all. Here's the thing we need to pack up and beat feet to our new home before today's ceremony. After the ceremony we will pack our bags for our extended leave."

A chorus of whoops and cheers erupted from the men.

"Let's get to it. Noel, you help Julio carry his bags. I will help Henri. OB3 is our barracks. North side near the Sub Caves . . . stop looking at me and get moving."

"OB3 . . . new home of the Ghost Commandos. I like it." Jojo said throwing his equipment bag on his shoulder.

The banter and laughter continued as the squad got to work, packing up their personal items, and equipment. Despite the urgency, the air was filled with happiness and excitement.

GHOST COMMANDO – Battle for Cavallo

As they entered the newly assigned home OB3 (Officer Barracks 3), the men's excitement only grew.

Each room already had a nameplate on the door, indicating whose room it belonged to. Surprised, Adélard walked down the hallway, pointing out the rooms.

"Julio, you're right here. Henri, your room's next door." Adélard said with a grin. "Obviously we were not the first to know we were moving here."

Jojo was the first to enter his room. His joyful yelling echoed through the hallway.

"Our Green Berets are here. Look at this, guys! " Jojo added strutting out into the hall wearing his.
"It's official . . . now We be Kraken."

Adélard watched with satisfaction as his squad members soaked in the joy of the moment. "Alright then my Krakens."

Adélard called, gathering the squad's attention. "Let's get settled in. Graham, take charge of the command office. We need all our gear and weapons sorted, stored properly and under lock and key before we leave this building."

"Can do!" Graham answered walking into the office.

"Everyone, lend a hand then pack your bags, the Bugatti helicopter will pick us up after the ceremony at 1800."

* * *

New Caledonia, South Pacific

New Caledonia is a group of islands located in the South Pacific, east of Australia and north of New Zealand.

The islands have been governed by France since 1853. Independence referendums were conducted in 2018, again in 2020 and a third and final referendum on December 12, 2021. Ninety-six percent of people who voted chose to remain with the French Republic.

* * *

Camp Melusine. Corsica

At commandant Gaston's request. The three officers, Vice-Admiral Vacheron, Commandant Gaston, and Commander Ross, gathered in a quiet corner of Camp Melusine.

"Thank you, Admiral, for taking the time to meet with us. Commander Ross and I need some guidance from you about the pacific mission." Commandant Gaston said, the moment they were away from the crowds of commandos and dignitaries.

"I understand, unfortunately I don't have much to tell you at the moment. Intelligence alerted command that there was an increase in suspicious bank transactions. Multiple multimillion Euro transfers between a maze of banks."

"At first, we considered the possibility that it might be dark money flowing through French banks in an elaborate laundering operations shielding oil payments to Iranian or Russia interest. Then aggressive protest by separatist factions within New Caledonia seemed a possibility."

"That's when you alerted us to prepare for a mission?" Commander Ross asked.

"Yes, but then one of undercover intelligence operatives was killed on Lifou Island under suspicious circumstances. Currently we are at a standstill."

"What do we know for certain Admiral?" Gaston asked.

"We know hundreds of millions of Euros are moving with no legitimate purpose. We know one of our best operatives was murdered and the killer has no past beyond 5 years that we can locate. We know violet protest are being funded by foreign interest on New Caledonia similar to what has happened in the United States. That is the sum total of what we know for certain."

Commandant Gaston listened intently than asked. "How do you want us to proceed Admiral?"

"I believe the forces at play here are violent in the extreme. I propose that we send a team of commandos undercover to New Caledonia strictly to gather intelligence, but with the authority to act in the best interest of France if necessary. Understood?"

Commander Ross and Commandant Gaston exchanged a glance, both understanding the meaning between the admiral's words.

"Yes Sir." Both Gaston and Ross answered.

* * *

Parade Ground, Camp Melusine
Under the bright sun of a clear day, the parade ground at Camp Melusine was transformed into a scene of national pride and honor.

All the squads that had fought on the island of Cavallo, their commandos standing tall and proud in their crisp uniforms waited. Each squad in its designated spot, standing in perfect alignment on the expansive field.

Alongside them stood Captain Renault, his officers and crew of the submarine Liberté, who had played an integral role in the island's defense.

At the edge of the grounds stood over 100 spectators. Fresh recruits, just entering their training along with all the staff, instructors, and officers that served at the camp.

The air was charged with anticipation as they waited, eager to witness the forthcoming ceremony.

At the front of the parade grounds, a raised platform had been built, the focal center piece as a symbol of national honor and respect. On this platform, under a canopy adorned with French flags that fluttered gently in the breeze, sat various distinguished dignitaries of the event. Commander Ross, Commandant Gaston, Commander Gérard Constantin, and Vice-Amiral Vacheron. Occupied their four seats side by side at the front of the platform, their expressions serious and solemn, well aware of the importance of the ceremony about to unfold.

Every person present could feel the gravity of the moment as they awaited the commencement of the ceremony. The air was filled with a sense of reverence and pride as the commandos collectively honored the sacrifices and heroism displayed by the men who had defended the island against overwhelming odds. The significance of the medals that would be awarded resonated deeply with all present.

A hushed silence fell over the parade grounds as the ceremony began. A military band played the French national anthem, setting the tone for the proceedings. The members of the squads and the crew of the submarine stood at attention, their eyes fixed on the platform.

Commander Ross stood up from his seat on the platform, a stern and proud figure in his crisp uniform. The assembled crowd fell into a respectful hush. As he began to address the gathered commandos and crew members, his voice carried with a weight of authority and appreciation.

"Today, we gather to honor the valor, sacrifice, and unwavering dedication displayed by the brave men who stood together in the face of danger."

Commander Ross began, his words echoing across the parade grounds.

"These medals that we are about to bestow hold more than just metal and ribbon; they represent the embodiment of courage and selflessness that define the spirit of the French military and of our sacred nation."

He continued to speak, his words resonating with every individual present. As he described the significance of the "Médaille militaire," a medal awarded for exceptional valor in combat, the audience's attention was fully captivated. He emphasized that this medal was a testament to their commitment to duty, their unity, and their unwavering dedication to the principles that the Commandos stood for.

With his description of the medal's importance lingering in the air, Commander Ross directed his gaze toward the table on the platform. There, laid out with utmost care, were the medals . . . symbols of honor, courage, and sacrifice. Each medal shone in the sunlight, its metal catching the glint of the day. The ribbons, carefully chosen in bold tricolor, added a touch of national pride.

As each squad and the crew of the submarine stepped forward, the ceremony became a poignant procession of heroes. One by one, they were presented with their medals. Each recipient stood tall and proud, their chests swelling with pride and a sense of belonging to a greater cause.

GHOST COMMANDO – Battle for Cavallo

Commander Ross personally affixed the medals to each recipient's uniform, his actions imbued with respect and gratitude. A handshake, a nod of acknowledgment. These gestures carried a weight that words alone could not convey. Each medal represented not only an individual's bravery but also the collective strength of a team that had faced death.

With each medal presentation, the applause from the assembled crowd grew louder, a heartfelt expression of appreciation for the sacrifices made. The atmosphere was charged with a mix of emotions, pride, honor, and a deep sense of camaraderie.

The ceremony concluded with the formation of the commandos and crew members, now adorned with their medals, standing in unity.

The sun cast a warm glow over the parade grounds, illuminating the medal-adorned uniforms. Commander Ross's final words resonated with everyone present. A profound gratitude for their service, their sacrifice, and their unwavering dedication to their duty and their country.

Commander Ross saluted the assembled commandos, his hand rising in a crisp and precise motion. As the applause from the crowd faded, he took his seat once again, his gaze filled with a mix of pride and reverence for the men he led.

Commandant Gaston rose from his chair, his presence commanding attention just as Commander Ross's had. The crowd fell into respectful silence, their attention fixed on the Commandant. Gaston's voice carried a deep resonance, carrying his words across the parade grounds.

"My fellow commandos, today we gather to honor not only valor but also resilience in the face of adversity." Commandant Gaston began, his voice holding a mixture of strength and compassion. "The Médaille de la Gendarmerie is a tribute to those who have sustained injuries while serving in combat, a recognition of their sacrifice and dedication."

As he described the significance of the medal, his words brought to life the immense value of honoring those who had borne the physical toll of their service. The crowd listened with a mix of respect and empathy, understanding that these medals were a testament to the courage required to continue fighting even when wounded.

Commandant Gaston then called for Julio, Henri, and Antoine to step forward. Their names echoed across the parade grounds, drawing the eyes of everyone present to their figures as they moved to the front of the formation. Each step they took resonated with a quiet determination, a reflection of their indomitable spirits.

The medals, carefully presented on a velvet cushion, glinted in the sunlight as Commandant Gaston held them up for all to see. The Médaille de la Gendarmerie bore the weight of history and tradition. The ribbons, deep blue and adorned with the emblem of the Gendarmerie, added a touch of solemnity to the occasion.

Commandant Gaston proudly pinned the medals onto the uniforms of Julio, Henri, and Antoine. The exchange was not just a physical act but a profound acknowledgment of their journey, their commitment, and the challenges they had overcome.

GHOST COMMANDO – Battle for Cavallo

As the three commandos stepped back into formation, their comrades' joy was visible to all in attendance. Commandant Gaston's final words resonated with a sense of unity, gratitude, and honor for all those who had sacrificed, fought, and persevered in the face of the enemy.

The crowd fell into a hushed silence as Commandant Gaston saluted the three commandos and resumed his seat. The gravity of the moment lingered in the air, a tangible reminder of the sacrifice and courage that these men had displayed.

Admiral Vacheron, a figure of immense authority and dignity, rose from his chair. The air seemed to change as he stood, a testament to the respect and deference he commanded. His presence alone spoke volumes, the parade grounds and everyone present was filled with anticipation as all eyes turned to him.

With measured steps, Admiral Vacheron made his way to the front of the formation. He carried himself with a regal air, a living embodiment of the history and honor that the Légion d'honneur represented. The crowd watched in rapt attention, their respect for the admiral evident in their attentive gazes.

"Commando Julio D'Parma please step forward."
The admiral's voice resonated across the parade grounds, carrying a weight of recognition as Julio's name echoed among the crowd with a sense of reverence.
The medal itself was a gleaming symbol of distinction, a reflection of the highest honor that France could bestow. As Admiral Vacheron held it up, the sun caught on its edges, casting a radiant glint that seemed to emphasize the medal's significance and bore the history and tradition of centuries.

In a voice that conveyed both authority and heartfelt appreciation, Admiral Vacheron described the Légion d'honneur, Chevalier Distinction. He spoke of its origins, established by Napoleon Bonaparte himself in 1802, and its role as the pinnacle of recognition for acts of bravery, selflessness, and service to the nation.

* * *

"As I stand before you today." Admiral Vacheron began, his words carrying a sense of gravitas that held the audience's attention. "I am honored to present the Légion d'honneur, Chevalier Distinction, to Commando Julio D'Parma. For his bravery under fire, his unwavering commitment to his fellow commandos, and to his selfless act of courage against unimaginable odds to protect his brothers."

Admiral Vacheron's words resonated across the parade grounds, capturing the essence of what the Légion d'honneur represented . . . a mark of distinction and an acknowledgment of the extraordinary.

The silence was profound, each person in attendance acutely aware of the magnitude of this moment. Julio stepped forward, his gaze steady and his demeanor composed, as the medal was placed around his neck.

Then Julio was overcome. A tear escaped and flowed down his cheek. "Forgive me Sir." He told the Admiral. "Nonsense young man, nothing to forgive. Be proud, you are the best of us." Admiral Étienne Vacheron whispered straightening the medal on Julio chest.

The assembled crowd erupted in applause, from the dignitaries on the platform, to the those watching from the edge of the parade grounds, and every single commando present.

None louder than Adélard and the men of his squad, their cheers a testament to their brotherly love for Julio and appreciation of the courage embodied by their youngest member.

Chapter 19: Recognition & Celebration

With the Navy band playing to end the ceremony the parade ground instantly transformed into a place of celebration.

Commandos who had stood side by side in the firestorm on Cavallo were now mingling with the all the spectators who joined them in the field, sharing stories and laughter.

Adélard's squad, their valiant efforts on Cavallo now well known, the story already becoming the stuff of legend stood together. Heros adorned with medals, they had become the center of attention. Recruits and officers alike approached Julio, extending their hands in heartfelt congratulations, recognizing the rarity and significance of his honor.

"Julio, you've made us all proud." Captain Philippe said, his voice tinged with emotion as he shook Julio's hand.

"Couldn't have happened to a nicer guy." Noel chimed in, a wide smile gracing his face.

"Seriously Julio, I am proud to call you, my brother." Jojo told Julio, shaking his hand, and pulling him down for a hug. "But this is all a bit much for wreaking Mr. Bugatti's car don't you think?" He whispered in his ear laughing.

* * *

The perfect blue sky, like a woman's pretty hat hung over the scene, as if nature itself was celebrating alongside them. The atmosphere was electric, the new recruits rushed out into the field to meet and be next to the seasoned commandos, while officers and staff mingled freely.

GHOST COMMANDO – Battle for Cavallo

As the celebration continued, Commandant Gaston approached Adélard, his expression a mixture of seriousness and warmth. "Adélard, may I have a word?"

"Of course, Commandant." Adélard replied, relaxed and smiling as he walked alongside Gaston.

They moved to a slightly quieter corner, away from the jubilant crowd. "I wanted to update you on the Pacific mission we discussed earlier." Gaston began, his voice carrying a note of gravitas.

Adélard's attention sharpened. "Yes Sir?"

"Things have changed. Recent developments have caused us to step back and reassess the situation and any possible mission."

Adélard stood quiet, his focus on every word the commandant did and didn't say.

"While the core objective remains the same, the how, where, and when are still in development as some strategic shifts are required." Gaston said in military speak.

"Sir, I still don't know anything about this mission, other than it might be in the Pacific Ocean. That's a pretty big place. Can you share any more details with me?" Adélard asked pushing a bit hard with his attitude.

Gaston smiled at Adélard recognizing why Étienne and Ross had so much faith in him, regardless of his age.

"Actually, no, I can't." The commandant answered. "Not because I won't Adélard, but because Toulon honestly does not know. All we really know is that something is going on in the South Pacific and that commandos will be needed to fix it."

"Thank you, Sir. Well, now I know that whatever it is. It is in the South Pacific which 100% more than I knew 5 minutes ago." Adélard said with a wink and a smile.

Gaston's face held a mixture of humor and respect. "I think I might be sorry for letting Ross talk me into you and your men being stationed here on Melusine Adélard. I would enjoy having you roaming the halls of Toulon with me."

"I'll take that as a compliment, Sir."

As their conversation concluded, Gaston's tone shifted slightly. "Before I forget, I look forward to seeing you at the Bugatti yacht party tomorrow night. Enjoy your 30 days of leave but be prepared to ship out the moment it's over."

"Sir. Yes Sir." Adélard snapped back into his role. "Thank you, Commandant. We will be ready."

With a final nod, Gaston rejoined the celebration, leaving Adélard to rejoin his squad. As the festivities continued around them, he couldn't help but feel a sense of pride in his squad and a deep connection with his fellow commandos.

With the sun beginning its descent and the celebration gradually winding down, Adélard turned to Graham and Jojo standing next to him.

GHOST COMMANDO – Battle for Cavallo

"Find everyone and tell them it's time to head back to the barracks and get our things packed. " Adélard ordered, his voice carrying a mix of authority.

Graham and Jojo exchanged nods and knowing glances. "We're on it." Graham answered for them both.

Jojo had no difficulty finding Julio. He was surrounded by dozens of recruits listening to his every word. Pushing his way through the crowd Jojo elbowed his way to the front.

"Calling Mr. Julio. Julio D'Parma . . . Celebrity roll call." Jojo called out, a mischievous grin on his face. Moving closer, Jojo pulled at Julio's good arm. "Sorry to take you from your adoring fans Mr. D'Parma but Adélard says we need to go."

Some of the men chuckled, and Julio rolled his eyes good-naturedly. "Oh, come on, Jojo. I was just answering their questions."

"Yeah, yeah, don't worry, we will make sure you're back to your humble self in no time." Jojo teased, playfully tugging Julio away from the crowd of recruits who had been surrounding him.

The recruits laughed, clearly entertained by the interaction, Julio shot Jojo a mock glare. "Thanks for the rescue, Jojo."

"Anytime, my friend." Jojo said with a wink, his arm draped over Julio's shoulders as they walked towards their barracks.

As the squad regrouped, Adélard couldn't help but smile at the easy camaraderie among his men.

"Ok you sons of Kraken, we need to get to the barracks, pack our bags, make sure everything is ship shape and locked up before Armands helicopter picks us up at 1800."

"Let's not forget, we won't be coming back for 30 days."

"I can't wait." Henri said smiling.

"We've got a yacht party, in our honor to attend, gentlemen." Adélard reminded them.

"Are we taking any guns Adélard?" Noel asked.

The squad members exchanged glances as Adélard considered the question.

"I think it would be acceptable to take our Baretta's that Armand gifted us. We can use the waist holsters; we need to be discreet. We don't want to make the guest feel uncomfortable. But no heavy guns, we're not invading the yacht. Ok Noel?" Adélard finished smiling.

"Fair enough." Noel answered with a grin on his face.

With a final round of laughter and good-natured banter, they headed back to their newly assigned officer barracks, ready to pack their belongings for the next chapter of their journey.

* * *

Parade Ground, Camp Melusine
Commandant Gaston, stood near the podium when he noticed Captain Philippe amidst the crowd, his presence a reminder of what had happened during the assault.

Approaching the captain, Gaston offered a nod of acknowledgment. "Captain Philippe, if I may have a moment of your time?"

Captain Philippe turned to face Gaston. "Of course, Commandant. I'm at your service."

Gaston gestured towards a quieter area nearby, away from the crowd. As they walked Commandant Gaston spoke in a measured tone. "You disobeyed my orders old friend."

"Did I? I do not recall it that way Gaston." Philippe answered.

"I ordered you to take Mrs. Bugatti and her children to my wife Genevieve's home on Corsica. Didn't I?" Gaston asked, raising an eyebrow.

"Actually Gaston. What you said was that you were worried of a secondary team of mercenaries lying in wait between Cavallo and Toulon and that you were willing to risk the secret that Genevieve was your wife to protect them."

"And?" Gaston pushed the question.

"And as Captain of my ship, I made a command decision to take the Bugatti's to the safest place in the entire Mediterranean. The bomb shelter here at Melusine, guarded by some of our best seasoned commandos."

"And ignoring my request to take them to Genevieve?" Gaston asked.

Captain Philippe's expression remained composed, and he nodded in acknowledgment.

"No old friend not ignoring Genevieve or your request. I was protecting Genevieve from her secret becoming public and putting her and your girls at risk."

"Gaston, if you wish to be mad at me then do so. But I used my judgement that night to protect both families. Yours and Armands."

Gaston's eyes held a genuine warmth as he continued. "You made a wise choice, Captain. As commandant I might have been mad, but as husband and father I thank you sincerely from the bottom of my heart old friend."

Captain Philippe's gaze met Gaston's with equal respect. "I appreciate your understanding, Commandant. With that out of the way, I have an exceptionally fine bottle of cognac in my locker. Please follow me Sir."

* * *

The Adélard squad stood on the tarmac of Camp Melusine as the powerful thrum of the Bugatti helicopter's engines filled the air. Anticipation filled the moment as they waited for their ride to Marseille and the start of their vacation.

The large Bugatti logo on the side of the helicopter gleamed under the sunlight, as the squad's luggage was efficiently loaded. The excitement was evident as the men quickly settled into their seats with smiles and bright eyes.

"Don't worry Noel." Jojo chided him. "We don't need to jump out of this one."

GHOST COMMANDO – Battle for Cavallo

"Good thing mon ami. I am wearing my good uniform." Noel answered smiling.

The flight was relatively short, and soon the skyline of Marseille came into view. The azure waters of the Mediterranean stretched out before them. The squad's amazement and anticipation grew as they spotted the elegant silhouette of the Isabella waiting below.

"Look at that beauty," Graham exclaimed, his voice full of awe as he pointed out the massive yacht.

The Isabella was a sight to behold, a 60-meter super yacht that exuded luxury and sophistication. Her sleek hull ready to cut through the water with grace, with three decks rising majestically above the water line. The yacht's exterior boasted clean lines and modern design elements, with a spacious swim platform extending from the stern and a touch and go helicopter pad perched atop the highest deck.

* * *

Dining Room, Isabella Yacht. Marseille France

As the helicopter descended towards the yacht, the squad members exchanged impressed glances. The precision of the landing on the ship's helipad was a testament to the skill of the pilot. After the helicopter touched down, the squad disembarked and were met by Bugatti staff.

"Welcome, gentlemen." One of the ships stewards said with a smile. "If you'll follow me, I'll show you to your staterooms." The squad followed their guide through the halls of polished surfaces, rich woods, and modern artwork adorned the walls within opulent interior of the yacht.

"These are your cabins gentlemen." The steward said, gesturing towards the staterooms.

The squad members exchanged appreciative looks. "Ok, it's official. I am impressed." Adélard said turning to his men.

Can you believe this, guys?" Noel added whistling his amazement. Just then Reine and Taber came running down the hall all but jumping on top of Noel laughing and giggling.

"Hi girls." Noel said, grabbing each in an arm and lifting them off the ground.

"Put them down Noel." Jojo said laughing.

"No, no, no." Reine said. "Carry us to daddy, he is waiting for all of you."

"Ok girls, but you need to show us the way, ok?" Adélard asked them.

"Sure." Taber answered jumping down, grabbing Adélard by the hand, and pulling him down the hall.

Laughter erupted among the squad members as they exchanged knowing glances. This moment, this unabashed love, punctuated everything they had done, everything for which they had fought. These two vivacious innocent girls brought it all home in an instant.

* * *

The narrow hallway echoed their footsteps as the girls guided Adélard and his squad towards the dining room.

GHOST COMMANDO – Battle for Cavallo

Reine giggled at being carried by Noel while watching Jojo making funny faces walking just behind.

Taber held Adélard's hand, leading them through the maze like corridors. "Almost there." Taber said pulling harder on Adélard's hand.

Reine's face broke into a huge grin. "Papa is going to be so happy." She added glancing up at Noel.

* * *

Armand and Isabella rose from their seats at the head of the table, their faces lighting up with genuine delight. "Ah, our honored guests have arrived!"

"Welcome, gentlemen!" Armand announced with genuine enthusiasm. "We are more than delighted to have you aboard the Isabella."

Isabella's eyes shimmered with happiness noticing Reine riding in Noels arms.

Isabella chuckled softly as she glanced at her daughter.

"Reine did you make Noel carry you the entire way?"

Taber laughed. "Yes, momma. Princess Reine wouldn't get down, she hung on his neck with both arms like a baby gorilla."

"Oh, I see." Armand interrupted smiling. "Well princess is Noel your personal bodyguard now?"

Reine giggled and leaned forward in his arms." Yes Papa, Noel is my hero." Her eyes curious as she looked up at Noel face. "Are you a superhero?"

Noel smiled at the question. "Not exactly, but I try to be brave."

As the group moved towards the dining table, Noel gently took Reine's arms from his neck. "And what about you, little lady? Are you brave?"

Reine's eyes widened in mock surprise. "Of course, I am! I'm a Bugatti!"

Laughter erupted around the room, including from Armand and Isabella. "Indeed, you are." Armand agreed with a chuckle.

Isabella gently chided. "Reine, darling, let's sit like a lady at the table."

Reine pouted playfully as she wiggled in Noel's arms. "But I want to stay here!"

"Sorry Reine. You may be a princess, but your momma is the Queen." Noel said, gently setting Reine down.

* * *

The dining room of the elegant ship was soon filled with laughter and the sounds of friends and family.

Isabella leaned towards Graham, a warm smile gracing her lips. "How did you manage to work in that grotto under the graveyard Graham? She asked shaking her shoulders.

GHOST COMMANDO – Battle for Cavallo

"Oh, I love it there. Father Paulo lets us run through all the tunnels." Taber spoke up and quickly lowered her eyes knowing her mother would not approve.

"Oh, he does, does he? I may need to have a chat with the good Father." Isabella said with her lips pursed.

Graham chuckled. "Well at first it was a little odd knowing we were in the same tunnels that the Knights Templar dug a thousand years ago. But then later it was fine, In the end it was an excellent command center for us."

Armand nodded approvingly then changed the subject. "The girls really liked that boat Captain Phillipe took them on. Taber says it is the fastest boat she has ever seen. What is it you call them . . . Requin boats?"

"Yes." Adélard answered. "And Taber is right. I doubt there is a faster boat in the entire Mediterranean."

As the courses came and went, the clinking of glasses and the merriment made the evening an enjoyable family event and not a lavish dinner aboard a billionaire's yacht.

* * *

Armand leaned back in his chair, a thoughtful expression on his face. "Gentlemen, in order to convince your superiors to give up a day of your vacation for the party. I did promise to transport each of you to any destination you wished for you vacation."

"I am sure I speak for all of us. We are all very grateful Mr. Bugatti." Noel said between bites.

"Absolutely Armand. Being here is amazing." Jojo added.

"I am curious Armand." Isabella said looking across the table. "After the recent event's, I want to hear where you brave men, the heroes of Cavallo would like to go."

"See I told you they were Heros." Taber whispered to Reine.

"Yes, please Gentlemen. Where is it you wish to go?" Armand asked, enforcing his wife's curiosity.

Graham cleared his throat, a smile playing on his lips as he addressed Isabella's question. "Well, Henri and I have talked it over, and we've decided to take our vacation together. We're planning on heading to Paris."

Isabella raised an eyebrow in curiosity. "Paris? That sounds lovely."

Graham leaned forward slightly. "You see, I grew up in the heart of Paris before joining the commandos. My parents have a lovely home with plenty of room. I want to show Henri the city in a way that no tourist ever would."

Henri's eyes lit up, and he nodded eagerly. "Yeah, Graham says we are going to cover that town from end to end. I am so excited. I don't plan on sleeping until we report back."

Armand smiled. "That sounds like a fantastic plan. Paris is a city of wonder and fun for those that know the real city."

Isabella chimed in, her eyes sparkling. "And don't forget to visit some of the dance clubs. They alone are worth the trip."

Graham chuckled. "Absolutely, Isabella."

As the conversation continued around the dining table, all eyes turned to Julio as it was his turn to share his vacation plans. Julio cleared his throat and looked at Armand.

"Well, Mr. Bugatti, I have thought about it quite a bit, and I've come up with a plan for my vacation. I'd like to start by returning to Corsica for the first two weeks. I went there for a 3 day leave and I absolutely fell in love with the mountains and the breathtaking landscapes."

"I think he met a girl in those mountains." Jojo interrupted smiling.

Julio sent a warning look at Jojo then continued. "I think spending some peaceful time there, maybe doing some hiking and exploring, would be the perfect way for me to recharge."

Armand nodded, showing his approval. "Corsica is indeed a paradise for lovers and nature, and what about the second half of your vacation?"

Julio's eyes lit up as he continued. "For the second half, I'd like to go back to where I grew up, just outside of Leon. It's been a while since I've seen my family and my childhood friends. Maybe visit some of our favorite spots, and of course, spend some quality time with my mother and father."

Isabella smiled warmly. "That sounds like a beautiful plan, Julio. There's nothing like going home to a loving family."

Armand raised his glass in a toast. "To nature, friends, and family. Your vacation plans sound wonderful, Julio."

Julio and all the commandos raised their glass as well, Julio's gratitude evident. "Thank you, Mr. Bugatti."

Noel shifted slightly in his seat as the conversation turned to him. He glanced around the table at the expectant faces and then back at Armand and Isabella. "Well, Mr. Bugatti, Mrs. Bugatti. I have to admit, I am still a bit undecided."

Armand leaned forward, his expression curious. "Undecided? That's perfectly okay, Noel. Take your time."

Noel nodded, appreciating the understanding. "You see, I didn't grow up with a family like most. I've spent most of my life in various foster homes, so I don't really have a hometown to visit or family to reconnect with."

He looked down at his plate for a moment before continuing. "But there's one thing I've always wanted to do, and that's to visit the Alps."

Isabella's eyes sparkled with interest. "The Alps? That sounds like an amazing idea, Noel. The mountains there are breathtaking."

Noel nodded, his eyes reflecting a mixture of excitement and uncertainty. "Yeah, I've always been fascinated by the mountains. I've seen pictures and read about the beauty of the Alps, and I thought it might be an incredible experience to see them in person. Maybe even do some skiing if I can."

Armand smiled warmly. "The Alps are indeed a magnificent, your idea sounds like a wonderful adventure, Noel."

Isabella reached across the table and gently squeezed Noel's hand. "And you know, you don't have to decide everything right now. Sometimes the best vacations are the ones that unfold naturally."

Noel flashed a small smile. "Thank you, Mrs. Bugatti."

Armand raised his glass in a toast. "To new adventures and the joy of discovering the unknown. Cheers, Noel."

As their glasses clinked and the laughter of the evening continued, Noel felt a sense of belonging he hadn't experienced before. It wasn't just about the extravagant yacht or the grand celebration; it was about the people who cared, the newfound friendships, and the possibility of embracing life's opportunities, even if they were uncertain.

Adélard cleared his throat, feeling a bit self-conscious as the attention turned to him. "Well for my vacation, I have a simple plan in mind. I want to go back home to my family farm in the south of France." He said, looking up at the Bugatti family.

Armand leaned forward in his chair. "I know your family has a farm Adélard, but you never mentioned if you liked it. What do you plan to do there?"

Adélard smiled, a hint of nostalgia in his eyes. "Well, it's been a while since I've been back. My father could probably use a hand with the spring pruning.

You see, we primarily grow vegetables and have some fruit trees, but we also have around 10 hectares of vineyards and with me gone I am sure my father is working day and night."

Armand's eyebrows raised, impressed. "Vineyards? That's quite interesting. What kind of grapes do you grow?"

Adélard's face lit up as he spoke about his family's farm. "We grow a variety of table grapes, but our better grapes are for producing red wine. It's a small operation, we produce about 1000 cases a year, but it's been in the family for generations."

Isabella's eyes glimmered with curiosity as she leaned in closer to Armand and whispered something in his ear. Armand's lips twitched into a knowing smile, and he nodded in response.

Adélard noticed their exchange, his curiosity piqued. "Is there something I missed, Mr. Bugatti?"

Armand chuckled softly. "It seems my wife is quite intrigued by your description of your family farm and vineyards, Adélard. She has a fondness for wine."

Isabella's cheeks flushed slightly as she grinned at Adélard. "Yes, I must admit, the idea of spending time in a vineyard sounds absolutely charming."

Adélard felt a mixture of surprise and amusement. "Well, you are welcome to visit anytime, Mrs. Bugatti. The countryside has its own unique beauty, and the vineyards hold a sense of peace. Just mention my name to my mother and she will treat you like a long-lost daughter."

Armand raised his glass in a toast. "To the joy of returning to one's roots. cheers, Adélard."

Adélard raised his glass in return. "Cheers."

As their glasses clinked, Adélard couldn't help but feel a sense of amazement at how the most beautiful moments in life were found in the simplest of pleasures.

Jojo grinned as the spotlight shifted to him. "Armand, for my vacation, I've got a plan that's a mix of relaxation and adventure. I want to head back to my parents' resort where I grew up. It's a beautiful place, nestled in the mountains."

Armand leaned back, intrigued. "Your parents resort? The one in the mountains where you were a ski instructor?

Jojo's eyes sparkled with excitement. "Yes Armand. Oh, it's got everything! It's a winter wonderland, perfect for skiing and snowboarding. And after a day on the slopes, there's nothing like warming up by a cozy fireplace."

Isabella's face lit up. "That sounds absolutely enchanting, Jojo. I've always wanted to experience a winter vacation."

Jojo chuckled. "Well, the season is almost over, so I am excited to hit the slopes. You and the girls are more than welcome. I did promise Taber to race her down the mountain."

Armand raised an eyebrow playfully. "Jojo, are you proposing that you a commando are going to race my 12 year old daughter down a black diamond slope?"

"Yes Papa. Yes." Taber said. "I want to race Jojo."

Jojo laughed, shaking his head. "Well, not exactly, but if we ever go there together, I promise we will enjoy some winter sports and relaxation, my parents' resort is the place to be." Jojo finished with a wink to Taber. "Besides, I wouldn't be so sure about the race. Taber is built to fly on the slopes."

Isabella's eyes gleamed mischievously. "I might just take you up on that offer, Jojo."

As the laughter subsided, Armand raised his glass. "To the joy of family and the thrill of adventure. Cheers, Jojo."

Jojo raised his glass in return, clinking it against Armand's. "Cheers, Mr. Bugatti. And thank you for this incredible opportunity."

As the last delicious bites of dessert were savored, Reine and Taber's excitement bubbled over. "Can we show you around the ship?" Taber asked the men. "We know all the best spots!" Reine exclaimed, her eyes shining.

Graham laughed warmly. "Lead the way, Princess."

The squad members chuckled as they pushed back their chairs and stood, ready to follow the enthusiastic sisters. Adélard exchanged a knowing glance with Armand, and they both smiled at the scene before them.

As the squad and the girls headed out of the dining room, Isabella rose gracefully from her seat. "I should attend to the preparations for tomorrow's celebration."

GHOST COMMANDO – Battle for Cavallo

Armand nodded with a fond smile. "Of course, my dear."

With a gentle squeeze of his hand, Isabella left the dining room, leaving Armand and Adélard alone. The ship seemed to embrace a quietness, a stark contrast to the lively chatter and laughter that had filled the room just moments ago.

As they sat in the comfortable silence, the sounds of laughter and exploration drifted in from the ship's corridors. Adélard glanced toward the door. "It seems the girls and your men are having a great time."

Armand's eyes twinkled. "Yes, Reine and Taber have a way of bringing out the adventurous spirit in people."

Adélard chuckled. "That they do."

The stewards had efficiently cleared away the remnants of the sumptuous meal, leaving Armand and Adélard alone at the table. A decanter of fine cognac and two delicate cups of espresso were now before them.

Armand poured the rich cognac into the glasses with practiced ease, his movements steady. He looked across the table at Adélard, his gaze thoughtful. "Adélard, my friend, let us have a more serious conversation."

* * *

Armand handed a glass of cognac to Adélard before raising his own. "To sweet victory Adélard and to France."

They clinked their glasses together, and the deep amber liquid swirled within the crystal confines. As they both took a sip, the warmth of the cognac spread through them.

Armand set his glass down, his expression contemplative.

"Adélard, what happened at Cavallo was nothing short of extraordinary. You managed to defend me, my island, and all its inhabitants with pure courage."

Adélard's gaze held a mixture of pride and gratitude. "The credit is not all mine, Armand."

Armand leaned back his gaze unwavering. "Leadership, Adélard is the factor that should never be underestimated. A squad like any organization is only as strong as its leader, and you have proven to be an exceptional one."

Adélard's humility was evident in his gaze. "I appreciate your kind words, Armand. But leadership alone would not have been enough to save Cavallo without the skills of my squad."

Armand nodded, his expression serious. "True, but it is a leader that cultivates those skills, and guides the actions of his team."

There was a moment of silence between them, the weight of their words hanging in the air. Armand leaned forward, his gaze intense. "So, Adélard, what's next for your team?"

Adélard took a thoughtful sip of his cognac, his gaze fixed on the amber liquid in his glass. After a moment, he looked up at Armand, his expression earnest.

GHOST COMMANDO – Battle for Cavallo

"Commander Ross and Commandant Gaston have informed me that my squad will be stationed at Camp Melusine. It's an unexpected decision, and while I understand the need for adaptability, I can't help but wonder what the true intentions behind this assignment are."

Armand leaned back in his chair, his fingers idly tracing the rim of his glass. "Ah, my friend, you're right to have questions. It is only natural to seek clarity when circumstances seem strange or out of place."

Adélard nodded. "Exactly. It's just that this arrangement seems rather odd. I'm concerned about the underlying objectives and what Toulon command envisions for my squad's future."

Armand regarded Adélard with a thoughtful expression. "You know, Adélard, in my experience in building and growing businesses, in management, there are times when you encounter something special, something unique in a person or a group of people."

"When you do, just like your father's farm, when you see potential, you work to nurture and guide its growth."

Adélard's curiosity deepened as he listened to Armand's words. "Are you saying that the Toulon command sees something unique in my squad?"

Armand's eyes met Adélard's, and he nodded slowly. "Yes, Adélard. Certainly, within the Commandos there are other squads with similar qualities and skills maybe even better than your own, but they are all older more mature."

"Agreed." Adélard added thoughtfully.

"Adélard, there is a synergy, a cohesion among your team that goes beyond the norm. The way you lead them, the way they work together, your willingness to reach beyond your arms to do the extraordinary."

"I have always believed in the strength of a team, was more than just the players." Adélard said looking back.

Armand smiled, a hint of pride in his gaze. "And that, my friend, is exactly what I'm talking about. There's an unspoken connection, a sense of unity, which sets your squad apart. It is possible that Toulon command sees that potential in your squad, and they are placing you in a position where you can continue to grow and excel."

Adélard took a moment to absorb Armand's words, the weight of their meaning settling in. "So, you're saying that this isn't just about our skills as commandos, but about the unique dynamics that we bring as a team?"

Armand's eyes sparkled as he leaned forward, his tone earnest. "Exactly, Adélard. Your squad is a force to be reckoned with, and you are just starting out, not just because of your combat skills, but because of the bond you share and the leadership you bring."

Adélard swallowed hard contemplating the wisdom Armand was sharing. "Armand, I think we need another cognac."

"Heard." Armand answered causing them both to laugh.

GHOST COMMANDO – Battle for Cavallo

"Remember this always Adélard, sometimes the most extraordinary endeavors arise from the most unexpected beginnings."

"Like you demanding my raw squad to protect everything you love on Cavallo Armand?" Adélard asked.

"Yes, well, I have made a fortune betting on people and businesses that I believed in. You mon ami are my latest."

"Thank you, Armand." Adélard said pouring another round of cognac for them both.

Adélard looked at Armand directly. "And what about you, Armand? What's next for you, for the Bugatti legacy?"

Armand's lips quirked into a thoughtful smile. "Ah, my friend, that is a question that leads down many paths."

"But for now, let's focus on the celebration tomorrow and your well-deserved 30 days of leave."

Adélard couldn't help but smile in return. "You are right, Armand. Tomorrow is for celebration."

Armand raised his glass again, a glint of mischief in his eyes.

"And let's not forget the promise of adventure that awaits your squad in the future."

Adélard chuckled, clinking his glass with Armand's once more. "Indeed."

La Fin

Index

Adélard Squad

Adélard l' ombre.

First name: Adélard. (Of German origin, meaning noble and brave.)

Last name: l' ombre. (Shadow, Ghost.)

Home: The quaint village of Saint-Étienne-du-Bois. Western France.
Mother: Noémie. Father: Bernard. Sister: Eléa. Girlfriend: Lorraine.

Graham

A bit older than the other recruits at 22, he is a short, stocky city boy from Paris. Raised by a well to do aunt and uncle after his parents died in a plane accident. Although pampered and shy he has a very high IQ and earned a master's degree in computer sciences from Sorbonne university by 21.

Noel

Orphaned at a young age, Noel bounced around between orphanages and foster homes until being put out on his own at 17. An imposing figure at well over 2 meters tall and as strong as an ox but with the heart of a teddy bear.

Jojo

A rail thin black haired young man from the village of Chamonix at the base Mont Blanc in the French Alps. Raised in his family's small hotel, he grew up doing odd jobs when needed since he had a natural almost magical understanding of anything mechanical. He also excelled at snow skiing which led him to becoming the best ski instructor on the mountain. Like Adélard he longed to leave his village and see the world as a Commando.

Julio

An 18 year old teenager, the youngest member of the squad. An Italian national from the city of Leon having immigrated to France with his family as a young child. Trained as a mason like his father, he possesses physical strength equal to Noel. His broad shoulders and callous hands are a testament to the hard work of his youth. Although reserved and at times painfully shy in nature Julio brings another element to the team being fluent in 3 languages besides French: Italian, German, and English.

Henri

Henri on the other hand, was older, nearly 25. Good-looking and quick witted. His upbringing in Caen near the English Channel had been far from conventional. Poor with little family support or guidance. From boy to man, Henri had made his way by any means possible in the seedy part of town.

* * *

Camp Melusine

Melusine: Fresh Water Goddess. Salacia: Sea Goddess.
Melusine Senior officer: Commander Ross
Sergeant Moreau
Training Squads: Adélard, Matis, Gilles
Melusine officers/Instructors:
Lieutenant Coeur nickname: Coop, Lieutenant Nickalos
Requin Boat Master: Captain Philippe Robart
Helicopter Pilot: Captain Auclair
Jump Instructor: Captain Margo Solitaire

Corsica Island Locals

Sisters Camille and Colette: Aldo the father.
Women in the woods: Helena

French Homeowner and her Children:

Homeowner: Genevieve Bernardone: (Gaston's Wife)
Daughters: Sylvie (Ginger haired), Arlette

Bugatti Compound on Cavallo

French Billionaire. Monsieur Armand Bugatti
Armand Bugatti's wife: Isabella Bugatti:
Bugatti's twin 12 year old daughters: Reine and Taber
Bugatti's Butler: François
Head of Bugatti Security. Luigi Battista

- Rohan Akhil COO, *COO Bugatti enterprises Indian Ocean*

Cavallo Island
Catholic Priest: Father Paulo of the church Eglise de la Mer
Elon Musk's American security men: Adam and David
Altar boys: Alex and Lucas

Toulon France. French Nacy headquarters.
Étienne Vacheron . *Vice-Amiral d'escadr of the Navy* VAE
Gaston Bernardone . *Commandement des Opérations Spéciales COSG*
Gérard Constantin . *Senior Operations Officer Bérets Verts SOF*
Counterintelligence
Lieutenant Dupont and Lieutenant Laurent.
Special Operations
Commander Audry Brielle

* * *

Submarine Liberté.
Captain: Louis Renault
Executive officer: Lieutenant Patel
Chief engineer: Lieutenant Donato

* * *

Congo
French operatives: Martine Boulanger, Mr. Secouer
Burundian Rebal leader: Aziza Samira
Chechen Mercenary Leader: Anzor Mayrbek

Moara Beach house, New Caledonia.
Korean Guest: Mina
French Homeowner: Thérèse

About the Author

Fabio Tagliasacchi

Fabio was born in Carmen de Patagonia, Argentina to Italian parents Achille and Guiditta in 1954. He contracted polio in 1955 in both legs while living in Argentina and is currently confined to a wheelchair.

In 1957 the family immigrated to the US.

Happily married to Rita, Fabio is blessed with wonderful loving children. Taber, Paul & Reanna and grandchildren. Cousins and near cousins on three continents.

He earned a degree in Mathematics from the University of South Florida and his Master (MBA) from Hodges University. Adding those honors to the unofficial PHD he earned from his father Achille Tagliasacchi.

Semi-retired Professor Fabio continues to teach Algebra at the local College, volunteer at the Elks Lodge, and when inspired writes Ghost Commando Novels.

Fabio enjoys sports, the ocean, or any body of water big enough to sail in, and all things mechanical or technical.

He can be found most weekends enjoying a movie or dinner with his daughter Taber, visiting the shooting range with his son Paul, playing in his garden, or pushing his wheelchair down the road pursuing a faster 5k time.

**Other Publications
by Fabio Tagliasacchi**

Ghost Commando
  Birth of a Kraken
  Battle for Cavallo
  In the name of the Father

Childrens Book
Kentucky Greens - The Adventures of Romeo and Juliet

Made in the USA
Middletown, DE
30 September 2023

39829862R00215